About The Author

Mohammad Reza Erfani is the pseudonym
or pen name of an English author who says:
'I would give anything to see my name in print,
for my writing to be appreciated but avoiding
the limelight may be the better option.'
The author prefers a life of secret anonymity,
not wishing to attract indulgent thrill-seekers
intent on promulgating a fatwa against him,
merely for asking awkward questions or for
not being a slave to the worst kinds of religious
dogma. Indeed, as a former Archbishop of
Canterbury once said in a triumph of optimism,
when greeting Muslim leaders for an interfaith
dialogue: 'We all worship the same God.'
So if it is Allah or the Son of God, Holy
Ghost and the Father, or Yahweh, or Mary,
one puts one's faith in, does it matter –
if God hears all our prayers?
Ask yourself the question.
What would you believe?

The
Margaux
memory

A PERSIAN LOVE STORY

What would *you* believe?

FIRST ENGLISH BOOKS

First Published in Great Britain in 2019 by

First English Books

The right of Mohammad Reza Erfani to be identified as the author of this work has been asserted by him in accordance with the Copyright, Designs and Patents Act, 1988.

ISBN 13: 978-0-9551437-9-3

Printed and bound in Great Britain

Cover design by Camilla Davis

Book design by Camilla Davis

Printed in 11.5pt

A CIP catalogue record for this book is available from the British Library.

* Translated from Horace's Odes by Giulio Galetto, with English translation by E. Segre and S. Carnell

**Unattributable to date

WHAT WOULD YOU BELIEVE?

THE MARGAUX MEMORY

A PERSIAN LOVE STORY

MOHAMMAD REZA ERFANI

First English Books
Great Britain
2019

Wine is the mirror to mortals…
Wine, dear child, and Truth….

Alcaeus *(c.620–c.580 BC)*

…You must be wise. Pour the wine
and enclose in this brief circle
your long-cherished hope.

Horace *Odes (65–8 BC) (I, 11)* *

Because we cannot know our days to come;
Because we cannot know our time to go;
Give up the gods. They're deaf and blind and dumb.
They answer no one's prayers – with yes or no…
…Give up your hopes, the endless dreams you seek,
And pour the wine in strong white streams that run
Away with life – yes, even as we speak.
Now, seize the day before the night's begun.

Horace *Odes (I, 11)* **

I

One

I WAS BORN NOT UNDER A WANDERING STAR BUT A MYRIAD OF them. As a child in our small house in the north of Iran, near the Caspian Sea, when my mother pushed shut the front door on a summer evening, as night fell, the sky lit up, not as lights are lit up in a theatre but in a gloriously wondrous arc that really *was* a theatre of the universe. I could see everything from my bedroom window, clusters of galaxies I suppose they were, millions of light years away, and yet somehow from such a distance they managed to impinge on our lives, and I was transfixed.

It seems an odd word to use, transfixed. Most of my friends think I am Anglo-Iranian, by birth even, as I lived in England for several years, and studied English literature, so I know with my small knowledge that the night stars did not actually 'transfix' me to my bed. I suppose as I gazed upward it's fairer to say they caught my boyhood imagination – well not exactly. The stars *held* my imagination in their imperceptible grasp.

Sleep was easy in the days of my childhood. The scent of almond and orange blossoms in our garden blew into my eager nostrils, not unlike horse whisperers when they breathe into the noses of their charges, and convey secret messages. In my case, nature blew into my bedroom the most exotic scents, perfumes even, that our womenfolk love to wear on their faces and sometimes behind or even under their ears. I am not sure whether I prefer the scent of almond blossom or orange blossom best.

Both provide an exquisite bouquet for the nose. We Iranians, as you may know, usually have large or prominent noses, as if to be enticed the more by perfumes of paradise.

Oh paradise! I still have not found it, not entirely, nor am I expecting to. Sometimes it is glimpsed in a garden, especially where there is clear running water. I suppose it is a bit like happiness; most of the time it passes us by, like a stranger, unrecognised. All this was some years ago now.

My mother was always preparing food in the kitchen. Often she sat on the kitchen floor, with a cloth spread in front of her. On the white cloth she would chop herbs like coriander, dill and parsley into ever smaller parcels of goodness. She seemed to prefer a cloth to a chopping board. The chopped herbs would go into various Persian dishes. Rice had to be steamed for what seemed hours under a cloth cover, with ghee added beforehand to be sure of crusts of 'toasted' rice called *tahdig*. This *tahdig* everyone loved and all wanted to be sure of a small piece of this crispy delight. If she was not cooking, after washing the cooking pans and plates, and after a little time to herself for prayer and resting, she would pick up her *jarrou*, a short-handled straw brush, and busy herself with it around our small house.

My father was more drawn to the Muslim faith than my mother but both prayed with tiny embroidered prayer mats, which helped them to concentrate more on their prayers. Very early on I grew tired of the – to me – dubious distinctions between what was *halal* and what *haram*. For those who do not know, such concepts of good and bad, acceptable or unacceptable, are a central tenet of the Muslim faith. I suppose much the same happens in other religions; Catholics eat fish on Good Friday rather than tasting carnal meat; on Saturdays Jews cannot even open the door of their refrigerators or turn off a light because they believe no 'work' is to be done on a Saturday, their *Shabbat* (Sabbath) day. It hardly seems logical. Jewish people don't eat meat and fish off the same plate. That seems to me very reasonable. No civilised person I am sure likes fish with the meat course.

Anyway, Jews are stuck with what is kosher and what isn't kosher, a bit like *halal* and *haram*. They are also stuck with the first five books of the Old Testament as revealed by God to Moses on Mount Sinai, the 613 rules of Jewish law, the Torah, and the Oral Torah, plus some 6250 printed pages of the Talmud, based on the teaching and opinions of many thousands of rabbis, these forming the basis for Jewish laws and practices. Jewish scriptures are so precious that if one is dropped on the ground, it must be picked up and kissed. A Jewish book should never be left open if no one is reading it, and never held upside down. If someone asks you for a book, you must always give it with the right hand, never the left.

The Jews were very lucky during their forty years of wandering in the desert on their long journey to the Promised Land, the land of milk and honey; it is recorded in both the Bible and the Qur'an that God provided food to keep them alive, known as 'manna', which had to be collected early in the morning before the sun melted it. Perhaps it was honey-dew from the tamarisk tree. When Moses died, so did the provision of manna. In the Qur'an, Allah sent the manna to the Israelites through the good offices of Moses. The original Ark of the Covenant inside the tabernacle contained a pot of manna. The Jews are still waiting for their Messiah.

I was not a very good Muslim student when I was going about my everyday business or when I put my head down on the floor in front of me to pray. I hasten to add not in the manner of Saint Denis, who had his head chopped off by a Roman soldier but calmly bent down to pick up his head, cradle it in his arms, and then walk six miles, preaching a sermon all the while. The spot where he collapsed and died became a shrine, which over time developed into the Saint Denis Basilica, in a suburb of Paris. Much later in life I discovered that Saint Denis is a saint invoked to guard against 'diabolical possession' and headaches. One can imagine that having one's head cut off might result in a severe headache.

But I have not explained myself clearly enough. I meant to say when I carefully placed my forehead on my embroidered prayer mat, I found it hard to focus on what I was supposed to pray about or for. Of course I was intentionally submitting to the will of Allah, peace be upon him. Even so I found myself jealous; well that isn't quite the right word, *envious* of my Christian brothers. The god to whom they addressed their prayers (in the form of Jesus) had a human face. Admittedly I didn't like to see the contorted representations of Jesus upon the cross, usually in a state of anguished pain as one would be with heavy iron nails hammered into one's hands and feet, let alone the ignominy of being lanced in the side, or having to wear an uncomfortable crown of thorns.

Of course, these 'cross-worshippers' as we sometimes call them have their own way of doing things but at least they can relate to humanity, to a human (even if incarnated into a god), a human with a mother and father. Furthermore, though this did not strike me as being relevant until later, they commemorated their god by drinking wine, if only a sip, as well as a very small piece of bread, more usually a paper-thin wafer that would not feed a starving mouse. The chosen wine was red; this was referred to as 'the blood of Christ' and the bread as 'the body of Christ'.

We were taught that Muhammad, who lived some 570 years after Jesus, was the last true prophet and that 'there is no god but God', *la illaha illa'llah*, sometimes written as '*La illaha illa Allah!*' (There is no God but Allah.) That always seemed to me to be rather an exclusive view of things, at a stroke cancelling out the gods of other belief systems. As I was saying, Christians had a god who briefly rode the stage of history as a human being, although I did question his genetic structure, only idly, as I was growing up. Presumably, the Christian God the Father must have assembled the necessary genes to make his Son, and of course to be 'fully human', we know that such a genetic composition must have included a scattering of genes from other early human species, like Neanderthals.

Still, Jesus was identifiably human but of Allah, and even Muhammad, there are few pictorial depictions to fall back on. Allah therefore for me had a nebulous nature; I could not 'pigeon-hole' Allah into any form of structure and I began to find a certain irony in that Islamic art in our mosques has all sorts of ways of creating obscure patterns into a kind of order, as if to find in this constructed order an order that was just not there when it came to making in one's mind an image of Allah. Of course this is forbidden in Islamic art but I thought it might have been helpful to find something to represent the unknowable, just as Christians have their wine and wafer-thin bread. These obscure patterns are supposed to represent the underlying, mathematical order behind God's creation, and of course when these mosaics are made and laid in their wondrous millions, the occasional error is made on purpose, since only Allah can make anything that is perfect.

My mother and my father both made the *hajj*, the pilgrimage to Mecca where, in the dusty heat of Saudi Arabia, they walked round in anticlockwise circles with a million or more other Muslims, threw stones at the devil, and considered it to be a pinnacle of their lives to stand before the monolithic stone known as the *Kaaba*. A lesser pilgrimage for Muslims is the *umrah* – a visit to Mecca at any time of year.

The original structure is said to have been built by Abraham, helped by his son Ishmael, for the worship of one God. But, such is the nature of faith; one can't question it. In any event, among conservative circles, one is not even allowed to question anything. For some, faith is everything, so much so that many people can't live without it – although some may side with the American journalist and critic H.L. Mencken, who described faith as 'an illogical belief in the occurrence of the improbable'.

If I may just mention it, I saw an image of the solid black cube only last week. It had black draperies over the top, with what appeared to be gold filigree work like the alluring eyes of a woman behind her veil, eyes that looked down on the fomenting multitudes. It was truly mesmerising, since the structure forms such an inherent, and major, part of my religion. Yet, when I dispassionately went through what were my reactions, it occurred to me, and I am unashamed to say it, that this monumental 'object' was in essence a giant kind of idol. As we walk round it, most reverently, remembering the teachings that depictions of idols are forbidden, I suddenly thought this is one of the greatest extant idols in the whole world! We Muslims worship this stone! Of the grand passions this stone excites in the breast of Muslims, there is no end. The thought frightened me, so I had no alternative but to banish it forthwith.

Even in my home country there are certain customs to be observed, and for some odd reasons many of these relate to the wearing of clothes, for which there are stricter rules for women than men. It is true that when my sister's friends return home from a visit to Tehran, almost as they walk through the front door, they begin to shed some of their dress, especially the *hijab* (headscarf), and kick off their shoes as if to be free from constraint. Restrictions to women's rights are common in Iran. If a woman wishes to play chess for the Iranian national team, a *hijab* must be worn or permission to play will be refused by the government. It's the same with finding a job or going to university. One day it is hoped all Iranian women will be free to unloosen their hair if they want to, even if only 'for the experience of the wind blowing through it', as told by the Iranian journalist and activist, Masih Alinejad in her book, *The Wind in My Hair*.

Many Iranian women have the most beautiful black hair; when young, and even when older, their hair shines. Can you imagine that? The colour of the hair is just that – *black* – but you would be wrong to imagine it as the colour of the *Kaaba*. It shines in a way I find difficult to describe to you. It glistens. Somehow, entwined with the *blackness* of their hair, of course if they have black hair, is a kind of steely dark blue, mysteriously compelling to the observer. As for their beauty, it rivals the famed women of Circassia. As soon as they enter our house, these girls will unloosen the great glory of their hair so it tumbles in curls and folds, sometimes peculiarly straight like a black waterfall. Of their eyes, I have no need to mention. They have the eyes of *houris*, shaped like black almonds, stolen from gazelles. I have always failed to understand the religious dictates about *modesty*. There is no modesty left in the world, or very little of it. Many women are naturally modest, even shy, like the gazelles. What need is there to cover head and hair, and wrap up in black sheets to look like wraiths?

My mother's favourite Persian dish was *fesenjān* (pronounced *fesenjoon*) made with young chicken (*joojeh)* with ground walnuts, pomegranate paste and onions, all simmered down into a rich, dark mixture, and served with saffron rice. The second favourite was *khoresh-e karafs,* a lamb and celery dish. At the table we drank chilled water, sometimes sprinkled with a few rose petals (to make homespun *golāb* or rose water), or fresh mint and thinly sliced lemons from our garden. After dinner, there was always *chaii*, black tea, without milk, kept hot by an old, cloth-covered kettle simmering on an ancient stove, as we did not own a samovar, or *samăvar* in Persian. Actually, now I come to think of it, perhaps we did have a samovar that belonged to my grandfather. It was too big for everyday use, which is why it was locked away in its own 'cupboard' in the kitchen.

Many times I have felt homesick for my country; I mean homesickness, that desperate longing or nostalgia to be back in the house I once lived in with my family. My mother and father have 'passed away', as they say in English. My sister, my dearest Bahar, is married now with a daughter of her own. I have an old uncle who lives in a small flat in Paris, an exceptionally gifted man, an academic no less. Why, when the Shah was alive, he himself, the Shah of Iran, 'King of Kings' (*Shāhanshāh*), whose other titles included *Āryāmehr* (Light of the Aryans) and *Bozorg Arteshtārān* (Head of the Warriors), Mohammad Reza Pahlavi came to the school where my uncle as a young boy was a pupil. All the boys had lined up for the visit because the Shah had offered free education for the brightest scholars. No doubt on advice from the school's head, he personally picked out my uncle for this honour. As a result of this incredible encounter with fate, my uncle was sent to France to complete his education in Paris. Some years later he was appointed, as Dr Amin Arvani, professor of marine biology at the Sorbonne. My uncle's family name was really Erfani but when he went to Paris as a young man, he changed his name to 'Arvani', for reasons which I have never fully understood.

The problem with my uncle was that he behaved to his family

(I think this is the word) like a martinet, a disciplinarian to be exact. His life was spent mostly with his head in books. When not at his studies, he liked to 'oversee' the lives of family, not just his immediate family but cousins, nieces, nephews, aunts and uncles. We Iranians are proud people. Our cultural diaspora stretches over the world yet my uncle wanted to control the lives of others. He was also devout or, if not, it was a very good pretence.

He would demand of me whether I had prayed the requisite times a day. Was I clean living, not wasting my time? Was I studying the hardest I possibly could? This did not fit in well with my character; I realised fairly early on that I disliked rules, proscriptions, 'moral urgings' to rid myself of 'bad' thoughts and unclean desires. Laziness for my dear uncle was perhaps the worst sin of all.

Alcohol was not to be tolerated, and even though my uncle spent many years in Paris, I soon realised that he had probably never ventured much outside academic (and some religious) circles, certainly never into the 'halls of corruption' as he sometimes called them. By this he meant fashionable and well-established casinos and dance halls, I would imagine including Moulin Rouge and the Folies-Bergère.

As a somewhat sheltered young man with virtually no knowledge of 'the opposite sex' – apart from glimpses of my sister undressing in our bathroom at home – the idea of risqué dancing by young women, flinging their long legs into the air, showing frilly underwear, and probably more besides, was an attractive proposition. I was sure their dancing involved a certain amount of discipline too, to get their routines synchronised, but it was not the sort of discipline that would have appealed to my uncle.

All this changed, by slow degrees, when I won a scholarship

to study at Oxford. I really don't know how I managed it. I had a flair for languages, and history. At my interview I contrived, by a kind of mental sleight of mind, to display an almost effortless precocity along with the naivety that often goes with gifts of the intellect. Having given the Master an overview of the Persian Empire from Persepolis to Marathon to Salamis, I was asked my opinion of Cecil Rhodes. I had no idea. I knew he was a potentate of sorts, a businessman of great wealth, so much so that in my country, in the olden days, we would have probably given him the title of *Khan* (leader, nobleman). As to the personal habits of the man, I had no knowledge. Quickly surmising that perhaps the Master himself might be a scion of a famous family of the British Empire, and seeking to ingratiate myself (which is actually one of the worst sins for an applicant to Oxford University to either admit or commit), I replied that I knew very little other than that I had no doubt he was 'a capital chap'.

Then I was asked what my conception of women's rights was. To be truthful, I had not given the idea much thought. Suspecting that this might be a kind of trick question, to set a trap for me, as in my country the rights of women surface only infrequently in conversations unless one is from a liberal family, I replied that whatever rights I enjoyed as a man, in whatever country, I would expect the same rights to be extended to women, whether in London, Colchester, or Tehran.

At the mention of Colchester, I did notice a kind of hooding of the Master's eyes. It was, looking back, very stupid of me to 'throw in' Colchester but I had remembered the history of that place is renowned for one brave woman's victory, the woman Boadicea or Boudicca, the Celtic Queen of the Iceni tribe. She torched Camulodunun, the Latin name for Colchester, then the provincial Roman capital of Britain, in a battle known as the Massacre of the Ninth Legion.

When her luck ran out a little later, the queen took poison rather than be captured by her Roman oppressors. Boadicea is portrayed as an early British heroine but she was none too merciful herself; captured women were sometimes impaled through the stomach on staves, or had their breasts cut off, and their mouths sewn over. If I am not clear I mean that the Iceni queen or those under her command cruelly stitched one or more of the cut-off breasts over the mouths of the captive women, a feat of barbarity not usually associated with women. Who could blame her? The Romans who had earlier captured Boadicea had her flogged and her two twelve-year old daughters publicly raped and tortured.

I don't think, historically, that the Persians were guilty of wanton cruelty but they did exact punishment for serious crimes. I am ashamed to say it is believed Persians invented crucifixion *c.*350 BCE.* A modern invention in the last few years has been to hang dissidents, activists and criminals from cranes mounted on trucks, most of these ordered by Iran's 'revolutionary courts'. Thousands of prisoners are currently detained in our prisons and at least 5,000 dissidents – men, women and children – were secretly executed in the late 1980s to eliminate political opposition. It is known as the 'Prison Massacre'. Amnesty International reported that 7,000 Iranian students, journalists, lawyers, environmental and women's rights activists and others were arrested in 2018 in a ruthless crackdown by the state. Many were imprisoned, flogged or died in custody. Nothing changes, it seems.

I know in much earlier times there is the famous story of the Roman emperor Valerian who was captured by the Persians and forced to act as a human footstool for the Persian king when mounting his horse. When he pleaded for his life, and had offered a vast amount of gold in exchange for it, the Persian king Shapur allegedly forced the captive emperor to open his mouth, and poured molten gold down his throat, saying, 'Here is gold for you!'

Goodness, I had not meant to stray from my story. In the event, I was offered a place.

* The author finds no objection to BC (before Christ) and AD (*anno Domini*) usage, and similarly AH for anno Hejirae, year of the hejira – when the Prophet left Mecca for Yathrib (renamed Medina) in 622 CE, and BH, before the hejira. Jews refer to AM, anno Mundi – the year of the world, or the year of creation in Hebrew. The date 2020 AD/CE in the West from the Gregorian calendar is 1441–42 AH; in Hebrew the 1st January 2020 is 4 Tevet 5780. The Buddha reached his final nirvana or parinirvana some 545 years before Christ's appearance. The year 2020 AD/CE is 2563 BE (Buddhist Era) in Thailand.

Two

I FELL IN LOVE WITH OXFORD THE MOMENT I ALIGHTED FROM the train as an undergraduate of one of the most famous universities in the world. Some say *the* most famous and I would have to agree with them. My luggage consisted of a rucksack and one old leather suitcase – a gift from my uncle.

Eschewing the desire to 'hail a cab', which is I believe what most Englishmen of some stature always do when in any important city and wanting to get from A to B, I determined to walk, you might say in the manner of a pilgrim. I was strong, with muscular arms and legs, 1.8 metres tall, with black hair and a very hairy chest. My features are, I suppose, typically Iranian but luckily my nose is straight, without those excessive proportions that compel some Iranians to offer themselves up to a cosmetic surgeon for 'a nose job'. I have brown eyes and a well-trimmed beard offset, rather nicely I believe, by even, white teeth. I have always been sure of my identity, likewise gender. In fact, in terms of sex and identity, I'd much rather be a man enjoying a woman than a woman being enjoyed by a man.

Resisting the urge to head straight to my college, whose name I have decided not to mention for fear of any ensuing scandal due to my writing, my literary ambitions notwithstanding, I walked the length of the main street, known as 'The High', scarcely daring to look at the grand, impressive colleges whose gates I passed with a sense of secret glee almost bubbling up inside every pore and bone of my body. I stopped only when I reached a familiar landmark, at least it was familiar from the small collection of postcards I had accumulated showing 'the sights of Oxford town', as I waited for the first day of the new term, and my new life that was about to begin.

This landmark is very familiar as it is brooded over by an even more famous landmark, the tower and spires of Magdalen College. I placed my suitcase on the pavement and took from my jacket pocket a handful of *tokhmeh*, tiny parcels of delight that we Iranians love to chew, one after the other. *Tokhmeh* are dried sunflower seeds and are eaten by carefully placing one between one's upper and lower front teeth, with the utmost precision. With a small amount of pressure, the sunflower seed splits open. The husk is discarded and the seed crunched to provide immediate satisfaction. One is so good that one has another, and another, and still another...until there is only a small pile of discarded husks on the plate, or in my case on the pavement of Magdalen Bridge.

It occurred to me that in the manner of one notable English tradition, namely Poohsticks, I could throw the remaining *tokhmeh* in my jacket pocket upstream, and then quickly see which was the first to emerge on the other side. (Should anyone not be aware, Poohsticks is played according to 'rules of the game', and there are even World Poohsticks Championships.) The traffic, however, decided against it. Instead, I leant over the bridge, throwing the white sunflower seeds like confetti for a bride – not an inappropriate analogy as I certainly wished 'to court' this incomparable city for the three years ahead of me.

Undergraduate life in Oxford was, how shall I say, congenial. A kind of *ancien régime*, laissez-faire attitude mostly prevailed. No one seemed in any great hurry, and the students riding around on bicycles seemed almost leisurely in their progressions through the narrow streets. I determined fairly early on to seek out a mosque for prayers. It was some time before I set foot in one for one reason or another. There are about seven or eight mosques in Oxford but several are simply prayer rooms in colleges set aside for that purpose. It was possible to pray in my room, and I decided I could follow my faith just as easily in my room, without the need for piously showing my face, as it were, in the nearest mosque.

I had only been there for about three weeks when I made the pleasant acquaintance of an English girl of the same age who was reading history in some obscure classical period, with an emphasis on the development of Sparta; I think she said her studies related to 'Dorian Sparta', around the 6th century BCE. As this period coincided with the so-called Persian Wars, the girl, whose name was Alice, grew increasingly keen on my company. Perhaps she considered she might elicit some unusual information about Ancient Persia – from 'the horse's mouth', so to speak – as I had announced to her that I was from Iran.

One day soon after, Alice invited me for a picnic. I can't say I knew very much about 'picnics' other than that the English enjoy seizing the opportunity for a little al fresco relaxation, and for students, this means a chance to escape from the confines of library or tutorials.

Alice, who had long blonde hair and blue eyes, a pretty face with a small rose-mole on her right cheek – I believe they are called 'beauty spots' – was highly organised. She had brought along a cane basket, like a fisherman's creel, and from this she managed to extract a thin, woollen shawl for sitting on, some homemade smoked chicken and mayonnaise sandwiches, and a strawberry tart.

I considered this very gracious of her. I suddenly realised that she had not even asked my name nor had I volunteered it, which must have been socially inept on my part. I will tell you my name a little later, but for the moment, let me tell you about our picnic. In my delight in taking in the late summer sunshine and the bucolic pleasure of striding through what I later knew to be Christ Church Meadow, seeing the park-like trees and long grasses of the meadow (such that I almost imagined we were in an English savannah, if indeed there were such a thing, which I doubt), that I had failed to notice a small shoulder-bag my companion had on her person. But I had noticed a rather ominous clinking sound that I surmised to be a flask of tea or coffee, together with perhaps cups, when she laid the shoulder-bag on the grass. I thought nothing further of it, as Alice ignored it completely at first.

After we had eaten the sandwiches, as well as a crumbly slice of the tart, Alice slowly moved her legs forward, as if to gain a new position, and I then realised she intended to lay her head on my chest. This she did somewhat abruptly but it was not an unpleasant feeling, even though I admit her left arm was thrown rather loosely in the direction of my lower body. It was not often that a girl's arm (if ever, really) had so casually lain across my groin but I decided to allay my concerns by concentrating on the idyllic nature, the innocence even, of two students relaxing together in the natural comfort of a late summer's afternoon.

'Tell me about Darius,' Alice said suddenly.

'To Persians,' I began hesitantly, 'we know him as Dāriush', using our pronunciation of his name. 'You know, I'm sure, it is said that one should never trust a Greek bearing gifts. The Persian army must have considered they so outnumbered the Greeks at Marathon that Miltiades, his 10,000 soldiers, and a handful of Plataeans were like a gift on the way to victory, a gift of course with a sting in the tail, since the Persians were routed.

The Immortals, their number was always the same. If one or one hundred were killed, wounded or got sick, their number was always replaced. I could tell you about his son Xerxes if you like but who could forget the greatest king of all, Cyrus the Great? We know him as Kourosh Kabir, the *Shahanshah* (King of Kings). He was gracious to the Jews in his country. He offered to rebuild Jerusalem and their temple. One day I should like to see where he is buried. It's not far from Shiraz, in Fars province.'

'Go on,' Alice urged me.

'The inscription on his tomb, it reads, "O man, whoever you are and wherever you come from, and I know you will come, I am Cyrus who created this empire of the Persians. Don't begrudge me this small patch of earth that keeps my bones." That's how I remember it.'

Alice was listening to me intently but I decided to say nothing more, not wanting to disturb the pleasant feelings I was getting being so close to a very attractive young woman. There was a silence between us that I interpreted as a mutual understanding of our thoughts – but before what seemed no more than a prolonged heartbeat, Alice turned, rolling herself on the grass, and then aligned her face over mine, whereupon she kissed me like someone who has been starved of a vital human need.

The sensation was exquisite in nature, being as I thought uncontrived, a spontaneous gesture of her feelings toward me. But I was already thinking of my uncle. Suppose he discovered me, carousing and revelling in a meadow instead of studying? If he stopped the small monthly allowance for my day-to-day living expenses, I would have to find a job of sorts, and there would be less time for my studies.

The kiss stopped at that moment. Alice appeared to remember something. 'Oh, I quite forgot,' she said. With this announcement, she dragged the shoulder-bag between her knees, and then sat up. 'Look, this is for us!' she exclaimed, undoing the clasp on the bag, and drawing out a large bottle encased in what looked like a sleeve for chilling drinks. Two glasses quickly followed. Instead of being tea or coffee it was a bottle of white wine. She looked at me with a playful glint, unscrewed the metal top, and holding out a glass for me, began to pour in a pale, straw-coloured liquid.

'Stop,' I said rather weakly. 'No...no...I can't—'

'Yes, you can!' Alice responded firmly. I took the glass. She poured some for herself in the remaining glass, saying, 'Bottoms up!' (This unusual toast is apparently favoured by some English types.)

Alice drained her glass, uttering a sigh of pleasure as soon as it was swallowed. My hand began to tremble.

'What's the matter?' she said. 'Don't you like wine?'

'It's not that I don't like wine...it's just that in my religion, it's...it's *haram*. You know, forbidden.'

Alice looked dumbfounded.

I began to tell her my name, as if this might explain something. 'My name is Mohammad...Mohammad Reza Erfani.'

'Oh Mohammad!' she said, almost reproachfully. 'You poor thing!'

Before I could reply, she screwed the top back on the bottle, and began to collect her things. I made a vain attempt to help her. 'It's all right, I have to go.'

'Alice, *please* don't go!' If like some dog I had a tail, I thought to myself, it would be curled up between my legs. 'Alice thanks so much for the picnic.'

Alice was already striding away across the meadow. All she said, shouting back to me, was, 'Hope you enjoyed the sandwiches.'

Three

WHY DIDN'T ALICE LIKE ME? I LAY ON MY BED IN COLLEGE, feeling quite miserable. I was sure I could still feel her lips on mine, so much so that I jumped off my bed suddenly, to look at my face in the mirror. I even ran my fingers over my mouth in case I might just find a reminder, a 'keepsake', like the palest of pale lipsticks perhaps (she did wear makeup). Sadly, there was nothing.

Perhaps it was my name. Of all the names my parents could have called me, they chose Mohammad! There are countless millions of Mohammad's all over the world! It was hardly original – when I thought of the many fine Persian names for boys, like Arya, Abbas, Bijan, Dāriush even, or Farzad, or Hassan, which the last is I recall now a fine play written by an obscure English poet by the name of Flecker.

If you can bear with me, for just the moment, while I go to my small collection of books I brought with me to college. Let me find *Hassan*. Of course, Persians have many great poets like Hafez, Saadi Shirazi, and Omar Khayyam. It is invidious to go down this route, I know, so perhaps, unless I remember some other lines as my story is written, I will mention no more. The Englishman deserves praise for it (though my heart will always be with Hafez):

Thy dawn O Master of the world, thy dawn;
The hour the lilies open on the lawn,

19

The hour the grey wings pass beyond the mountains,
The hour of silence, when we hear the fountains,
The hour that dreams are brighter and winds colder,
The hour that young love wakes on a white shoulder,
O Master of the world, the Persian Dawn.

But I was named Mohammad. Of course I know, this is the name of our great Prophet, peace be upon him. The name is also written as Muhammad (for the Prophet), Mohamed and Mohammed. Mohammad is the popular spelling in Iran. The number of boys in the world with my name is no less than 150 million, I believe. I suppose if it was good enough for our great Prophet one must be content.

My second given name Reza is no doubt a nod from my uncle to the Shah of Iran, since it was he who plucked him from obscurity and gave him his place in life. (It is pronounced more like 'rezZA' than 'razor'.) I determined in the future, since my first name seemed to have shocked Alice out of her daydream on the grass, to announce myself thereafter, proudly I admit, as Reza! I would no longer 'stand on ceremony' and give my full name. I had to become like everyone else; everyone I overheard seemed on 'first name terms'.

I had nothing that evening to do, after dining in hall. I don't know if I seemed out of place with my single glass of water when most of the other students ate their meal with a fine glass of red wine. I had no idea of the nature or quality of the wine on their tables but it did not escape my notice that the long-stemmed glasses into which the red wine was poured were more elegant than my plain tumbler.

As I lay on my bed thinking of the day's events, a sudden creeping chill came over me. Surely Alice did not take exception to my refusing to drink the wine she had so kindly offered me? It was as if by that one refusal I had been marked out, assessed even.

Let me explain, just a little. Before the Arabs came to conquer our lands, Persians strongly held their own beliefs and unique way of life, a culture derived from Zoroaster, an ancient Iranian prophet who lived 3500 years ago. He was the founder of Zoroastrianism, and the phrase, 'Thus spoke Zarathustra', borrowed by Nietzsche, is another name for Zoroaster. We were fire-worshippers – my uncle said originally we came from Sogdia or Sogdiana in the long distant past. I'm not certain my uncle was correct about the fire worshipping but I do know the Zoroastrians worshipped communally in fire temples. They believed in the four elements (fire, water, earth, air). Fire was especially revered as representing God's light or wisdom. The god of the Zoroastrians was Ahura Mazda, the creator god of the universe, and their 'Wise Lord'.

Even now, Iranians still jump over fires they have lit in the countryside, even in their back yards, to celebrate our new year, which in our native Farsi we call *Nowruz* – literally 'new day', the first day of spring. So we must have been 'fire jumpers' more than fire worshippers. (Fundamentalist Muslims consider our *Nowruz* and its joyful celebrations as 'un-Islamic'.) It takes place on the day of the vernal equinox, in March. When we jump over these small bonfires, usually we sing a favourite song, '*Zardi ye man az to, sorki ye to az man.*' The meaning is like, 'Take away all my aches and pains, and instead give me your health and energy.' We dress up in our best clothes and exchange gifts. At the family table, we must set the '*Haft Seen*', seven things whose name begins with an 's', like *sabze* (sprouting lentils in a dish), *sib* (apples) and *somāq* (sumac berries). We also love, on a day we call *Sizdeh Bedar*, the thirteenth and last day of *Nowruz*, to go to the countryside for a big picnic with friends, even better if the location is near a lake or river as we can throw in our sprouting seeds (*sabze*), to symbolize new growth and life, and to wish for good luck. (The Jews also have a similar number of symbolic foods, eaten at the time of Passover, to celebrate their deliverance from slavery in Egypt, and bread has to be 'unleavened'.)

If we ever feel the need to ward off the 'evil eye', we burn *Esphand* seeds. These Syrian or wild rue seeds we hold over a hot flame until the seeds pop and crackle, releasing smoke which one should wave around one's head. The smoke lingering in the air will cleanse the home and all the family living there, and keep the evil eye away. Before I forget, there is one more important celebration at the time of the winter solstice – *Shab-e Yalda*. It's all about the longest night of the year, the victory of light over darkness. In England the people seem to make more of the longest day – the summer solstice in the midst of summer; a festival associated with merrymaking, the fruits of summer and such like, June roses, and fields of plenty. In one famous play, this involves sprites, fairies and a mischievous jester called Puck. At the time of *Shab-e Yalda* we make a spread of red fruits like pomegranate and watermelon, with nuts and sweet pastries. We may even lay a thick cloth on a low table (with a heater underneath the table) in a public park, sharing our treats and lighting candles late into the night. Someone usually brings a book of poems by Hafez. Each person may take the book, hold it close, and make a wish or wishes. Then, he or she will open Hafez's book at random, and slowly read out whatever poem is found there.

Iranians generally don't like Arabs (our Muslim conquerors) as they forced Islamic practices upon us. We call Zoroaster, in Persian, Zartosht or Zardushst. His precepts were very simple: in life there is but one path and that is the path of Truth; if

22

one does 'the right thing' because doing that is right, rewards will come.

Luckily we Persians held on to our beliefs, though we were forced, compelled to follow the precepts of Islam, gradually at first, and then there was really no escape.

I know you must be thinking, why? Because Islam brought its own rules and cultural mores, quite alien to us proud Persians. I suppose what I meant to say is that cultivating the grape to make alcohol is a sin. Persians had a flourishing wine trade for thousands of years, think of the Shiraz grape, like the Syrah grape, said to have originated from that most wonderful of cities. After the Islamic revolution in 1979, vineyards were torn up, dug out, destroyed. Once there were 300 wineries in my country; now not a single one is left. Our great poets like Hafez and Omar Khayyam would be most upset, don't you think? Religion can do so much good but rooting out vineyards, whether one drinks wine or not, seems to be a pointless assault on nature. Hafez had words of wisdom to say about most things in life, in fact I remember he wrote, 'The great religions are like ships, Poets the life boats. Every sane person I know has jumped overboard.'

Never mind the making of it, drinking alcohol is a major sin because Muhammad says so. Furthermore the sin is so great that eternal punishment is promised. Various Imams have proved this. A person who drinks alcohol cannot be a believer as believers do not drink alcohol. In fact, I remember the verse from the Qur'an: 'O you who have faith! Indeed wine, gambling, idols, and the divining arrows are abominations of Satan's doing, so avoid them, so that you may be felicitous.' Satan wishes to create enmity and hatred through wine and gambling. These things hinder the remembrance of Allah, and get in the way of our prayer.

Goodness me! Perhaps I was lucky to escape Alice's embrace with the wine, proffered before me, an invitation by Satan (we call him *Shaytân*). I wondered if Alice had been drinking a Californian white wine, in which case the wine itself would have been made in the country of *Shâytan-e Bozorg*, the Great Satan – America.

When I awoke the next morning, I scarcely knew which country I was in, I was so confused. I did know that young love had not wakened on my shoulder, and the Persian Dawn – oh! my beloved Persia – was a pale, damp, misty morning in Oxford.

Four

IN THE MORNING I IMAGINED, FOOLISHLY AS IT HAPPENED, that I was lucky. I awoke with my eyes fully open, my mouth 'mint fresh' – because the sin of alcohol had not tainted me. Nevertheless, there was a bad taste of sorts in my mouth. Alice's kiss had awakened the devil, I thought in my innocence, because all night long I suffered a peculiar kind of suffering. Perhaps to you it is nothing unusual but not having been close to a woman for as long as I can remember, and truthfully, that goes back much further, since the closest I ever came to woman, metaphorically you understand, was when I was ejected into this world to make my own way in life. Alice's arm seemed to have kindled something not unlike a fire; it burns hesitantly to begin with, and then oxygen, if someone waves a small sheet of cardboard as if trying to light a barbecue, fans the flames.

Most of the night I felt disturbed. Whichever way I tossed and turned in my bed, I seemed to be followed by some part of my anatomy that was grossly inflated, in the manner of an obstinate flagpole – I will spare the detail.

For much of that day I resorted to comfort food and dared not venture to a single lecture. My sister had given me a small packet of dried mulberries, we call them *tut*, a favourite Iranian snack, a bit like *tokhmeh* in the habit of eating them, except *tut* has much more body, and is juicier.

It didn't matter too much, I thought, if I missed the occasional lecture; history was my strong point, but my degree was essentially concerned with English Literature. Trying to make a start with my studies, I picked out the book that formed part of my first year's reading. Of course I knew the title, but had been remiss in starting at the first page, or even reading the reverse of the front cover.

The more pages I read of this book the more disturbed I became. At first I could put up with the odd, niggling sense of unease, a frisson not of pleasure but an emotion of disquiet and even fear. I began to wonder at the peculiar power of this strange story. A man wakes up one morning to find himself transformed into a gigantic insect-like creature. Overnight the travelling salesman Gregor Samsa metamorphoses into a sort of monstrous vermin. Finding himself covered in hard, bony scales with his six legs waving in the air, eventually he is able to roll over onto the floor of his bedroom but gradually his segmented body expands, so he is hardly able to move between the furniture. It is a horrible story. He is rejected by his parents and sister. I don't think an Iranian could possibly have ever composed such a gruesomely bizarre tale that is supposed in some ways to reflect the existence of 'modern man'.

Not long after finishing the story I began to experience a series of very troubling dreams. The plot was nearly always the same. I visited my uncle's flat in Paris but when I had climbed the stairs to arrive at his front door, even though I had a key, I found it difficult to push open the door to his flat. It was always as if a great weight lay behind it, and each time as I opened the door a little more, I could see an unreal structure (I am ashamed to say) like a grotesque insect. My poor uncle! He has been so kind to me over the years that it seems now sickeningly unfair. The dreams always ended in the same way. I was unable to enter my uncle's flat but I could hear his cries of despair.

I made up my mind, not long after this episode, to visit a mosque in Oxford not just for prayer but to try to speak to an imam for guidance. I could confess my shameful feelings towards Alice perhaps, narrate my troubling dreams, and have my faith in not drinking alcohol strengthened by a considerate imam. I knew that Catholics could unburden themselves through the confessional, simply by going into a dark box and confessing their sins, whether mortal or venial, to a priest. When a Catholic emerges from this box I was sure, they feel, well, not exactly transformed but certainly renewed in faith and hope.

The idea of metamorphosis, that is a sudden transformation from one state to another, or even a series of changes, seems to me a way that nature has engineered to enable a creature not 'to get stuck' in one form but to develop, anew, into another creature altogether. I suppose that one might have metamorphoses of mind too, such as a sudden 'conversion' to a religious belief. I thought there must be some good metamorphoses too (for myself, at that time, this was an unusually positive way of looking at things). A metamorphosis might be seen as a sudden change for the better, a new way of understanding, or of doing things, which had previously seemed immutable, or immutably fixed. There was no reason to suppose that all changes were somewhat 'grisly' or macabre in concept, such as happens with flatfish. They are born 'bilaterally symmetrical', with an eye on either side of their body, but during metamorphosis, 'one eye moves to join the other side of the fish', so both end up side by side on the upper part of the fish. Having an eye move in such a way can surely not be the most welcome of experiences. But consider the butterflies in flight – dancing in tandem, in the sunlight – when before they were just rubbery grubs, crawling from leaf to leaf.

I did find a mosque, off the Cowley Road, where I prayed

with a handful of other worshippers. The imam leading prayer was quite young, I thought, with a beard like mine – not too long and straggly, which I always consider somewhat unsightly, in the manner of an obstreperous billy goat.

After prayers, an exchange of *As-sālamu 'alaykums* and *Wa-Alaikum-Salaams,* and a Persian *Salām* from me, a touching of fingers in a kind of abbreviated handshake, I introduced myself to the imam. He seemed very self-contained, with a guarded smile that was, nevertheless, welcoming. I began by explaining my recent arrival, the length of my studies, and that I wanted to find an imam with whom I might discuss some problems of a personal nature.

'Well,' he said, 'we all have our problems but luckily Allah is there to guide us on our journey.' His deeply-set eyes seemed to look right into my soul, such that I felt almost 'naked' – what I mean is that I felt vulnerable. Perhaps it was not such a good idea to confide in the stranger before me.

'Tell me about your problems,' he said, this time with an ingratiating tone as if to entice me to open up.

'It's about adjustment,' I replied, 'to this new society. All the temptations, you know, that any young man meets at this time of his life…'

'Oh,' the imam said, as if affecting deep surprise. I saw his eyes narrow ever so slightly. 'What kind of temptations?'

'The temptations,' I said, 'are chiefly on the subject of young women. That is my main temptation. I have not been tempted to drink alcohol as yet but maybe, in the future, a glass will be thrust into my hands, and as a matter of courtesy, I am thinking I might not be able to refuse this generosity out of hand, and upset my guest.'

'The religious law on these matters is quite clear. Sex outside of marriage is not tolerated. Drinking wine, any alcoholic drink, is playing with fire. You would be gambling away your life, your health, and risk punishment from Allah. Muhammad, our great Prophet, peace be upon him, instructs us not to consume this evil if we want to avoid eternal punishment. Imams have proved this, beyond any doubt.'

I waited to see if there was more. The imam had picked up a small sheaf of papers, and was riffling the tops of the pages to find what he wanted. 'It is good to settle these things early,' he said, his neck suddenly appearing to extend itself in height, as if to add authority to his coming words.

'Imam Baqir, and I quote,' he said somewhat pompously, I thought, 'has written that "disobedience to the order of Allah is mostly due to alcoholism. The alcoholic abandons prayer. He can even commit incest under its influence; he loses his senses!"'

For a moment there appeared before my mind's eye a picture of a beautiful afternoon, and Alice was handing me a glass of straw-coloured wine...I coughed as I felt a lump of anxiety reveal itself in my throat.

'Imam Jafar Sadiq provides us with all we need to know about alcohol. Even swallowing only a mouthful of wine, at that very moment, the angels, the Prophets, and the righteous believers send their curses upon him.' He paused before continuing. 'And when he drinks enough to become intoxicated, the spirit of belief leaves his body, it is replaced by the dirty, accursed, devilish spirit.'

As if to punch home the message, he added, 'All these things can happen with alcohol – never mind the health problems, like damage to the brain, numbness of hands and feet, impotence, and even blindness! And let's not forget kidney infections, high blood pressure, and liver failure.'

'I don't think I have anything to worry about from alcohol,' I said. 'It is true that I have been disturbed somewhat in the past week – by a young woman I met. I found it difficult to deal with the sexual urges I felt at the time, and still afterwards.'

'You had better tell me about these temptations then,' replied the imam. 'Young women, women of mostly any age are a great distraction. The physical urges can be very strong. Premarital sex is absolutely forbidden in Islam. Have you forgotten that *zina*, fornication, whether with a girlfriend or a prostitute is completely *haram*? As for masturbation, that is an indecent act. The believers protect their sexual organs except from their spouses. The end for all fornicators is *Jahannam*!'

'Well, I have no desire to marry just yet.' Suddenly, I thought it was none of the imam's business to start probing me for details about my encounter with Alice. According to Islamic law, provided a girl has reached puberty, a man can marry her if she is nine years old. I wanted no lectures about morality. I had read of very rich sheikhs visiting London's Park Lane, staying with a retinue of servants, cooks and butlers in one grand hotel or another. One sheikh booked an entire suite on one floor for his wife, and another suite two floors down for his mistress, and only he 'was the wiser'.

'I will try to follow Allah's will,' I said lamely. 'Personally, however, I believe that whatever happens consensually between a man and woman, if they are acquaintances, should not be subject to the scrutiny or jurisdiction of others.'

The imam stood up abruptly, as if to say our conversation had ended. There were the obligatory, polite salutations one uses when saying goodbye to a fellow Muslim; I was pleased the imam had the grace to bestow some sort of blessing on me as he said, in words translated to English as: 'May the peace, the mercy and the blessings of Allah be upon you.'

It was not long after this that I suffered my first nervous breakdown. Back in college, in my room, I should believe that if I had merely a sip of wine, I would bring down on myself howls of execration from angels, the Prophets, and other righteous believers. And if I attempted even the thought of gratification with Alice, I would be in *Jahannam*, The Fire, or The Pit of Blazing Fire, in no time at all.

Five

TO BE HONEST, IT WASN'T JUST THE DUBIOUS MORALITY OF chastity and the avoidance of alcohol that had unnerved me. It was also my attempted accommodation with Gregor's peculiar metamorphism into a horrid, nasty bug; the way the insect became trapped in its solitary room, had bits broken off, the restrictions to free movement, the alienation Gregor (lest we forget his name) experienced at the hands of his own family!

I had made some friends at the university, some good friends but on the whole I felt I had not yet become, or reached that realm of togetherness that modern British society knows as 'inclusiveness'. I felt there was some irony in that many Muslims do believe in peaceful co-existence with their neighbours who are not believers (only until the day the disbelievers lose the battle waged by Allah's followers) but that assimilation must be rejected at all costs – a view to which I could not subscribe. I was not included in the various wild parties, where alcohol flowed more freely than the Cherwell under Magdalen Bridge. I did attend some of these student gatherings, usually with a soft drink in hand, but although my 'swarthy looks' gained some attention I was probably, in the early days, not that far removed from that unfortunate soubriquet used by the English, namely a mere wallflower.

Oh my god! I have just remembered the Flower Garden of Isphahan. We Persians know it as the '*Baghe Golha*'. The roses there are stupendous, though I suppose they do not come close to the roses you will find in Shiraz, the resting place of a nightingale of a poet, Hafez. Persians learn his poems by heart. His full name, Khwāja Shams-ud-Dīn Muḥammad Ḥāfeẓ-e Shīrāzī, still excites my heart. Hafez's tomb, among flower gardens, orange trees and streams is illuminated at night. By day visitors can take refreshment in a tea house in the grounds. For someone who celebrated wine so much in his poems, even I, as a Persian, who also loves tea and tea drinking, can see the irony. In fact, should you visit his resting place today, 'official' guides will inform you, 'No, Hafez did not drink wine! He would only drink sweet, coloured water.' I think this was a decision taken by censors from the Ministry of Culture and Islamic Guidance. 'Moral policing' has always been a complete waste of time, and is usually initiated by the institutionally religious, as for example by cruel, psychotic nuns (and priests) in some children's homes and orphanages.

By night my dreams wrecked what sleep I could get. Once I dreamt that I was at one of these student parties; there was a mirror into which I glanced with pride, expecting to see a handsome Persian prince. Instead, my upper body had been transformed into the head of the ugliest beetle imaginable and, what was worse, two of my 'legs' went in another direction from the others, holding themselves over my crotch, as if either to protect myself from wrongdoing, or to shield others from the sight of my bare genitals. I wished I had never had to study Kafka. I had enough problems of my own to worry about, without the existentialist nightmare of poor Gregor's fate.

By this time, the end of my first term was approaching fast. The Oxford streets became chilly, and I felt they were full of ghosts, admittedly some very famous ones, students who had passed through, like Matthew Arnold and Shelley (how strange to be called 'Percy' and 'Bysshe' all in one breath). One night I put on my overcoat and headed out of town. I had researched the opening times for late-night surgeries, where one might go in an emergency to seek medical help.

I found the surgery on the corner of a junction. Once inside, the doctor called me in. He was a tired looking man about sixty with the appearance, and the cough of a heavy smoker. When I politely asked about his health, as he had mine, he said he was continuing to work that night even though he had a collapsed lung.

What mysteries I revealed to him about my anxieties I was never able to find out. Sitting in his dimly lit surgery in my long dark overcoat with rings under my eyes and a rather dejected mien, the patient would not have looked promising. After eyeing me cannily (I think he was Scottish), the doctor scrawled a note and sealed it inside a small envelope. He handed me the envelope, saying, 'Take this to the nearest hospital.'

As I had not been diagnosed with any infectious disease, I feared the diagnosis had been of the mind rather than the body. As soon as I stepped outside, ignoring the words 'Private and Confidential', I gingerly opened the envelope. Under a poor street light, I read his handwriting: '*Please admit to hospital urgently. Patient suffering from severe psychosis.*' Of course, I never went to hospital. With such a note in my hands, how could I? I was frightened I might be declared mad, insane.

Turning into the grounds of my college half-an-hour later, I saw Alice talking to two male students; I partially hid my face in my coat, as if to keep out the cold. But Alice must have seen though the feint. She ran over to me, crying out, 'Hey, Mohammad! How's it going?'

'Okay, everything is fine,' I lied. 'You know, please, I prefer to be known as Reza.'

'Oh *Mohaammmad!*' she exclaimed, turning my name into a kind of grotesque parody of itself. 'I'll always remember you as Mohammad. Still, if you prefer, Reza it is then.' She leaned over to kiss both my freezing cheeks – even so I immediately felt the softness of her lips, the sweetness of her breath, so close to mine.

Alice stepped back a little, as if to inspect me, and after a moment she said, 'Reza, have you ever had a stiff one?'

Horrified by my interpretation of this peculiarity of the English language, where to express oneself fully, one might use a euphemism or French term over an English one, as in a 'double entendre' – I believe it is much the same with 'French leave' or 'French letter', although in this case the words she used were in fact English but could have been interpreted, by the salaciously minded, quite differently – I attempted to splutter an indignant, if somewhat embarrassed, riposte. 'Alice, that kind of language is not really called for.'

'Reza!' she exclaimed, 'I know it. You've never really had a stiff one, poor chap, have you?'

With this, Alice took my left arm in hers, held it tightly against her, and started walking away from college. 'Just follow me,' she said, showing firmness. I was dragged some yards, quite a few hundred probably, until we were standing outside a very old, almost dilapidated building, but I could tell from the voices coming from inside that it was full of students.

I followed Alice through the entrance. Clearly, I knew this to be a pub, one of those unique institutions in Britain that are found the length and breadth of the country. It had a flagstone floor and a maze of little side rooms and a narrow but long seating area. At the tables sat crowds of young people cradling what I supposed to be pints of beer or lager, most of them animatedly talking, each seeming, or so it seemed to me, to be shouting over the other to be heard. Finding a spare corner, Alice pushed me into a seat, with a firm 'Sit there!', then went up to the bar.

On my small oval table, I noticed a leaflet from, I think, the branch of religion that call themselves Jehovah's Witnesses. Idly, I glanced at it, noting to myself that it had probably been left there for that purpose – that someone would pick it up and read it. The message was about 'turning away from sin' and avoiding evil. In fact, printed in bold at the top, it read: 'When wickedness wins, it is God's alert to evil.' I remember thinking how kind of God to alert us to bad things, and that for the past several thousand years, the number of alerts sent out by God must be in the millions, if not trillions, as human beings seem to have propensities in that direction. I mean why else would they drop bombs on innocents and gas them to death? Or torture them with cigarette ends, electrical devices like 'cattle prodders', suspend them upside down from rafters, or use pliers to pull out their toenails? We should not forget all those poor souls who are forcibly 'disappeared' – a euphemism for murder. The tortured, raped and imprisoned scream out to us in their thousands but their screams might as well be silent, as no one hears.

The world must have ears to hear them – the political prisoners, the oppressed – the vulnerable writers at risk for being too honest or outspoken. Indeed, far better to try to reach out to make their cries heard than strive to catch the ear of Allah with dumb, fruitless requests.

My introspections were abruptly ended when Alice sat down next to me, placing two small glasses, each with a solitary ice cube, of an amber-looking pale liquid on our small table. 'That's a stiff one for you,' said Alice alarmingly, 'and a stiff one for me – one of the finest malt whiskies in the world!'

Already weakened by the knowledge of the doctor's diagnosis I had just received, my nerves making my fingers shake, I sat back, resigned to sorrow and sadness – what was I to do? Alice looked at me with compassion in her eyes. She said, 'Think of it as medicine.' She sipped her glass. 'Oh, god that's so beautiful,' she purred as a cat will with a dish of cream.

Before my eyes danced djinn and white-eyed whirling dervishes, obviously intent on leading me astray. I had two conflicting thoughts; either I had no choice through my own weakness but to drink it or I had the option either to drink or not to drink of my own free will. In that moment's suddenness, a minor metamorphosis for me really, I decided I would exercise my own will, my own choice, my own free will...

Alice watched amazed as I slowly picked up the glass and brought it to my lips. First my nose inhaled peaty odours, then the first sip brought a bite to my tongue, my eyes smarted slightly, and I coughed. The second sip was warmer, a little softer. It was not an unpleasant taste. I then closed my eyes and drained the rest of the glass.

'Wow Mohammad, I mean Reza,' Alice exclaimed, 'you finally did it! Wait there a moment.'

Then a second glass (this time 'a double') was placed before me. As in the British expression 'in for a penny, in for a pound', there was now no going back. I drank half of the second glass before a slow warmth moved through my body. I no longer felt cold. My toes weren't numb from the winter frost. My shoulders suddenly relaxed downward as if held up beforehand by an invisible coat hanger. I pulled a note from my jacket pocket, saying 'Look, let me pay.' She accepted after I insisted I was paying until the bitter end, as Persians do. We use an expression that translates as, 'I would rather die before you than allow you to pay.'

Dare I say that I began to feel more content with myself, with the world? That I actually felt happy for the first time in weeks.

We talked for a while until Alice had to go. I finished the last of the whisky, and kissed Alice goodnight.

'You should sleep well after that. Sometimes you've just gotta take the medicine!' She smiled like a beacon of good hope in that damp and frosty Oxford night.

Six

ON THE WAY BACK TO MY ROOM IN COLLEGE, I REALLY FELT AS
if I were half-floating along the dim, narrow streets. If I saw
a gargoyle, it smiled back at me, as all seemed 'at one' with
the world. I felt possessed by inner warmth! I could understand
why some call this firewater, even 'The water of life'. Hurriedly
I brushed my teeth with strong toothpaste, and rinsed my mouth
several times. I had risked punishment from Allah! Quickly,
even though it was late, I washed myself as Muslims do, and
then placed my prayer mat on the floor. In such haste, I even
forgot to face the direction of Mecca, which the Arabs know
as *qiblah*. Originally, it was the holy city of Jerusalem that
Muhammad revered above Mecca but the Prophet later changed
the direction of prayer to Mecca. I am not ashamed to say that I
asked Allah for forgiveness. I then went to my bed, and within
minutes fell into a deep and untroubled sleep.

Early the next morning I awoke. Incredibly, a smile crossed
my face. As yet I had escaped eternal punishment. I rushed to
the mirror and found I looked quite well, even slightly 'jaunty'
for so early in the morning.

In our first year in halls of residence, breakfast is available at
minor cost, so I availed myself of strong English tea and scram-
bled egg on toast. I paused before a tray of sizzling hot bacon
but firmly rejected taking a second major risk to my well-being.
I might have escaped so far but I was surely tempting the devil

41

if I placed a few slices of bacon on my plate. We Muslims consider bacon (pork), like dogs, unclean, near the top of the *haram* scale of things. I accepted this without question. I understood that other religions have their prohibitions too. In Pakistan, a Hindu can be beaten to death for eating cow meat – and for eating buffalo or goat meat if the mob mistakenly thinks it is beef. The cow is sacred in Hindu religion. I have to say nevertheless that bread dipped in beef dripping from a roast is so very tasty – good enough to be offered as a sacrifice to the lesser gods. The animal is seen as the mother of prosperity, and the ghee (butter) they make from the milk gives them strength. It is common for Hindus to drink the cow's urine and even bathe in it. That's just the way things are, although on reflection, it does not seem very logical.

But lots of things are not logical. Think of Mashal Khan, a brilliant student from Pakistan murdered by a mob for his secular and religious questioning. Lying in bed in his dormitory, he often brought up 'arcane subjects', such as whether the offspring of Adam and Eve might have married each other, thus suggesting the taboo topic of incest. He was not encouraging incest but asking a philosophical question (indeed as one Philip Gosse asked whether Adam and Eve had navels, as presumably they were never attached to an umbilical cord). Fellow Muslim students dragged Mashal from his bed and beat him to death for blaspheming, and insulting our Prophet, peace be upon him (and Mashal). And let us not forget Qandeel Baloch and Sumbul Khan, two murdered female singers from Pakistan or Avijit Roy from Bangladesh, hacked to death by a mob with machetes for penning an atheist blog. Or Asia Bibi, a Christian woman accused of blaspheming our beloved Prophet (peace be upon him) while out plucking *falsa* (a kind of edible purple berry). The Supreme Court of Pakistan, the highest court in the land, exonerated her but the mobs are still baying for her blood. She will be very lucky to escape with her life – even though the court has set her free. She had to stay in prison immediately after the verdict, where she had been for eight years awaiting trial, because if she stepped outside the mob would kill her. If anyone was guilty of blasphemy it was her fellow Muslim workers in the *falsa* field who conspired, malignly, to misrepresent her.

I wish it were possible to petition our beloved Prophet about these grave injustices but alas he seems to have no ears to hear our prayers. Why, of late, I have been thinking the unthinkable – that a new universal law must be passed to make insulting any religious figurehead *legal*. Or at least allow it as a defence to a charge of blasphemy. It is the only way to defeat extremists who demand *death* in all its gory, inhumane ferocity and finality – for insulting our beloved Prophet – as the only possible outcome. In Pakistan, there are groups of lawyers who believe death for blasphemy is mandated. Some work pro bono, offering their help to prosecute blasphemers. One lawyer says this work brings him 'a lot of peace', and in any event, even if he does this work for free, then Allah will reward him in the hereafter. How they poison the idea of just, wise counsel, and discredit their noble profession! Allah is just. I don't think he will be a greengrocer weighing the merits of human souls in the hereafter – but of course only Allah knows what he will do, and Allah knows best. Sometimes I believe it wise to believe there is much that will always be unknowable to humans, and trying to convince oneself otherwise leads to hocus-pocus piety, flim-flams, and the worst kind of humbug.

For the record, defence lawyers in Russia have a hard time of it – only 0.34 per cent of cases in Russian criminal courts result in not guilty verdicts. In China conviction rates are 99.9 per cent, no doubt helped by torture and other coercive methods. Perhaps one cannot blame the lawyers when their legal systems are inherently corrupt, state managed, *ab initio*.

A second universal law would be to repeal the idea that suicide bombers are martyrs en route to paradise. Instead these butchers should be condemned to *Jahannam*! In perpetuity and into the fire that is blacker than tar!

A third to allow peaceful dissent and freedom of expression without being imprisoned, beaten and left to rot in jail, as happens in many Muslim countries, such as Bahrain, Saudi Arabia and the UAE in the Gulf region, to name but a few. In the UAE and other Muslim countries the BBC, that harmless paragon of British broadcasting known as 'Auntie', is blocked. One must also include Egypt where journalists are jailed for objective reporting (second only to China and Turkey), which the state determines as 'fake news' – as with Mahmoud Hussein, an Al Jazeera journalist who has been detained for more than two years without charge. A woman wearing a mildly sexy dress may be charged with 'inciting debauchery', and even 'spreading microbes' to those viewing the dress. Only the state's narrative of 'truth' is allowed, which means that reality is only what is officially sanctioned. Kafka, Orwell and Alice are all at the Mad Hatter's *chaii* party!

Peacefully and even politely expressing a personal view on social media – only vaguely critical of government, or a single tweet asking for democratic elections – can result in solitary confinement, lengthy prison terms, torture, and denial of essential medical assistance. How can these countries be truly 'Muslim' when Allah himself would not forgive them for such injustices! Citizens of any country should be free to criticise their governments if the authorities fall short of generally accepted norms of human behaviour. These changes must come about through proper human governance – we cannot expect Allah's intervention to sort out the mess. Whatever Allah wills happens or doesn't happen, and Allah knows best. Unfortunately his guidance is often none too apparent.

What is the price to pay in some countries for speaking out and writing about it? Remember Jamal Khashoggi – the Saudi journalist who 'upset' the kingdom's crown prince, Mohammed Bin Salman. Khashoggi had taken a call from a member of the Saudi royal court telling him to 'stop writing' his column for *The Washington Post*. The bone saw, allegedly taken into the Saudi consulate in Istanbul by a 15-man murdering hit squad from Riyadh – what could that be used for? To cut off Khashoggi's fingers one by one whilst telling him, 'We told you to stop writing but you didn't and this is your punishment.' Anyway, *Allah will avenge his death.* I am sure of that. Did not our great Prophet say, 'God has no mercy on one who has no mercy for others'? I was also comforted by the fact that Almighty Allah in our Holy Qur'an tells us that the murderers will face justice because it is written, '…if ye distort justice or decline to do justice, verily Allah is well-acquainted with all that ye do.'

I regret one must take these religious sayings lightly. I believe one of the psalms in the cross-worshippers' bible (Psalm 11) has these lines – and still the wicked prevail, and murderers escape justice…

> On the wicked he will rain
> fiery coals and burning sulphur;
> a scorching wind will be their lot.
> For the LORD is righteous,
> he loves justice;
> the upright will see his face.

It's all very well for the cross-worshippers to claim, as they do, that God sent his only son to *save* mankind. By that very act millions of people as yet unborn would be condemned to death and hideous torture – martyrs for the warring, squabbling Christian churches. Pope Francis said in one of his Christmas messages (*Urbi et Orbi*) that the Palestinian and Israeli land was 'chosen by the Lord to show his face of love'. *What went wrong?* Of course I know that we Muslims also kill and are killed for the sake of Allah. It is indeed a pity that the 'Arab Spring' became as painful and bleak as Eliot's description of April.

Certainly the cross-worshipper's son will never be allowed to save the natives of the Andaman Islands (and their souls) – mainly in the sense of receiving 'the word'. Anyone who lands there is likely to be speared to death or riddled with lethal arrows. In the ancient world, the Cycladic island of Delos was so sacred that no one was allowed to be born or die there. In the Andaman Islands no outsider is allowed to land by law as any contact with modern humans will inevitably result in the islanders' destruction by diseases to which they have no natural immunity.

Is it not strange that one man can kill another but refuse to eat a slice of bacon? I believe a Muslim can eat a slice of bacon in a case of very urgent necessity, if, for example, one was about to die of starvation, say in desert or jungle, and there was no other food available to sustain life. Of course, the chances of finding a slice of hot bacon, waiting to be eaten, in the Sahara Desert or the Brazilian jungle are equally remote, and this does not take into account whether the meat was *halal*. To be *halal* meat, a prayer must be said before slaughtering the animal, invoking the name of Allah, and it must be killed in a certain way, by having its throat cut so the creature bleeds to death. This has a practical purpose since the carcass is drained of blood, and consuming blood is *haram*. Sadly, animals subject to 'religious slaughter' in this way suffer pain as they are still conscious. Meat cannot be deemed *halal* if the animal is humanely stunned first. Of course, if one is hungry in the jungle or desert, just about any food can become *halal* or 'permissible'.

On the subject of remoteness, I won't forget the prayer meeting held by a mullah in Iran; there was a 'discussion' about premarital sex. The mullah said if as a man you were in a hotel on the fourth floor, and on the third floor, exactly under you was a woman lying in her bed, if there was a sudden earthquake so that you fell through the ceiling and landed on top of the woman, and inadvertently penetrated her by virtue of falling on top of her, that would not amount to a sin, as it was the earthquake's fault and not one's own lustful thoughts or actions.

After this moment of musing to myself on improbabilities, I am ashamed to admit that there passed through my mind 'in very quick order' a question as to whether earthquakes had ever occurred in Oxford. To my surprise, on Googling, I discovered there had been a small one in 2016, but on the Richter scale, it measured only 2.3, enough to shake houses but not bring down ceilings.

With my mind seemingly cleared of emotional debris, I set about my studies with renewed determination. I wanted to please my uncle with a First. In no time at all, I came to terms with Gregor's unfortunate demise, followed the trail of Coleridge's imagination from the Antarctic to the equator in *The Rime of the Ancient Mariner*, and began a study of Baudelaire's poems. This last was especially difficult. Who could read *Les Fleurs du Mal* without being shocked to the core by its morbidly erotic content? After reading *Les Bijoux* (The Jewels) and another, *L'Ame du Vin* (The Soul of Wine), I suffered another nervous lapse. I actually longed for another shot of whisky to force the demons out of my head, as it appeared I had managed to do so with Alice. Suppose I followed Baudelaire and sank into the abyss? I would never walk in the straight path, as we are instructed by the Qur'an. Don't we all know that the spirit is willing but the flesh is weak? This being a quote from another 'holy book', namely the Bible.

You might wonder why I mention this but we Muslims share much with Christians. In the holy Qur'an, Mary the mother of Jesus is mentioned almost seventy times. She was the 'most perfect of all women'. She even has her own Chapter of Mary (*Surat Maryam*). The angel Gabriel appeared to her in the 'annunciation', a miracle foretelling the birth of Jesus (*Isa*), and the same angel Gabriel (*Jibreel*) appeared to Muhammad at least twice, and guided him on his famous night journey towards Jerusalem, of which there is no need to tell further since the believers know the story well.

It was the angel Gabriel who brought *Al-Burāq* to Muham-mad, a white 'steed' from heaven (smaller than a mule and bigger than a donkey, with a pair of wings on its back), which transported our Prophet from Mecca to Jerusalem and back in one night, a journey (to Jerusalem) that would take a fast camel team at least 40 days at 25 miles per day. If the angel ever returns, he would find it easier to travel on the Haramain train, the new 300 km/h high-speed link connecting Mecca and Medina.

I considered myself very lucky to have escaped from the dolorous snares of Baudelaire. He himself felt wounded like the albatross in his poem of the same name, forced to drag his feet on the boat's deck with his wings flapping like useless oars when all he wanted to do was to fly on the poet's wings. Being so hobbled to earth, he amused himself on hot, torrid nights with the naked landscapes of languorous women, succulent as pears, their exotic perfumes and intimate scents trapping him as surely as birds in a cage, who still sing as they can.

About this time I began to realize that my little flirtations with Alice were nothing to worry myself about. I had offended no one, and certainly in my mind I knew that God himself could hardly have given me any 'black marks' for my behaviour. Of course, had I been living as Baudelaire, or Gauguin or many of the other great artists of the past, 'up to my eyeballs', so to speak, in laudanum or opium, or in modern times smoking crack cocaine or chasing the dragon of heroin, and falling into the arms of numerous women for the purposes of sexual gratification or conquest, that would be another matter all in all, for the judgment of the lord of the worlds, the compassionate, the merciful to whom all praise belongs – God. *Allahu akbar.*

Seven

TIME PASSED SO QUICKLY OVER THE NEXT TWO AND A HALF years. I embraced my studies diligently, knowing that it was the best route to success. For sport, I played tennis after a fashion, and had a rowing 'taster day', after which I was able to join a novice rowing crew. I was a Novice D, so I trained only at weekends (Novice A's trained four or five days a week). After only a few weeks, I abandoned hopes of ever making 'Summer Eights'. I had some degree of athletic ability but I concluded fairly early on that the top rowers are almost a breed apart, with the lungs of lions, the strength of staying racehorses.

I did not revisit the mosque but instead prayed in my room. I failed in regularly making *Namaz*, the Muslim way of prayer for Persians, five times a day, as is God's word for Sunni Muslims, three times for Shi'as, though this last rule is not absolute. Originally we were commanded by God to pray fifty times a day but Prophet Muhammad reduced this to just five times, after a consultation with Moses, who had said praying so many times a day was unrealistic. I found even three times too much, even if it is one of the Five Pillars of Islam. Anyway, I concluded that all Muslims would be questioned about prayers and whether they had fasted according to the rules of Ramadan etc. on the Day of Judgement, so I decided to let myself be 'accountable', when that day came.

Some Christians, I believe, do not allow themselves to drink alcohol, and thus impair their judgement, because they feel they must be 'ready' for their Lord, if he should suddenly turn up one day, quite literally, on their doorstep. They must prepare for his coming. When I reflected on these things, I could not help concluding that 'patience' plays a significant part in the lives of the believers. The almighty God 'Bigbanged' the universe into existence about 13.8 billion years ago then waited another 9.2 billion years for the Earth to form. He/She/It then waited another 4.6 billion years minus 2000 or so years before the prophet Jesus was born, announced by the angel Gabriel. Then another 570 or so years passed until Prophet Muhammad, the last true prophet was born and some 40 years later, *Jibreel* (the angel Gabriel) appeared to him in a mountain cave, and some few years after this accompanied Muhammad on his special night journey. The patience involved in waiting so long for God's word to take root is surely on a monumental scale that makes the pyramids nothing more than mere mounds of dust, not even molehills, in the grand scheme of things. It was beyond my simple human comprehension.

The world lived a long time without either Jesus or Muhammad. In the chapters of life on earth, both are hardly more than the beginning of a page turning, even a paragraph. How strange that a visitor to earth today would find more books and pages from the Bible, the Qur'an and other religious books, scattered in towns and cities, than all the books or scrolls ever kept in the great library of Alexandria.

I felt reasonably sure that nowhere in our holy book is anyone *forced* to do anything. Verse 256 of Al-Baqara in the Qur'an states that 'there should be no compulsion in religion'. If one missed a few prayers, one missed the benefits, but I doubted that the inevitable consequence would be that one ended up in *Jahannam*, the Pit of Blazing Fire.

The passage of time did not unduly concern me as I was young, with the promise of some kind of gainful employment waiting at the end of the graduation line. I did once reflect that everything moves on in life, everything changes, as a skyscape is a series of scudding clouds, driven by inexorable forces. These changes I categorised in my mind as 'mini-metamorphoses', all necessary for the progression of life. The seasons catalogued them. In some college gardens, if you looked over walls or through iron gates, one saw magnolia, pink cherry blossom or wisteria grace ancient college walls. I had heard that Iffley Meadows was the place to catch sight of the rare snake's head fritillary, with their nodding burgundy or white bells humbly bowing toward the green meadows beneath. But I never made the time to see them. It had occurred to me that I might invite Alice to view them one April day and that perhaps she would be amused to learn of one of the other names of this flower, sulky ladies, but the idea came and went and I forgot to ask her. I did meet Alice from time to time, however, but throughout, our friendship remained platonic.

Looking back I shudder at the convoluted thinking, if you can so call it, I used. For example, the rules of ritual ablutions for Muslims are quite complicated. One must not forget initially the *niyyah*, making in one's mind the *intention* to perform cleansing for the sake of Allah. There is a minor (*wudhu*) and a major form of washing oneself in order to seek the pleasure of Allah before prayer. *Wudhu* goes in a certain order: the right hand, then the left hand, three times (use the left hand to wash the right hand and vice versa, and include between the fingers); the mouth washed or brushed with a toothbrush three times; water to be splashed in nostrils three times (but once is acceptable); wash face three times, spread hands to wash from right ear to left and from hairline to chin; then forearms from wrist to elbow, making every part wet, washing right arm with your left hand three times and vice versa; then wipe down hair, then wash back of ears and inside and out; then the right foot with the right hand and the left foot with the left hand. Take care to wash between toes. There are variations between Sunni and Shi'a (for example, Sunnis wash their forearms from fingertip to elbow but Shi'as wash theirs from elbow to fingertip), and this is only the briefest of descriptions, and does not include the various prayers that can accompany each stage of *wudhu*. It has occurred to me more than once that this ritual would suit someone with an OCD complex rather well.

Once *wudhu* is done it remains valid as long as it is not nullified. Events that nullify *wudhu* are natural emissions from the body (urine, stools, wind, vomiting), and falling asleep. In such case the ritual cleansing must be done again before prayer (*salat*) takes place.

There is another form of cleansing called *ghusl*, the major ablution; washing the whole body becomes necessary after sexual contact with a woman, the emission of fluids, discharges from the genitals or anus. If the ritual is faulty, to the smallest degree, it's all invalid and one must start again...one must not touch a wet dog either. Minor ablutions are for lesser cleansing...one must be clean for prayer or Allah will not accept the prayer. I know that I have not detailed everything about our ablutions nor have I really described some of it correctly but, to be truthful, I am past caring. God's word is God's word, is it not? There are imperfections in my description, akin to the sonnet (no. 116) I had to study in my dismal room:

...Love is not love
Which alters when it alteration finds...

I believe faith is much the same. Could I not say, 'Faith is not faith which alters when it imperfection finds'? Allah is no less Allah just because I got my prayers wrong. What I meant to say at the outset of this strange confession is that, had I had sexual relations with Alice, the more time I would have had to spend on *ghusl*! What a hopeless way of excusing my lack of success with her. Even so, I liked her as my friend. There was no pain as fortunately I did not have the chance to love her. Doesn't everything happen for a reason?

Luckily for me there was no question of imitating the Duke of Dorset in his forlorn quest for Zuleika Dobson, the 'heroine' of a book by the same name by Max Beerbohm. I can tell you I had no idea who Zuleika Dobson was until my English tutor gave me a copy, saying that I would find it amusing. I was still hoping for a First but by then considered it unlikely, especially in view of my aversion to Kafka. The upper division of second class honours would justify my uncle's sacrifices; and a BA from Oxford means the degree of MA (Oxon) may be conferred not too long after.

At the end of three years of study, along the byways and cul-de-sacs of English Lit, I duly took my place in the Sheldonian Theatre to receive my degree, and I passed out into the world, coming down from Oxford with a 2.1.

Eight

IT WAS STILL SUMMER, *TABESTAN*, AND OXFORD IN THE SUMMER
has none of the miasmal air of winter that seems to abound
there, with few students, and many tourists. I may have 'come
down' from Oxford but I was not sure what to do with my life
in terms of finding a career. I had carefully saved some of the
monthly allowance from my uncle, so I had sufficient funds to
rent a room whilst I 'found my feet'. Having time to spare, I
wandered around the Oxford streets and lanes, often reading the
inscriptions above doors, or on 'foundation stones', and noting
that a foreigner might think that many titled people spent much
of their time 'laying stones', which is doubted since the weight
of many such cornerstones would defy the lifting (or laying)
strength of frail dowagers, crotchety old bishops or a Lady
Windrush or Wimborne.

My mind seemed to flit back quite regularly to scenes in my
head of poor Gregor living out his brief life, confined to one
little room, with an occasional sortie outside, which resulted in
him being pushed back, the door shut in his face. Clearly any
metamorphosis such as he endured was a state of being con-
summately to be avoided at all cost. The change wasn't for the
better; it was unimaginably for the worse. I admired the meta-
morphic changes in some insect species, for example the may-
fly, *Ephemera danica,* which lives for a year or so in lakebed
or river as a nymph, and suddenly launches itself towards the

surface, and climbs the air on its great wings but the shortness of its life on earth is unbearable. After enjoying freedom following hatching, and finding a mate, the females, known as 'spinners', return to the water to lay their eggs, lightly skimming the water, dipping their abdomens through the surface film. The result is always the same – death. Spent of energy, their huge wings weighing them down, the river that nourished the creatures as nymphs finally claims them. Death may be faster if a gorging trout sucks it down. No, what I wanted was a good change, a lasting change for the better not fifteen minutes of fame or glory followed by an eternity of nothingness.

My first 'change for the better' was one of two that were to result in immeasurable life changes. Not for the first time would I sing the praises of my dear uncle. He wanted me to go to Iran – to a house he kept there. The house was empty, only occasionally attended by an old woman who dusted and minimally cleaned, since its owner had been absent for several years.

I was to retrieve a family heirloom; those are my words, not his. The thought of returning home, having been away for too long, made the hairs on the back of my neck tingle – I shivered with the excitement of it. I could see my mother, as she was still alive at that time, and my cousins and various family friends. In Iran, very few people live alone because we believe family is everything worth having in life, so it's like having a large, extended family always ready to be by your side. When you return home, it's a uniquely special party where everyone belongs, and no one is shut out.

I still have the ticket, my portion of it. LHR-IKA, that's London Heathrow to Tehran Imam Khomeini International Airport by Iran Air, leaving London 5.00 p.m. and arriving Tehran 2.30 a.m. That was an 'ungodly' hour to arrive but it meant that I would surely not be denied my first glimpse in a long time of a Persian dawn.

My 'mission', if you can call it that, was to travel to my uncle's house in the north of Iran, to the town of Bandar-e Anzali, a port on the Caspian Sea, close to a large city, known as Rasht. The housekeeper was to give me a key to a bureau in his long-abandoned study. It was not gold or jewels he wanted – in case you may be thinking I was being commanded to retrieve a 'treasure trove'. No, it was something much simpler. It was our 'family tree', made by my uncle and listing various forebears, some illustrious, some unknown much beyond the town that Reza Shah had changed to Bandar Pahlavi, only for it to be renamed Bandar-e Anzali after the revolution in 1979. Before I forget the Pahlavi dynasty was the last to wear the Imperial crown jewels of Iran, a priceless collection of bejewelled swords and shields encrusted with precious gems, tiaras and crowns with diamonds, emeralds, sapphires, and rubies, and a chest full of pearls. You can still see much of this incomparable treasure today in the Treasury of National Jewels in Tehran.

At the beginning of this chapter, I told you about the female mayflies, called spinners, which come to an untimely end in the river that brought them life. Just before I forget, I think (and because I am a storyteller myself I tell you this) that some of the biggest 'spinners' of yarns come from the various organised religions. It seems they cannot resist embellishment on a preposterous scale – such as Saint Denis carrying his head in his hands and giving a sermon at the same time – when medically he must have been dead. Aristotle commented that without a windpipe, St Denis would not have been able to say a single word. The Catholic Church loves to make up miracles so saints can be canonised – a vision of the Virgin Mary, stigmata in the hands, when in fact the Romans drove nails into crucified victims through the wrist, because if they were in the palm of the hand, the weight would simply tear the flesh.

You cannot read any religious work for long before there is some preposterous yarn, yarns that really belong in the realms of magicians, shamans and witch doctors – religious prattling on a grand scale. A list of miracles performed by saints would run into tens of thousands of pages. One of the greatest of the miracle workers in the Catholic Church was St Vincent Ferrer, with over 873 miracles, one of which was raising 28 persons from the dead. The saint is often pictured with wings because many people witnessed him, in the middle of preaching, 'suddenly assume wings' and fly off, with the aim of helping some poor suffering person elsewhere. Some time would elapse before the saint flew back to his preaching position, and carried on with his sermon.

As well as promulgating fantastic notions of miracles and saint workers, the Catholic Church banned or suppressed notions that were true. The teaching of the existence of sunspots was banned, since the sun had to be a perfect sphere, without blemish. Heliocentricity, as suggested by Copernicus and Galileo, was rubbished. Galileo was formally ordered to 'abandon completely…the opinion that the sun stands still at the centre of the world and the earth moves…'.

Many are these stories. Jesus turned water into wine, walked on water, and, three days after being crucified, was resurrected – brought back to life – but didn't stay long as he ascended into heaven. As for walking on water, we have a Persian proverb for that: 'Whoever can walk on water is probably made of straw.' And where is heaven? We say 'Heaven is under the mother's foot.'

Muhammad, peace be upon him, 'split the moon in two', made barren sheep give milk, and on his approach, palm trees walked towards him. Gautama Buddha had miraculous powers. Wherever the baby Buddha's tiny feet touched the ground, a lotus flower bloomed. In the same era Confucius lived. I can't think of anything miraculous attributed to him – other than his thoughts, which included, 'Roads were made for journeys not destinations'; and he believed good social relations with our neighbours are more important than living our lives based on absurd predictions of rewards or punishments after death.

The Mormons believe in a star called Kolob, where God now lives, and they refrain from swimming in the sea as the Devil controls it. The full name of the church is The Church of Jesus Christ of Latter-day Saints (LDS), dating from the 1820s. Their founder Joseph Smith, who had 40 wives, the youngest being 14, was visited by an angel named Moroni. The angel told him where to find secretly cached gold plates on which had been inscribed all sorts of gospel truths, and accounts from pre-Columbian civilisations, written in a strange language. Smith, having found the plates, decoded their meaning, studying them with the aid of two 'seer-stones', and a stovepipe hat over his eyes in order better to decipher the inscriptions on the gold plates. I surmised, secretly and perhaps cruelly, that a dyslexic Mormon might spell their acronym as LSD – which from a rationalist point of view is, very conceivably, not far from the truth.

Mormons wear sacred, magic 'undergarments'. Young male and female missionaries sent to European seaside towns for training won't go swimming even at popular beach resorts. Most admit this is because Mormon elders instruct them not to swim 'for safety reasons' – especially in the case of young male missionaries – in case they might get 'distracted'. If the thought of a bikini or two might be too much, and stop them from following God's wishes, I don't know why they don't go down for a swim in the very early morning. They never seem to think of that.

Scientologists believe in a madcap galactic ruler named Xenu. He was a genocidal maniac overlord who brought billions of humans to the earth 75 million years ago and then destroyed them with hydrogen bombs. All the problems of present day humans stem from 'brainwashed alien soul remnants', according to a Scientology spokesperson. As far as I can see the only 'brainwashing' is conducted by 'training routines' and 'auditing' by Scientology misfits. If you get to the top of the hierarchy or near the top, like actor Tom Cruise, you will be known as an 'OT', or Operating Thetan. As with the cost of becoming declared a saint by the Roman Catholic Church, reaching the top of the Scientology church may cost a million or two dollars.

Amongst this miracle working, is not simplicity itself something an honest soul might seek for? I know that Jehovah's Witnesses are themselves witness to some strange beliefs. The present world order is under the control of Satan. God's kingdom is in heaven where 144,000 chosen people will rule with Jesus (since 1914 and, invisible, return to earth), and ultimately the earth will be transformed into Paradise, with no crime, sickness, death or poverty. Some refuse blood in medical emergencies because of doctrinal beliefs. I hesitate to mention all these vile heresies for fear of offending our great Prophet, peace and blessing be upon him. I don't really consider these heresies vile myself but some fundamentalists would.

The Garden of Eden myth is undoubtedly a universal story that every tribe of the human race recognises. The perfection of childhood dreams metamorphoses into the stark reality of adulthood. A person can make up a picture of this garden exactly as he or she pleases. I think Eden was not a garden, more likely a cool forest where light dappled through green leaves and where translucent streams of pure water ran beneath. If there were beasts, they looked like Rousseau's tigers.

I continued with these religious musings, sometimes to amuse myself. I decided that the Church of England will spend years debating whether (God forbid) one man's rectum is law-fully ever the business of another man; one could gamble successfully, if one might obtain the odds, that there will never be a female Archbishop of Canterbury in one's lifetime; that postulators would continue their scouring of the earth on behalf of the Roman Catholic Church in search of proof for very dubi-ous 'miracles'; and how very generous it was of Muhammad in allowing a man to have four wives at once, even 'tempo-rary' wives too, although there are, I feel, many people in the west who consider looking after one wife quite sufficient. It is not just in the Muslim world that there are odd arrangements or adjustments in dealing with sexual matters. Church of Eng-land clergy, for example, are allowed to form same-sex civil partnerships as long as they go separately to bed. Celibacy might suit saints but is never really appropriate for the average human being.

One miracle no longer accepted by postulators, when assess-ing candidacy for sainthood, is the idea that the dead body of a saintly person could be *incorrupt*, as happened to St Catherine Labouré and many other saints. These saints were so especially holy that the normal forces of nature, such as decomposition, maggots, and rotting flesh, were miraculously suspended. If this were true, and not just a fabrication by the Catholic Church, it would be easier for their bodies to be resurrected 'at the end of time' – as is the belief of the cross-worshippers and many other religious belief systems.

For once I was glad I had to study English Literature, which included even the knowledge of Gregor Samsa's fate, and the doomed albatrosses, for my degree, knowing that – apart, just possibly, from the Qur'an, the King James Bible and, the Talmud, etc. – none of it was really 'God's word'. If I had studied theology I would undoubtedly have gone mad, having to read an endless library of fodder for the proselytisers.

But enough of this! There is no arguing with religion. It just *is. Allahu akbar.*

Let me return to my story. I know some may refer to this outpouring of mine as a nothing more than a mere 'yarn', the 'gut-strings' of an idiot or *flâneur*'s meandering thoughts. The phrase 'to spin a yarn', a sailor's expression, was first recorded in 1812. It was to tell a story, usually sitting down, whilst engaged in yarn-twisting. May I say to you now, I tell this story from my heart? I tell it as truthfully as another fine Englishman, whose existence I became acquainted with only through my English studies. He was a writer, and one of his works is entitled, *'The Story of My Heart'*. I quote here a few of his words. At the time I first read them, I dismissed them as idealistic daydreams without substance. Only later did these words take on a new meaning. I fear this is not the time to explain, not yet. It would be impossible for you to guess the connection I was able to make in my mind some months later but such is the nature of change, for which read metamorphosis, as no one knows what can emerge from the mind of a man who has been transformed by coming into contact with some elemental thing, which lays a hold on his being, his very soul.

> *I was utterly alone with the sun and the earth. Lying*
> *down on the grass, I spoke in my soul to the earth,*
> *the sun, the air, and the distant sea far beyond sight.*
> *I thought of the earth's firmness, I felt it bear me up:*
> *through the grassy couch there came an influence as if*

I could feel the great earth speaking to me. I thought
of the wandering air, its pureness, which is its beauty;
the air touched me and gave me something of itself.
I spoke to the sea: though so far, in my mind I saw it,
green at the rim of the earth and blue in deeper ocean; I
desired to have its strength, its mystery and glory. Then
I addressed the sun, desiring the soul equivalent of his
light and brilliance, his enduring and unwearied race.
I turned to the blue heaven over, gazing into its depth,
inhaling its exquisite colour and sweetness. The rich
blue of the unattainable flower of the sky drew my soul
towards it, and there it rested...

When I arrived in Tehran after a tiring flight of more than six hours, still carrying the same rucksack and old leather suitcase I had left with, I was met by a group of relatives and friends, and in the middle was the diminutive figure of my mother, her arms already open to embrace me. The expression on her face was one of imploring gratitude. *'Khodaier bozorg!'* she cried, wiping tears from her eyes. Again and again she repeated the words, *'Khodaier bozorg! Khodaier bozorg!'* (Great god! Great god!) She kissed me and blessed me at the same time, and I held her tightly in my arms. She kept calling me her *'gol pesar'*, her good boy. *'Muma!'* I exclaimed, *'Muma, haleh troubeh?'* (Are you well?) I think everyone cried with happiness.

A cousin whose name I now forget drove us back on a journey that lasted several hours. My mother handed round *nabaat* to keep up our spirits, pure sugar crystals infused with saffron. These miraculous little 'jewels' settle the stomach and the nerves. As we passed villages on the way home, there were so many wonderful colours in the early morning sky; they reminded me of the Pink Mosque in Shiraz, the Nasir al-Mulk

Mosque. If you go there in the early dawn, when the rays of the sun penetrate through the stained glass, it's like a kaleidoscope of colours more breathtaking, I imagine, than taking LSD. The Persian carpets below the windows are colourful enough, when suddenly a cascading riot of colour splashes over them. (If you buy a Persian carpet, say from Kashan or Kerman, note that by tradition a single flaw is woven into each one, because 'only Allah is perfect'.)

So it was on that morning, my first in Iran for some years. The Persian dawn was rising before us.

Nine

THE MOMENT I FIRST SAW OUR HOME MY EYES WERE BLURRY with tears. It is strange that deep joy or deep sorrow does this. What brings tears to the eyes is not whether we are happy or sad but the strength of the emotion. I am sure Muhammad wept when he returned to Mecca from Medina, just as I know from my studies that the Greek hero Ulysses did, when he saw his green and lovely Ithaca.

When we arrived, even being so fatigued after the long journey from Tehran, my mother went straight to the kitchen to make tea. Before anything can be planned for the day, there must be hot *chaii* on the table (and often *ghand*, or sugar cubes, placed in the mouth and sucked with each sip of tea). I believe it is much the same in Great Britain; certainly it was so in Oxford, especially among the older generation. Once there was something called 'high tea', but nowadays most ordinary folk express their liking for this national drink by announcing that they are 'dying for a cuppa', and reach for a teabag. Most Iranians dislike teabags. They like loose tea that can be measured accurately enough between thumb and forefinger.

Iran is such a big country – seven times larger than Britain – and so there are many different kinds of living. Some live comfortably in old-style villas in the north, others live in caves cut into rock, and make sheep's head soup (*kale pache*) in winter. People like to say they come from the north of Iran because the further south you go the hotter it gets, and the people get slightly darker in skin tone.

I almost forgot to tell you that same evening we had the most wonderful party. There seemed to be mountains of jew-elled rice, known as *zereshk polo*, *zereshk* being tart, dried bar-berries; *ghormeh sabzi*, a favourite Persian dish, a herb stew; *khoresh bademjan* (a stew made with aubergines, and so much better with dried limes), and *kabab koobideh* (minced lamb kebab). My mother liked to prepare as well a large bowl of plain yoghurt with freshly chopped mint. When I used the word 'stew', it's not really the right word for some Persian dishes. The British usually make unimaginative, tasteless stews as dull as their weather. They like thick, tasteless gravy made with dried 'granules' or stock cubes. Persian 'stews' are delicate and nutritious, infused with a multiplicity of subtle flavours, freshly chopped herbs, spices and tenderly cooked meat.

I missed my sister, the lovely Bahar, but there were many relatives and friends to meet, including some beautiful cous-ins – fine-boned creatures with long, shiny, blue-black hair, and big, almond-shaped eyes stolen, as I mentioned earlier, from gazelles. Of course, this is a poetic interpretation – just like we refer to Hafez as the 'nightingale' of Shiraz. Every now and then one or more of the girls would get up and dance. Persians love dancing; through it we give expression to our unique culture. I danced too as dancing comes naturally to Persians, old or young. We drank soft drinks and *chaii*, of course, but nothing stronger. I did think about Alice that night, wondering how she was, but I had lost touch with her soon after gradua-tion. Momentarily my tongue remembered both her lips and the burning whisky she put before me in the pub in Oxford but the memory of both evaporated in the happiness of the moment.

When I went to bed I found the sultry heat oppressive. I

did not sleep well. Nor did I pray that night although I know my mother earlier had taken out her little prayer mat. Instead, I looked up, just as I had done in my childhood, at the night full of stars. Even if each star represented one human being on the Earth, there would be countless billions of stars left over, including every ancestor who ever lived. As well as the stars, most nights had the moon, not like I imagined they were in dark Africa, full or gibbous moons hanging luminous over jungle or savannah like a fat yellow eye, but silver slivers of crescent moons, young and fresh, clear as water, virginal and lovely.

Forgetting the unknowable before long, I began to wonder why my uncle had sent me to find the 'family tree'. Perhaps he wanted to show me how illustrious our family had been because I knew he had talked of several 'khans', or leaders, who had become powerful overlords. One had three hundred men in his charge, a brigand-like figure, while another was said to have been the governor of a province and he didn't just have four wives, he had at least forty. Perhaps it was all the fault of Genghis Khan, since one in every two hundred men alive today is his relative (his wives numbered over one thousand). Genghis Khan had the choice of the most beautiful women, captured as spoils of war, and he reserved these bounties for himself. It was just as well I did not mention this to the imam in Cowley Road.

The next morning my mother packed a lunchbox for me; sandwiches made with local *paneer* (cheese), fresh tomatoes (*goje farangi*) and cold chicken (*joojeh*). I had decided not to return home after visiting my uncle's house but to make my way back to Tehran, and get a direct flight to Paris. My old leather suitcase and rucksack were both filled with gifts of food from my mother; pistachio nuts and lemons from our garden, slices of freshly cooked *ghormeh sabzi* wrapped in foil, two moist chunks of *kuku* (egg and herb fritter), and a plastic container brimming with *khoresh bademjan*.

My throat tightened as I embraced my mother. 'Mohammad,' she cried, 'Mohammad, *joon-am*', and in words I translate to English, 'May god go with you, my dearest, my best, my darling son! *Khoda hafez! Khoda hafez!*'

'*Muma*,' I cried, kissing her, '*Dooset daram, Muma! Khoda hafez!*' I told her to look after my little sister, my *khahar kuchulu*, next time she came home. Sometimes I called my mother Mama but usually only if I was very upset.

My mother was crying, tears running down her cheeks. As I turned back to wave goodbye, if I had known – yes, if I had known – I would have rushed back to hold her once more. I never saw her again.

Not far from our house I hailed a passing taxi, remarking to myself at the time that it was much as I might have done in London or Oxford except that there were two other people already inside with the driver. I guessed they must have been heading towards Bandar-e Anzali because when I told the driver where I was going he nodded in agreement without demur. My fellow passengers were not very talkative, acknowledging my presence with little more than a flicker of an eyelid, the lifting of an eyebrow. One of the passengers was a middle-aged man, with a pot belly and a week's growth of beard, who languorously flicked worry beads between the fingers of his left hand.

The other passenger, a younger woman, wore a full-length black *chador*, her face revealing two smoulderingly dark eyes. Inexplicably, as I closed my eyes, preparing myself for the journey to my uncle's house, the mysterious eyes and dark clothing of the woman suddenly became a gigantic black beetle. The Iranian woman had metamorphosed herself in my mind into a weird ghostlike apparition of Gregor Samsa, sitting next to me, that is, before he became too large to fit in his room.

Luckily, this reverie, which I fully admit shocked me, came

to an end the moment the young woman turned in my direction, her large black eyes charged with gentle inquisitiveness. She asked me how I was. '*Haleh shoma chetor ast?*'

'*Man khoobam, merci,*' I replied.

'Welcome,' she said quietly, switching to English. 'Are you from Bandar-e Anzali?' The freshness and directness of her enquiry took me by surprise. I expect I blushed the same colour as the Pink Mosque. I decided not to label her as *foozool*, which in my language means a nosy person. (We also refer to such a person as *nokhode har ash*, someone with a chickpea in every soup.)

'No. I'm originally from Rasht, but as the bird flies that is only 25 kilometres away. I have an uncle who lives in Bandar-e Anzali, well actually, he stays in Paris now but keeps a house there. I am going to visit it today.'

The woman smiled, as if appreciating my candour. 'Is your uncle famous?'

The man with the worry beads stopped his incessant fiddling as if wanting to overhear. 'No,' I laughed, 'he's not famous but he is well known in the groves of academe.' The woman seemed puzzled by my remark so I continued. 'He is notable for his work as a marine biologist, and as a professor. He knows absolutely *everything* about caviar, about the life history of the sturgeons in the Caspian Sea.'

'Oh,' she responded. 'That's amazing.' Then she said, 'I think I know him. The professor...but I forgot his name.'

'Dr Amin Arvani,' I replied proudly.

'Exactly him,' she said, excitedly. 'I have met him.'

'You mean Dr Arvani?'

'Yes. His house is near mine. He always used to visit when he needed something for his kitchen.'

'Truly the world is a small place,' I responded.

'Yes, she said, '*Damet ghan!*' (A Persian expression of agreement.)

A short time after we arrived in Bandar-e Anzali. The driver followed the woman's directions so that, quite magically to me, the taxi soon pulled up outside my uncle's house. I took out my old suitcase from the boot, thanked the driver, whereupon there was some discussion about payment but it was resolved after a little haggling. My woman friend stepped out with me, saying her house was near enough.

We walked together for a few steps, when she suddenly said, 'You can go now. You are home.' I thanked her profusely and promised to visit her before I left.

In a courtyard behind my uncle's house, which was of moderate size and shuttered up – a pity I thought since an agreeable prospect of the Caspian Sea was visible in the distance – I found an old man sitting in a chair. I dread to think how old he was as his hair was whiter than the snows on the mountains to the north of Tehran, like Mount Damavand in winter, and his eyes were cloudy with cataracts. Yet, I also observed how nimbly his fingers worked a set of *tasbih*, or worry beads, so there was still some life left in the old fellow.

'*Salaam!*' the old man cried. '*Khosh-amad*' or welcome. Without a moment's hesitation, he handed me a rusty key, beckoning to the front door of my uncle's house. As soon as I gingerly stepped inside, I was greeted by the smell of books, piled in rows. I like that smell, dusty pages contriving to outlast time itself, if just for some decades. There were so many papers, box files, drafts I supposed, and most of them, as I pulled each down to ascertain my uncle's fondest thoughts, about fish. Not just fish, I mean, but that grandest and most noble object of desire, the sturgeon.

This royal fish, heralded by Greeks in their banquets with trumpets and flowers, twenty-four centuries past, valued for its exquisite, small black eggs remains treasure from the Caspian Sea. Black gold, best eaten with a wooden, or plastic, spoon (not metal) and consumed with ice-cold vodka, or so I am told. (*Red gold* describes the best Iranian saffron.) The consumption of alcohol with this black magic might invite the Devil to sup, though the Devil would sup remarkably well, I must only imagine, with the slippery cold vodka rinsing down the pearls of plenty – as I envisage they were so considered by the fishermen. 'By these eggs, you will feed your family.' Of course, I know that Jesus, Isa as we know him, fed five thousand people with five fish and two loaves – oh no, I think it was two fish and five loaves of bread. What matter? There were said to be twelve baskets of crumbs left over, that is, bits of bread and fish.

Why would anyone pick up all the broken bits except to make fish soup? I have in my short life decided not to question anything to do with religious belief. Jesus turned water, miraculously, into wine. That is truly a miracle, as I discovered later that wine is not so easily made from water. It is instead formed by what I now know to be beyond the wit of the old alchemists. For now I am saying nothing. Muhammad worked miracles too; he multiplied food, split the moon, and when he 'went abroad' in the desert and there was no water, either to drink or for ablutions, he caused wells to erupt. He spoke to the dead, healed the sick, and cured blindness, as Jesus did, just by his touch. Trees walked towards him, one supposes not grand old oaks or giant sequoias but date palms. 'Take up thy roots and walk,' he might have said, our Prophet, peace be upon him for ever.

Now that Arabian deserts are largely devoid of water sources, one wonders why Allah, or our great Prophet, chose wells to erupt for the sake of ablutions. There may have been camels in want of water. But, as I said before, nothing can be questioned, except within the purviews of Islamic scholars. Many Muslims say no one should question these things. In Shi'a texts I have listened to, praise is heaped upon peacocks in one sermon, though anyone who has had to listen to peacocks 'of an early morning' is likely to be severely tried for patience. The smallest bird, killed unnecessarily, will complain to God on the day of resurrection, which is described as 'nearing the end of time'.

What should one expect at the end of time? The Islamic (and Persian) scholar known as Imam al-Bukhari, who lived from 810 to 870 CE, and who claimed more women than men would be found in hell as they are always ungrateful to their husbands, narrated that a fellow Muslim reported, having heard the Messenger of Allah speak (peace and blessings be upon him), 'Allah, may he be blessed and exalted, will take hold of the earth and will roll up the heavens in his right hand, then He will say: "I am the Sovereign, where are the kings of the earth?"' Of course no scientist can confirm this. Even if Allah knows best, any scientist, not being a professed scoundrel or a scurrilous mountebank, would consider the Messenger of Allah to be talking out of his hat. I mean where does truth begin and flummery end?

At the second blowing of a trumpet, 'all creation from the beginning of time till the end of time' will be resurrected. There will be people standing around, not knowing what to do, and they will be naked, barefoot and uncircumcised. The first human to be given clothes on this day of resurrection, which lasts for 50,000 years, will be the prophet Abraham. Only after this day will a person be admitted to Paradise or cast into Hell. Naked men and women will not bother to look at each other (Aisha, one of Prophet Muhammad's wives, known as 'Mother of the Believers', asked this question, being concerned for modesty, one supposes). She was told that the situation for all humanity would be so grim that no one will have time to take any notice of naked women or uncircumcised men. I supposed this meant that a man who preferred not to have been circumcised might be content in the knowledge that all that was taken would be returned one day. It is most confusing, like life itself often is. Not for the first time have I held my hands up in despair. Anyway, Allah knows best.

For my part, I have to say that the idea of a 'Day of Judgment' is a gross fiction, a very gross fiction. In every culture, throughout history, ordinary folk have been averse to courts, where justice, of one sort or another was dispensed. They feared courts, feared to go anywhere near them. The clerical authorities used this motif of courts, retributory punisher par excellence, where 'the buck' or even the toman stops, to say that one day God himself would judge every human on earth, according to his works. No one could escape this final authority to be dispensed by the divine court on the very last day of all.

I think we each have to carry out own 'can', and whatever is inside each one, we alone are responsible, and must answer for alone. To be fully human, we must be our own masters, master of our souls. We are not slaves, and indeed in the national anthem of my late adopted country, we sang out that we should never, ever, be slaves. God will not say, 'Look at your can, what a mess inside. I gave you your can and look what you have done with it!'

The only last day anyone will ever know is the day or night when death comes. Everyone who has a life is under sentence of death. Every living thing that crawls or swims or flies has the same final fate. For the seed to find the egg how many chases, displays, fights and rutting there is, how much frantic, orgasmic coupling – for new life to begin – to create the next set of genes.

Much the same I fear to say is with the 'honour' of our dear Prophet, peace and blessings be upon him. I mean absurd notions of blasphemy, no doubt addressed by my dear old friend Voltaire. Of course the honour of our beloved Prophet is plain for all to see but we should not seek to silence by brute force a person holding their own opinions as to what constitutes honour or dishonour as invariably human weaknesses – being as they are – lead us to become judges in our own cause and blind us to the truth. Indeed, what is truth, as Pilate asked before Isa? Those who claim to know ultimate truths are not to be trusted.

All this haranguing of others, defending 'honour', stoning adulterers, beheading *kafirs* or unbelievers in extreme examples, is largely a complete waste of energy and time, and achieves nothing. Mobs citing moribund blasphemy laws on the streets of Pakistan, intent on killing men and women with their bare hands, are by their religious beliefs turned into mindless, bigoted cretins. The cross-worshippers believe in 'turning the other cheek', which is indeed valiant, and so improbable a method as to invite comparison with that most honourable of true knights – Don Quixote. And Isa's idea of whoever is without sin should cast the first stone is admirable, so much so that I wish our own dear Prophet – may Allah bless him and bring him peace – had thought of such an idea.

My eyes were then drawn to a somewhat primitive looking bureau. Inside no doubt was my quest. Fighting back the urge to look inside, I was overcome, naturally, by a desire first of all to refresh myself with a cup of black *chaii*. Inside my uncle's kitchen, I found some black looking tea leafs, aged and crumbly. I made the tea carefully with an old kettle with a whistle on the spout. I waited for it to brew. I glanced around my uncle's living room-cum-study, all dusted and clean but with no obvious signs that anyone had lived there recently. The tea satisfied

me, as it always does; the tea leafs had gained the maturity of
age; the taste hung on the edge between bitterness and satisfaction, with my thirst edging it in favour of the latter.

It was with trepidation that I made my way to the bureau
where, as my uncle had informed me, I would find our family tree. Of course they are but names on a piece of parchment
or paper. Yet all of those ancestors had lived, much as I do,
and as everyone else, but these names were personal because
their genes had touched me, or bits of them, through all their
long struggles and triumphs in every generation. How far could
one go back? I feel certain some of them were horsemen in
the steppes of Asia, others merchants on the golden road to
Samarkand. Go back further and perhaps Alexander had swept
through some part of Persia. For all I knew he might have rav-
ished a girl, as lovely as my mother when she was like a green
shoot, or in Sappho's example, like a red apple on the topmost
branch that somehow the invader finally managed to reach, and
topple into his arms.

I believe that Donne, a poet of some renown in Britain, was
right. Love's mysteries, yes they grow in souls but the book,
where things are written, is the body and its miraculous issues
too. These codes are like locked libraries that only scientists
know how to open. In the midst of this reflective musing, I suddenly recoiled – as if I had found a truth, discovered a reality
just as that man, whoever he was, who unlocked the Rosetta
Stone. Actually I felt a sigh of relief. Relief that 'beliefs' and
'creeds' cannot follow down genetic lines. One might be born
'irretrievably' Catholic, or Muslim, Christian or Jew. There
would be no escape. Imagine if that baggage – I can find no
other more apt word – if that baggage survived in genetic cod-
ing. One might be called to prayer subconsciously whilst still
asleep; feel an urge to decorate an altar tapestry, fall in front

of a cross, or worship an elephant. Man might be made in the image of God, as the cross-worshippers allege, but oh so luckily man's genes were his alone, and not God's. But of course God has no genes.

Which is probably just as well. There would be no free human choice, or free will, although the latter is very intangible, since most humans are slaves to one kind of system or another, even if they don't realise it. Some people, I know, would demur at my uncle's primitive bureau. I think it was roughly made from local wood, and had not been attended to by a master of carving such as Mr Grinley Gibbons or Mr Thomas Chippendale – well known for his chairs and tables, designing in mid-Georgian, English Rococo and Neoclassical styles that have, all of them, never seen 'the light of day' in Iran, except in rare collections made by such spendthrifts as the Shah.

It might seem that I have spent too long describing this old bureau. It was just that I was struck by the simple expression – 'of wood'. How it can be shaped, using its intrinsic qualities. Moulded, even, as that poet said (one of his translators), 'nearer to the heart's desire'. Actually, no one read Omar Khayyam's poems in our household. None of us knew that he was a great mathematician, a solver of quadratic and cubic equations, and undertook a three-month journey to Samarkand when he was just 20. He was remembered for his longing for 'A book of verses underneath the bough', and a 'jug of wine, a loaf of bread' and the person he was with, or God, that was paradise enough.

Hence, we did respect the man, because his legend in Persia has always been strong, but of his wine-bibbing or supping, we disapproved. Allah dislikes alcohol; I mean our great Prophet advised against it. As a consequence of prohibitions on alcohol use, many Muslims chew khat leaves instead.

I began to reflect further, on things of the soil. We are in the habit of saying things like, 'He is the salt of the earth', just as Isa or Jesus declaimed to fishermen. He also talked of sowing seed on good or stony ground, and what happens if you choose the former over the latter or vice versa: things that grow from the earth, like wood (trees), plants, grass, fruit, and vines – a vineyard being so often a metaphor of plenty in the literature of the Christians. Isa also said that he was 'the true vine', which is really an extraordinary thing to say.

Of course it is true to say that the cross-worshippers have some extraordinary beliefs too, such as transubstantiation. By this, the bread and wine offered during Mass undergo a change in substance or essence, and become by 'an unknown mystery' the *body* and *blood* of Christ, although the bread and wine still retain their normal appearances. The cross-worshippers of the Roman Catholic persuasion take their faith ever further by crossing themselves with the mark of the cross at every opportunity, almost as one might say in English, 'at the drop of a hat'.

I wondered about things that grow from the earth, all the fruit and the crops; how real these living things were, directly connected to the soil. Man strides over the loam, and often thinks nothing of it, though his ashes may be scattered there eventually.

So it was with the bureau, fashioned by human hand yet ultimately born, made, from the earth.

Ten

I OPENED THE BUREAU. LUCKILY IT WAS UNLOCKED, SO I DID not need to ask the housekeeper for a key. The hinged sides opened smoothly to reveal what I supposed was the writing desk that my uncle had used to pen his various theses on *Acip-enseridae* – the family of sturgeons with its 27 species. I know of course that you don't want to hear about sturgeons – why should you? What matters is the life now, with fish, without fish. Could I beg you to listen just a little more? We Iranians are not so proud we cannot beg anything, especially the hearing of a story. But sometimes a Persian is too proud to ask even for a hair that drops from the head of the beloved. Nothing moves a Persian when his mind is made up. He will not alter his position for all the gold you offer. We are so proud, we will die for the sake of it. We think we are stronger than mountains. The gods know us for that. Man is a god some say, especially for the cross-worshippers because they believe man is made in his image – but a Persian God, think on that!

I know you've heard similar before. But try me. *I am Persian!* My heart – it's made of gold! Of course not literally but in the deep well of the most noble of human emotions. I can bring you riches, wealth beyond the facile, the fanciful – you can keep your dreams of El Dorado. *I am Persian!* Destiny is in our Persian genes. From the beginning. So hear me out while

I tell you about these monsters in the deep Caspian. Then you will know my uncle's work.

This extraordinary fish can live for 100 years or more, and has an evolutionary history dating back to the Triassic era, more than 200 million years ago. Some beluga sturgeons found in the Caspian Sea, if indeed there are any such leviathans left, may be 18 feet long and weigh 2000 kg (4400 lb). My uncle must have known more about this fish than just about anyone after studying them for forty years but standing at my uncle's desk, I knew the sturgeons in the Caspian Sea were at that moment the very least important thing to me, even though I felt captivated by such a miraculous survivor. Where was it – 'the scroll' of characters to whom I was related?

When I spread the scroll open after discovering it rolled up at the back of the bureau, it seemed such a small affair, about a foot wide, and just slightly larger in height. I counted some eighty names in neat, black lettering. I soon saw I had aunts, uncles, cousin after cousin, great aunts, great grandfathers, and great grandmothers and there he was, right at the top of the tree – Ghorbali Khan!

He was, to me, the fabled leader of a political movement fighting against invading communists. He had taken to the hills, the 'jungle' in some mountainous area to the north with about three hundred men armed with ancient rifles. All that is left now of this great warrior is his name on the family tree, and a black and white photo of him standing proudly with a rifle at his side, wearing shiny black boots. On his head is perched a tall, brim-less black hat, made from Persian wool. Scanning the names at the foot of the page, a sudden chill came over me. My uncle had left no male heirs. Of the related male lineages, I was the latest and the last! Upon my shoulders rested the continuation of our little 'family dynasty'.

I felt so proud of my ancestors! I had no idea then how much this ancient scroll mattered to me or what was my uncle's real intention in asking me to retrieve it for him. I paused while I felt a shiver and a silent tingling beneath my scalp. It was my future I was making but I didn't know in what way. I would press on, I resolved, until all became clearer. With great care I rolled up the scroll of names, putting it back inside its cardboard holder.

A knock on the front door roused me from the reverie of my ancestors. It was the old man I had met in the courtyard earlier. Standing behind him was the woman I had met in the taxi. After the usual pleasantries of meeting, she stood in front of me holding a bowl of soup. I knew what it was – *ash reshteh* – made with herbs, beans, and noodles, sometimes called 'builder's soup'. It fills you up quickly and afterwards it is hard to move far from one's chair.

'*Aali ye*', I said. '*Kheili mamnoon.*' I told her the soup was wonderful, thanking her.

'Just like your mother makes, I am hoping,' she said, smiling like one of those cats, said to come from a county in the northwest of England.

'*Befameh,*' I said. Come inside.

'Please eat,' she implored, 'while it is hot.' Despite asking her to stay, the woman, whose eyes I noticed were like two black coals, no that can't be right; I mean they glowed in a way I suppose that a gazelle's might if it had lingered by a fire, so that its eyes were so burnished by the flames of the fire that they too were lit in return – this gazelle of a neighbour whose name I didn't even know had blessed me with the gift of her soup – moved towards the door, excusing herself for interrupting me! Oh, we Persians have the politeness of princes in our blood. In a moment she was gone, and I sat down to eat a rather lonely meal but after a few spoonfuls I felt my insides warming, and after finishing the delicious soup fell fast asleep on my uncle's bed.

In the morning I awoke refreshed. I dreaded to think what it must be like for those poor people so addicted to alcohol that they awoke with sore heads. I believe they describe the sensation as being 'hung over', something I had never experienced, and praise Allah, hoped I never would. By this time I seemed to have stopped daily prayers in the direction of Mecca – or even any other direction. I found no harm in simple prayers expressed with a contrite heart. Allah I felt would not mind to any great extent. Of course it is possible I am entirely mistaken in this belief but I proposed to take my chances. For such slight error I hoped I would be confined to the edges of the great pit of blazing fire, *Jahannam,* singed rather than burnt alive. I had to commend the present Pope, whose titular names include 'Bishop of Rome, Vicar of Jesus Christ, Successor of the Prince of the Apostles, Supreme Pontiff of the Universal Church, Primate of Italy, Archbishop and Metropolitan of the Roman Province, Sovereign of the Vatican City State, Servant of the servants of God,' and so forth, for reportedly saying he did not believe in hell. So much for the great pit of burning fire! He suggested that the souls of bad people don't end up in hell – they 'simply disappear', which is remarkably convenient. If there is no hell, is there no *Jannah*?

Thanks to Milton, the English have a word, Pandæmonium, for a place in the middle of hell where all the cursèd demons live. This is the grand palace built by Satan – 'the high capital of Satan and all his peers'.

The Pope announced recently that capital punishment is 'unacceptable in all cases'. One thinks of that proverbial English phrase, 'the pot calling the kettle black'. Think of the legions of people tortured, burnt, and executed by the Catholic pre-Reformation state, and in Protestant countries of Europe. The Church considers it has a duty to inveigh against moral shortcomings but, as nearly all the old shibboleths have passed away or been debunked in recent history, there is little else left for the Church to set its sights on.

It is very odd, now I come to think about it, that this idea of mine of being singed rather than burnt I put down almost entirely to the English education I had so fortuitously gained through my studies. Being at heart a Persian but also 'an Oxford man', I surmised, had not led to conflicts of interest. Instead I had gained a broader view of things, or so I believed. A rounded education at Oxford had the effect of opening more 'windows' in one's reckonings of life, in the imagination, and in the essence of more restrained, if no less logical, thought.

We Persians are almost too enthusiastic about many things in life, like the Greeks. Being rational is not part of it. The only reason we sometimes appear rational is that so often we so precisely dig down to the heart of the matter, to the very essence of the thing under discussion, that we appear to be nearest the truth. The ancient Persians had one remarkable rule of government. If an important decision was taken when sober, it had to be reviewed once more when drunk, and vice versa. The motion passed if the general consensus was accepted in both states. Of course Allah would have disapproved of such behaviour though its empirical validity cannot be questioned.

Before I let this pass, let me say Persians sometimes can have too much pride. Frequently as a boy I used to remind myself of great King Xerxes who built a bridge over what was called 'the Hellespont' for his army to cross. A storm came, whipping up waves, which destroyed the bridge before it was finished. The king ordered the sea be punished. The chief engineers were beheaded and his soldiers instructed to lash the sea three hundred times. He also demanded that chains or fetters be thrown in the sea as if to restrain it. The soldiers were to abuse the sea while whipping it, and some of these words were recorded by the historian Herodotus, such as, 'Bitter water, our master thus punishes you, because you did him wrong though he had done you none. Xerxes the king will pass over you, whether you want it or not…'

I had to clear my mind of this matter. How could I go through life being worried about being thrown into a burning cauldron of fire just for *not* praying to Allah? I decided to walk down to the lake and offer up a prayer there. A lake! *Haha*, as my friends say in England. It's no wonder it is called a 'sea' – being the largest lake or inland sea in the world by area, bounded by Kazakhstan, Russia, Azerbaijan, Iran, and Turkmenistan. It has about one third the salinity of sea water, inflow from over 130 rivers, a shoreline length of 4300 miles, covers an area of 143,200 square miles, and until the 1970s you could find Caspian tigers roaming its shores. Because of shifting tectonic plates and falls in sea level it became landlocked over five million years ago. So many birds live there – including exotic white pelicans, bee eaters, flamingos, sea eagles and the weaving, tumbling swifts and swallows.

Before I let this pass, I have a problem with my country's 'authorities'. They seem to imagine there is a spy under every tuft of grass. 'Spies' are everywhere – and this includes conservationists in Iran who have an interest in preserving the wildlife – just like you will find around the Caspian Sea. A number of these innocent scientists are now in prison, charged with 'sowing corruption on earth'. What was their crime? Using camera traps. These essential tools of science help the study of endangered species worldwide yet the conservationists, including Niloufar Bayani, who was studying endangered Asiatic cheetahs in Iran by following their tracks, face the death penalty for 'undermining the national security interests of Iran'. If you have the misfortune to be detained in the infamous Evin Prison, you might decide it's better to commit suicide – like prominent Iranian-Canadian environmentalist Kavous Seyed-Emami. Who do you believe? Iran's paranoid judiciary or his family, who reject the idea of his suicide as a blatant lie and cover-up. There are other dual nationals locked up in my country for no good reason, as is true of Nazanin Zaghari-Ratcliffe but there is not space to name them all, and in any case I must continue with my story.

But just a moment! Nasrin Sotoudeh, 55, is a fine, decent, intelligent Iranian woman who works as a human rights lawyer offering legal counsel to women charged with removing their headscarves (*hijab*) in public. In 2019 a newly appointed judge, perhaps anxious to make his mark in more ways than one, sentenced her to a total of 38 years in prison *and 148 lashes*. The charges included 'inciting corruption and prostitution', 'openly committing a sinful act by...appearing in public without a *hijab*', and 'insulting supreme leader Ayatollah Ali Khamenei'. I think that judge should be brought before a court and sentenced to be publicly lashed for making such a stupendously absurd, inhumane and obscene judgement. The mullahs just don't like an intelligent woman with the courage to stand up, think on her feet, and 'speak truth to power'.

The walk to the shoreline took me about fifteen minutes. As I walked towards the lake, the size became apparent. It just filled everything except the sky and the land I was standing on. The shore was rocky with sparse and scrubby vegetation. I took off my sandals and walked up to my knees in the water. In no way was it anything like a lake; it had the majesty of seas, a huge impenetrable presence that opened to allow me to stand in it, and it moved against my skin as if it were alive, a being of immensity and power.

If I wanted to offer a prayer to Allah, I thought I could use the water surrounding me for *wudhu*. The water had to be *mutlaq* (pure and unmixed), clean and *mubah* (lawful) – this is, either I was the owner of the water or I had permission to use it. I certainly did not own the Caspian Sea but I felt it 'belonged' to me, if only for sentimental reasons but I decided that I had not broken the existing *wudhu* from my earlier one that same morning, so I was okay to pray without making it again – no discharge from the genitals or anus, touching the genitals or falling asleep. I had not fainted or become intoxicated, had not bled from a wound or touched a wet dog.

I said two short prayers, one in Arabic and one in English. The first was Surat Al-Ikhlas (Qur'an 112), which begins '*Bismil-laah irrahmaan irraheem/Qui hoo Allahu ahid*'…In English:

> In the name of God, Most Gracious, Most Merciful
> Say: He is Allah, the One and Only!
> Allah, the Eternal, Absolute;
> He begotteth not nor is He begotten,
> And there is none like unto Him.

My second was:

> Righteousness is not that we turn our faces to the east
> and west; but Righteousness is that one believes in Allah
> and the Last Day and the angels and the Book and the
> Prophets…Ameen.

I promise you at that moment I began to cry. Is it not complicated being a human being? The full sea in front of me, even if it was only lake water, the Caspian Sea had brought me to this. There was this great body of water, coursing this way and that, alive with fish, seals, birds, gazelles on many of the small islands, yet I was worried if I had sufficiently cleaned behind and inside my ears, because if I had not done so properly, I would have failed in my attempt to offer pleasure to Allah. Suddenly, these archaic rituals seemed trivial. I cried because of the complicated nature of human existence. I had begun to hate proscriptions. When I was a child growing up in my village I know that some small girls were beaten for swimming in the Caspian Sea; not so much for swimming but for swimming either on the wrong day or in the part reserved for men. One small girl was beaten so severely that she was paralysed.

For the sake of that small girl, whose 'sin' was to bathe in the part of the lake reserved for men only, and whose name I do not know but know that she was cruelly hurt and maimed by religious piety, I decided to exact my revenge. I tore off my clothes, all of them, and ran into the water. I would swim for her, and to hell with piety, I would swim as naked as Adam. Regrettably, there was no one there to arrest me.

When I emerged from that water, an unangry and still glimmering sea, I felt as if my whole body had been cleansed, not just my body either but the soul or spirit within me. I was made new. Henceforth, I decided – as much as it is possible to decide anything in this life – to look at my existence on earth from an aspect not so concerned with the religious dimension. I would continue to offer prayers to Allah but on my terms. I would attempt to be more sanguine in spirit, to accept slings and arrows of misfortune gladly if they came my way, and principally abandon the idea of being negatively dictated to by a fictional deity. No longer would I view prayers through the closed prism of obligation (*fard*). As for *Fajr*, *Dhuhr*, *Asr*, *Maghrib*, and *Isha'a* (the five daily obligatory prayer times of dawn, midday, afternoon, sunset, and night), I should by their abandonment become an unholy sinner fit only for the great pit of fire. Anyway as a Shi'a, I was only abandoning two of the five daily prayers, and allowing myself leeway on the other three.

At the same time, my life took on an aspect of urgency. What on earth was I doing swimming naked in the Caspian Sea? It was time to get on with the business of living, and I supposed this meant I had to find work to make my life liveable, viable. I thought it was good to have something real in life – not only dreams. Without wasting any more time, back at my uncle's house I packed my clothes, took the precious scroll my uncle had asked for, and locked up the house. The old man was still sitting outside with his *tasbih*. The woman who had so kindly brought me some soup was a slight problem, as I was unsure exactly where she lived, so I gave the old man the house key, and the clean bowl, and asked him to return it to whichever neighbour it might be. I think, *inshallah*, he would have known its owner.

By the way, the prayer beads usually have 33 or 99 beads, because of one Hadith that calls on Muslims, after prayer, to repeat short phrases, like '*Subhanallah*' (Glorious is God) 33 times, as this pleases Allah especially if one carries on throughout the day. One might also try '*Al-hamdu li-llah*' (Praise be to God) 33 times, and *Allahu Akbar* (God is Great) another 33 times, making 99 in all, just like the names of Allah, peace and blessings be upon him. The scholars have written much about whether it is better to use the fingers, most saying it is better to use the fingertips to count, as one might be showing off with an expensive set of beads, and using beads or *tasbih* can allow the mind to wander. You can use left or right hand but it is better to use the right hand. Personally I prefer the Greek way of using their *komboloi*, solely for relaxation, fidgeting and quiet reflection and, dare I say it, not just pandering to please Allah.

Six hours later I was back in Tehran, my flight to Paris booked for later that day. Wandering outside the airport, I was surprised to see how busy the streets were – but no dogs, as it is forbidden to walk them in Tehran's parks or public spaces, and if you drive a dog around in your car you will be arrested if caught. I think there was a political meeting of some sort going on because there were several groups of women holding up posters of the President of Iran, Hassan Rouhani. Most of them wore dark chadors; many covered these with loose black coats that we call a *monto* in Farsi. I confess that their appearance was more like a gathering of black ghosts. Women also wearing glasses were the most forbidding of all, as if their eyesight had shortened from too much studying of our beloved Qur'an. I do not like the colour black, always reminiscent to me of the funereal, the dismally sombre, the darkling night which extinguishes light – and hope, though I do not mind and actually quite admire the blackness of jet, Tahitian pearls, black sapphires, black zircon, opal, and onyx, all mineral-like objects created in the cauldron of earth. Black is legitimate for extreme grief and loss but to dress women in black for the sake of religious piety is demeaning, like covering a lily with dross.

If any Iranian says he likes leaving his country, he is surely lying. No one really ever *likes* leaving the bosom of home. In Iran, there was once a great Persian prophet named Mani, who posited a dualistic view of the world. He believed there was an eternal struggle between the light of the spirit and the darkness of the material world – like a battle between good and evil. Manichaeism has long since fallen out of favour but the struggle goes on. Politics and power mean that some are forced to leave their own countries and seek asylum elsewhere to escape persecution, and even death. Sometimes there is no option but to try to escape one's homeland in order to find a better way of life. Exiles must bear the pain of homesickness. Yet citizens of numerous countries are not free to leave, and in any case can be subjected to lengthy 'travel bans', restricting free movement for many years. Indeed if they try to flee abroad, they are often forcibly kidnapped, on the flimsiest of false charges, and brutally 'returned home' – like Skeikha Latifa al-Maktoum, an Emirati princess, a prisoner in her own home. On a previous escape attempt in 2003 her father Sheikh Mohammed, the ruler of Dubai, allegedly had her beaten and held in prison for three years. And the same father, on a separate matter, wrote that he preferred to follow the instructions of Prophet Muhammad, who said: 'A wolf only eats sheep that leave the flock.' Happily she is alive and safe but she has effectively been silenced from taking part in any public debate.

One thing that really matters to the princess is the human right to have 'freedom of choice'. To lead a prescriptive life – to be forced to live a prescriptive life – does not amount to freedom.

II

Eleven

The freshness of Paris made me lightheaded. I noticed people walking very freely, dressing gaily, and generally exhibiting an elegance of living one would not find either in Oxford or Tehran. I believe the French word that fits this idea is one that is often ascribed to the attributes of the great Frenchman Cyrano de Bergerac, namely, panache.

To tell you the truth, I could not wait to see my uncle. I owed him so much and I had really done little to deserve his continued support. His flat was minutes away from the Champs-Elysées, very tiny and on the top floor. I passed the concierge without incident and ran up a very long flight of stairs. When I reached my uncle's door I stopped to catch my breath. There was no 'flashback' of the earlier dreams I had when I imagined trying to push open the door against the horrid carapace of a metamorphosed Gregor Samsa.

I rang the bell and heard footsteps.

'*Monsieur Mohammad, mon brave!*' my uncle exclaimed on seeing me. 'You are welcome. Please, please come in.' He embraced me warmly.

'Uncle, I am pleased to report your house in Bandar Pahlavi, I mean Bandar-e Anzali, is kept well by your housekeeper.'

'Did you bring it?' he asked.

'Yes, Uncle. I have it.'

'Then bring it to my table. We will discuss.'

I followed but he insisted, like any good Iranian, that I go before him. My uncle had the same handsome features he had as a young man but he looked older, and even a little tired. Age is like a donkey that sits on your back and refuses to get off.

'Sit down,' he said with a voice that had not lost its strength. 'Have you rested?'

I said I had slept on the flight back.

'Are you sure?' he asked. 'Certain?'

'Yes, *Amujan*,' I said, reverting to Persian.

'Then you will be ready for lunch. We will eat first and discuss things after. Go and wash, leave your things in the bedroom next to mine.'

I did so, catching a glimpse of rooftops from the small window. I took the scroll from my suitcase, and carried it to the kitchen table.

'Leave it there,' he said, almost harshly, pointing to the sideboard. 'We will have the best *chelo kababs*, and salad.' There was a noticeable pause. 'Tell me, are you a good Muslim?'

I had not expected my uncle to bring up the subject so quickly.

'Perhaps I am, perhaps I am not,' I answered evasively. 'I have been going to *Namaz* less than usual. In fact, following some thought on the matter…'

'…I understand,' my uncle interrupted. 'There is no need to say more.'

In the short silence that followed I swear I could hear the *oiseaux rapide*, the swifts, over the Parisian rooftops. As they fly they scream like disembodied spirits. Actually, I think these swifts cry out to their friends, to use an old chestnut of a cliché, with simple *joie de vivre*, no prayers necessary, and no ablutions, other than rain from the sky gods. The change in my uncle's demeanour startled me. I had expected a lecture at the very least.

'You will find in the refrigerator a small dish for two. I have already opened the tin. Wait a moment – let me bring some bread, some butter.' My uncle placed these on the kitchen table, and I went to the fridge. One doesn't find too many black things in a fridge other than blackcurrant jam or blackberry jam, or jelly, and certainly never, ever, black pudding. I knew straightaway what it was, and perhaps it was from the Caspian Sea.

Caviar!

The precious pearls were not black, when brought out of the fridge but an olive, greeny, golden brown, with a hint of dark grey.

My uncle insisted the caviar sit on the table for just a minute or two and in that time, I saw his brow pucker up, as if considering a matter of some importance. 'Fetch two small glasses, Mohammad.'

I did so.

'To consume the finest beluga caviar, we must add what is necessary,' he said with unusual gravitas, 'nothing more, nothing less. Go to the freezer compartment.'

Again I did as I was told but could find nothing there, other than a few packets of dried fish, atop of which sat an enormous litre bottle, a plain bottle but with an unmistakeable label, which seemed to scream silently at me, if one can imagine such a thing. *Vodka!*

'In Iran,' he began, 'caviar goes with vodka and vodka goes with caviar, like…strawberries and cream. Or beef with horseradish. Rice and *chelo kabab*.' I digested this revelation in silence: My uncle, the martinet, had suddenly become more human than I had ever expected.

'Mohammad, fill the glasses!' he said. As I did so, my hand trembled slightly. I was trying to question him for this extraordinary change of character but he would not allow me to interrupt him. With a broad smile, he said, '*Salamati,*' my good nephew. 'Your health!' For the first time in months, I remembered Alice. I took the small glass of the cold vodka and 'downed it', as I had with Alice. My throat caught any breath there and held it. There was little taste, unlike the malt whisky, but it was seductively warming in a mild way.

'Delicious, Uncle,' I said, wishing that Alice could have seen me. The English have a quaint expression: 'Out of the frying pan and into fire.' *Jahannam* was coming for me!

'You see, Mohammad, when one Persian meets another, family especially, we must keep our customs. Please have another, while I bring the spoons.' With caviar, mother of pearl or glass spoons are recommended but my uncle said his plastic spoons were as good if not better – just avoid spoons made of metal as nothing must adulterate the flavour he said, and the eggs should be unbroken when placed in the mouth.

'Just take a small amount first, to savour. As I am sure you know, my dear nephew, let the caviar dissolve slowly on the tongue, with gentle pressure. Actually no, you crush the eggs between tongue and palate to create a small explosion of exquisite taste. I have made some small pieces of thin toast if you like.'

I tried a quarter-spoonful, dipping my spoon into the oily sheen of the tiny eggs with care, and exerting pressure between palate and tongue, as my uncle had said. It takes about twenty years for the female beluga sturgeon to mature enough to produce the roe. The processes the roe goes through after being 'stripped' from the fish number about twelve, all having to be made by a 'caviar master' in about fifteen minutes. The master taster and grader has to measure bouquet, colour, size, firmness and the like and then decide how much salt to add to ripen roe to caviar. Almost like a fine wine blender, or a tea blender, the expertise needed is formidable.

I was perturbed by the presence of vodka in my uncle's flat, yet I had to concede that it added piquancy to the taste of the caviar, as is the ancient custom not only in Iran but in Russia too. After lunch we sat down to the usual black *chaii*. I could see my uncle's eyes on the scroll and before long he got up to examine it. 'Mohammad Reza Erfani,' he said aloud to himself, 'born nineteen so and so…mother, father, sister…various relatives, your uncle, back and back and back…to the khans… and the great Ghorbali Khan.' Then he looked up at me. 'You know, I spent so many years studying fish, my head in books, papers, and I am still called to lecture to university students at the age of seventy…but I made so little time for family life. My wife died in a skiing accident. We had no children, and I never remarried.' I wondered what my uncle was pondering. 'My nephew, at the moment you are the only male heir bearing our family's name, *mashallah*. What do you intend to do with your life?'

The question stunned me. 'I know that, Uncle. I have no plans at present. It is not said to be so useful to have a degree in English even, as it will be, an MA from Oxford. I am not sure yet.'

'I think,' said my uncle in a firm voice, 'you need to find something to do. Years can pass and be wasted, and as they say, "The clock is ticking". Now you have your degree, I will not be able to support you much longer.'

'Yes, you are right,' I told my uncle. 'The question is what? I had presumed my time at Oxford, with its progressive and liberal ways of doing things would grant me, *inshallah*, a path to follow afterwards. Yet this doesn't seem to be materialising. I am certain I do not wish to become a schoolteacher, explaining

such things as Baudelaire's torments or Kafka's existentialist ordeals.'

My uncle stared at me. 'You will forgive me, my nephew, if
I say *merde alors!* Baudelaire and Kafka led desperate lives.
Wretched lives for the sake of a few words on paper. Poems of
licentiousness and novels explaining life as a nightmare.'

I began to feel uncomfortable.

'Fresh air – do you like it?'

'Of course, Uncle. I love it. In fact in Christ Church Meadow
and the nearby Botanical Gardens in Oxford I found respite...'

'...No more about Oxford, please, Mohammad! I am thinking of landscapes, such as you have never imagined. I went to
Oxford once and found the atmosphere oppressive. I know you
love it but you would benefit from a change of scenery. Wider
horizons beckon.' He still said the word 'wider' like an Iranian,
the '*w*' sounding more like a '*v*'.

By now I had begun to wonder just what my uncle was driving at. I hoped he did not have in mind working on a fish farm
breeding sturgeon.

'During my forty years here in Paris I have made many
friends. I am able to introduce you to a family, a family I have
known for half that time. There may be work there too, if you
put your heart into it.'

'Uncle,' I said, getting worried, 'if what you have in mind
is anything to do with fish, I would have to refuse.' My uncle's
balding head, I suddenly thought, was completely unfurrowed.
His domed forehead, holding so many secrets about the life of
sturgeons, showed no signs of his academic labours, the long
hours of lucubration.

'The purpose of life, I have realised all too late, is to have
children. They become the torchbearers for the next generation,
and those to follow. My dear nephew, you have chance to do

what I could not. You are young and good looking. You have prospects. The family I have in mind owns an estate near the Gironde estuary.'

At this I think my mouth must have dropped open. Perhaps my uncle knew a family there with a fish farm. All day long I would tend sturgeons perhaps, and then every now and then extract the black pearls after years of maturation. 'Uncle,' I said, raising my voice, 'I don't want anything to do with fish, even if you are a world renowned authority on Caspian beluga!'

My uncle merely smiled a half-smile, and then I knew it was not about fish. 'No, Mohammad, this is on dry land. Fertile, stony land given over to the production of small parcels of… which become changed into something, something our great poet Hafez would have praised!'

I guessed it was something to do with France. At the mention of Hafez, I began to get an inkling. It was not going to be about harvesting rose petals to make rose petal jelly, rose water, or running a fish farm. I did not need to be a divinator or a finder of Jamshid's sacred cup to understand that *wine* might be at the heart of the matter. Perhaps I was to be sent grape picking.

Twelve

I SAID I WAS CERTAINLY FREE TO UNDERTAKE SOMETHING NEW.

I did not hesitate. 'My dear Uncle, you have been so kind to me over the years. I am most willing to try.'

'Many years ago at university, I became friendly with the owners of the estate. Now it is owned by Madame Saintoissant. As the wife of Monsieur Saintoissant, ownership passed to her upon his death, which, regrettably, is only recent.

'It's not a big estate but still it takes many hands to run it, and her family is small – one daughter. They will need someone with brains, and strong enough to do other kinds of work. Let me be clear from the outset, this will involve things…things incompatible with our Muslim religion!'

'If it's about prayers, Uncle, I have lapsed. Whatever work I do would therefore not have to accommodate time for *Namaz* several times a day. Of course I pray to Allah in my heart, and our great Prophet, peace be upon him.'

My uncle lifted his face up and then down slowly, rolling his eyes too, a gesture that conveyed to me he had no interest in whether I sent my prayers to Allah. In fact, though formerly he had been strict, the secular life he followed in France seemed to have lessened his religious piety to a great extent.

'Nephew, I don't care whether you go to *Namaz* or not. I am not yet an apostate but as I have become older, some things

101

seem less important, less valid. I am concerned that *you* may have objections because of your upbringing.'

Once again my uncle paused, as if assessing my commitment.

'You can't afford to be too choosy in this life,' he said.

'Uncle, I could not agree more. The English have a very good word to describe such a view. Pernickety – fussy and fastidious.'

'I don't doubt it. The meaning of obscure words is not the reason why you were educated at Oxford University. No, I am talking about the big, fundamental issues. If Muhammad can't call the mountain, Muhammad must go to the mountain. We all have to adapt in life, and sometimes this means conflicts with our trusted beliefs. Today we had Iranian caviar but we also had vodka, which our Prophet would have roundly condemned.'

I assured my uncle that I had no regrets when it came to the vodka. In fact, it loosened my tongue somewhat so I blurted out, 'I have drunk whisky in Oxford and had relations there with a very pleasant English girl.'

My uncle's face showed surprise but nothing more, whereas I felt slightly ashamed of my conduct – until a sudden thought saved me from further abashment. If I were a sinner, Allah would count me among the very least of his problems. The amount of alcohol I had consumed at university was to be measured in billionths of millilitres compared, say, to the countless gallons of water flowing daily under Magdalen Bridge, and the Jeroboams of wine consumed at summer balls. As for the girl, a few kisses are hardly toxic to Islamic rules of sexual propriety.

'I think the problems stem from the sexualisation of everything that occurs between man and woman in our society.' I felt emboldened by this remark so I continued, my uncle listening intently. 'I see little harm in the occasional drink – certainly two or three vodkas should never be enough to condemn anyone to eternal punishment. In order to reach the heights of fanatical extremism there have to be bridges, stepping stones. Fundamentalist beliefs and attitudes are often the bridges that lead to extremism.'

I surprised myself by these remarks. Only a year or so before I had been an upright person of faith, willing to eschew alcohol in any of its hydra-headed manifestations, and premarital sex was high up on the *haram* list.

'The drunkard deserves no respect,' my uncle said sternly, in the manner of his old self. 'Britain is full of binge-drinking youths, I believe. They are almost proud of their drunken stupidity and worthless lives. Their women, brash street girls do the same on Friday nights! They want to ape the foolish males and get drunk together and lie in the gutters. Eventually the police arrest them. Never once do they think of their mothers at whose breasts they were succoured. They profane the air with their taunts and lewd propositions, and think nothing of crouching down shamelessly to urinate in the streets. Meanwhile the youths tear off their shirts and fight like demented idiots, knowing nothing except the most atavistic hatred for their fellow man, a hatred that erupts from their innermost selves like a fountain of distilled vitriol from the violent depths.'

My uncle's lucidity as I recollect it now was quite remarkable. I had not heard such a way with words since leaving Oxford. But he calmed down soon after. He sighed deeply. '*Irani hastam. Bebaksheed.*' My uncle said he was Iranian and that he was sorry for the outburst.

For a while we sat in silence, a silence broken only as it happened by the *oiseaux rapide* swinging past my uncle's flat, their screams calling out to me. 'I think you can be trusted,' my uncle said.

I did not understand what my uncle meant.

'You will go the vineyard,' he said, rather prophetically as I recall it now. 'You will help Madame Saintoissant with her estate. You will learn.'

It was my turn to feel all kinds of emotions welling up inside me. Vineyards meant vines and vines meant wine! The cultivation of vines and the making of wine were acts forbidden by the conservative clerics in my country. Yet I did not seem to care. Any kind of 'gainful employment', as long as it did not harm others or other living beings was to be welcomed. I could not earn my way in life by swimming naked in the Caspian Sea to avenge the paralysed young girl or by pointless musings. I had to become involved in the world!

'That is something I would welcome,' I told my uncle truthfully. What else was I to do? What else could I have done? If I could escape from having to teach in a fusty classroom, cataloguing the dolorous thoughts of Baudelaire or the chronically paranoid Kafka – though I supposed I could leave room for Coleridge's 'Kubla Khan' – I would be happy. I felt, strangely, as if my uncle were 'the man from Porlock', who interrupted Coleridge's reverie and his dream of the sacred river. But this 'interruption' was perhaps a key to a new life. My life would find a new reality and if it was to be with grapes, with vines, with the soil of the earth, with making and nurturing, I would openly choose that path.

And anyway, who can know the future? Sometimes it must be made. The Persian poet Nizami, whose full name we write as نظامی گنجوی, and who penned the beautiful story of Leyla and 'crazed' Majnun – as doomed in their love as Romeo and Juliet – wrote that '…the future is veiled from our eyes; the threads of each man's fate extend well beyond the boundaries of the visible world'.

The next day my uncle took me to the station. He also gave

me 500 euros, which I tried to refuse with a very weak effort. It was enough for the fare and would get me to Madame Saintoissant's home, the address of which he had carefully written out for me on one of his professional cards.

I embraced him and he wished me luck. I was about to burst into tears but he held my shoulders firmly, looked me in the eye, and told me that it was now up to me. '*Amujan*,' I said, 'I can never thank you enough. *Kheili mamnoon. Sharmande kardin.*' I had thanked him from the bottom of my heart.

With that, he turned with almost military precision and walked smartly away but after a few steps, he turned back to me, his face smiling, and he called out, 'Remember Ghorbali Khan! Don't forget him.'

Thirteen

I WATCHED MY UNCLE DISAPPEAR AMONG THE PEOPLE AT THE station until the last moment when I could see him no more. With my ticket bought, and waiting on the platform to board the SNCF train, I composed in my head an imaginary letter to my mother. 'I am standing on a platform at the Gare d'Austerlitz, Muma, and I am going to a new job here in France. I have a train ticket all the way to Bordeaux…let me read it…"Bordeaux Saint-Jean".' I stopped short when it came to mention of a vineyard, however.

The journey was just over four hours. I had time to reflect on the way, but the scenery distracted me most of the time, especially when the train followed the banks of rivers, skirted green forests, crossed more shining rivers, and stopped in cities en route. At Orléans I could not help thinking of the maid, La Pucelle d'Orléans. Although her hair was short, she did not feel obliged to cover it, except under a helmet, this brave woman burnt to death by the English for 'cross-dressing' and other heresies when aged only nineteen after her spectacular lifting of the siege of Orléans and still more victories over the English. Whatever god spoke to her in her visions, the advice she received was very effective. She rejected all heresies herself, and for her this included Islam, but I did not mind that. An illiterate peasant girl would have known little about the reality of our great Prophet, peace be upon him. I cannot hold that against her. How discomfiting it must have been to endure a private inspection to determine her virginity. It was believed that if Joan was a virgin she could not have made any pact with the Devil.

As for the cruel duplicities of the English at her trial, in Iran we have an expression to describe this. When the English want to dispose of an enemy, they kill them very slowly with *cotton wool* round their necks. Even if it takes thirty years, they get you in the end and you'll never notice it until it is too late! *La Perfide Albion…*

When I alighted from the train, I felt as if I had already begun a new life. If only I had known more about Bordeaux at that time, I would have stopped longer to see something of the city, like the palatial Place de la Bourse and the mighty Garonne, a river as stately as the Thames but almost 160 miles longer.

Only minutes from the station the aromas of newly baked bread from the *boulangeries*, freshly ground coffee, and a melange of olfactory delights invited the idea of a market full of cornucopias but to all these I dare not succumb for a moment. All I wanted was to get to the address my uncle had given me. I got a taxi. We were soon out of Bordeaux heading north. After a drive of about twenty miles the scenery dramatically changed – rows upon rows of vines, occasional clumps of tall trees hiding large houses behind tree-lined drives – chateaux I suppose they were – until we reached Margaux village. It was very quiet.

A few shops were open selling wine! This felt to me like stepping into the unknown. I knew that the imam I met briefly in Oxford would be 'turning in his grave' at the thought of so much potential for producing alcohol. The value of Bordeaux wine each year I discovered is in the region of two billion euros, with some 900 million bottles awaiting a thirsty mouth.

When I ran over these figures in my mind, I felt as if I needed to sit down. A rusty old blue chair outside a wine shop was vacant so I almost crumpled into the seat. So much wine! Enough to quench the Blazing Pit of Fire, I thought, to a great extent. If, as the imam had suggested, taking one mouthful would mean the angels, the prophets and the righteous believers would send down their curses, the air must have surely been blue, beyond Caspian Sea blue, with their imprecations. There would be time for nothing else but a perpetual stream of curses. As for the sins committed as a result of drinking alcohol, the Pit of Blazing Fire would be full to overflowing (admittedly a paradox).

I decided to offer up a prayer to Allah for forgiveness. Allah has ninety-nine names and whoever memorises all his names, and is mindful of them, will enter *Jannah* or Paradise. I could not recall all of them, however, so I began badly. To pray day and night and constantly ask Allah for forgiveness regarding the repentance of sins, that is what my mother told me as a child. Unfortunately, I did not know any prayers to petition Allah to forgive others (for consuming all that wine) but I know there must be prayers for that purpose.

'Allah! Forgive us our sins and efface our bad deeds and take our souls in the company of the righteous…Allah! We have sinned against ourselves and unless You grant us forgiveness and bestow Your mercy upon us, we shall most certainly be lost.'

All the prayers we offer to Allah are supposed to please him, though he has no need himself of our prayers. The closest we are supposed to get to Allah is reputed to be in the act of prostration, in prayer. In fact, our great Prophet, peace and blessings be upon him, taught that the first of all a man's deeds in this life for which he will be called to account on the Day of Resurrection will be his prayers. If a believer has conducted his prayers according to the Islamic laws, he will be safe and successful;

but if not – if a man is defective in his prayers – he will be unfortunate and a loser.

At that moment the sun came through into the square in Margaux village. I forgot about praying. As there are almost two billion Muslims in the world today, Allah might be sick of listening, especially times five a day times 365 days a year. Shrugging off any need for further prayers, I set off in the direction of Madame Saintoissant's estate, after an old man with about three teeth and a typical Breton hat had without hesitation pointed the road to take at the mention of '*Monsieur, excusez-moi mais je cherche la maison du Madame Saintoissant.*' He watched me I thought with some curiosity as I thanked him and marched off. I had by this time dispensed with the old leather suitcase. I was travelling light with just my rucksack. It now seems extraordinary that one could possess so few belongings and need so little other than the clothes I was wearing and a few dozen euros. But such is the courage and audacity of youth.

I was so excited at the prospect of my 'new life' that I felt no hunger. A fountain in the town had supplied me with fresh water. After each quarter mile or so, I imagined being a Roman soldier, a redoubtable legionary, marching all day to reach the next camp. I counted the quarter miles and the half miles, and then the miles, all very approximately. By mile five, or eight kilometres at a guess, I was still feeling relatively fresh, and after ten miles, I felt I could go on all day, and I even supposed this might have been how the great Ghorbali Khan had marched in Persia almost a hundred years before, excepting for the fact that he had three hundred men under his command, and I was there on the road, completely on my own and had neither gun, nor boots, nor his black hat made from Persian wool.

I saw the sign. I can't tell you what it read, just as I could not reveal the name of my Oxford college. Some writers suffer unjustly and are punished for writing truthfully when others have their own idea of the truth. One man's truth is another man's lie. For the sake of Madame Saintoissant, whose name appeared on the bottom of the sign as 'Propr. Émile Saintoissant' (her late husband), I cannot reveal it. Instead I will choose 'Chateau La Comtesse de Margaux', for it was an estate in the Margaux area, and still is.

On arriving at a place of some stature, of some standing in the wine region of Bordeaux, there is a sense of history, of continuity, of worth. It is more than a sense of place. I felt humbled by the long drive towards a distant prospect of a chateau crowning a small elevation of land. There were some machines in the vineyards, and people moving almost silently over the earth. Because I knew so little about wine, this unseen grandeur only lightly touched me. Farmers of the land have all sorts of crops – potatoes, swedes, turnips, corn – but these are mostly just dug up or cut down, washed and sold. They are only stored for freshness and must be eaten quickly. I knew nothing of the long maturation, the turning of the seasons, of the soil's contribution, heat of the sun, even the wind's contribution from breezes carried inland from the sea. I knew nothing of wine, the varieties of grape, and all the processes that changed the juice of grapes into – well, Hafez would have known – into something rich and 'passing strange', and strangely lovely, as I would discover.

I reached the main house and for a few minutes just stared at it. I had never seen such a large house in my country, although in Oxford nearly all the colleges are very grand, beyond imagining. The windows were large and long, almost in the style of a Georgian manor house in England. It had a circular gravel approach in the middle of which was a green, trimmed lawn with a sundial in the centre. The house, I call it, but a small chateau might be more accurate, was built with beautiful yellowed stone. A flight of stone steps led up to a white-painted door.

'Monsieur Mohammad Reza?' An unmistakeably French voice called out. I looked up to see a middle-aged woman at the window above me. I had by then counted all the windows I could see, sixteen in all, including three dormer windows in the roof.

'*Oui, Madame, c'est moi!*'

'*Attends,*' she said, disappearing from sight. Some moments later the front door opened. I have to tell you my heart was beating quite fast. Madame Saintoissant was so welcoming. '*Bienvenue à Margaux!*' We exchanged a Gallic kiss.

'*Bonjour Madame,*' I said nervously.

'*Mon anglais n'est pas bon mais mon farsi est désespéré. Alors, parlons en englais. C'est mieux.*' Of course I understood her completely. All the world manages, or most of it, to converse in English. I suspected her English was better than she made out. A tall, graceful lady, she looked like so many French women – the epitome of style and elegance, even so far from Paris.

'*Bon,*' she said, 'Let's go and talk. Do you like tea? *Thé* Earl Grey?' I was going to suggest black *chaii* but thought this would only confuse things so I simply said '*Merci beaucoup.* Of course, thank you.'

The brief 'bones' of what I was supposed to do were explained over tea, which a maid had brought to our table, seemingly without any request. I was to take charge of the accounts and be granted the status of 'stagiaire' or trainee for management. I would need to learn all the varied aspects of running the estate, including a lengthy introduction to the work done in the vineyards, so I might become conversant with the production of their wines, though in truth the making of the wine was always left in the expert hands of their *vignerons* – those who closely follow the life of the vines, watch over them like a father, and are involved in the whole process from harvesting the grapes right up to the bottle.

I was given a room at the top of the chateau, one of the rooms with a dormer window from which I could see the extent of their estate. I found it extraordinary to think later, as I surveyed the vineyards, how the vines were all, as it were, groping into the soil beneath for sustenance and using the sun's energy above to sustain and develop their growth, how all these processes combined to furnish the climax of each year's efforts, the *vendange*, the grape harvest.

I was so tired that I went to bed early that night. Once again I looked out from the dormer window at the fading evening light. A car, a white car, drove up and parked somewhere near the outbuildings. Then there was silence but moments later I heard footsteps on the gravel. A girl was walking towards the main entrance, carrying a bouquet of white roses.

Fourteen

MY INDUCTION BEGAN SHARPLY AT SEVEN O'CLOCK IN THE morning. As I left by the main entrance I caught the strong, sweet scent of roses, I presumed brought in by the girl of the previous night.

My guide for the morning was Antoine, a boy who seemed even younger than me. He said little, but he did take off his French cap from time to time to give me an odd stare, scratch his head, and then replace it. '*Allons monsieur, suivez-moi.*' Dutifully I followed him across a yard into a large building holding huge stainless steel vats, with pipes and gauges, and an army of mysterious machines of one kind or another. I confess that it took several months before I began to understand the processes and various stages. In essence, wine making is simple, all because of what happens during alcoholic fermentation. As a language student, I was hopeless at science subjects so I don't really understand it:

$$C_6H_{12}O_6 \rightarrow 2\ C_2H_5OH + 2\ CO_2$$

Anyway, yeast starts it off and produces fermentation of the natural sugars found in the grapes.

After the annual harvest, the grapes are separated from the leaves and stems. The grapes are then lightly crushed, the resulting 'must' is placed in a fermentation vessel, whether vat, barrel or tank and the yeast produces carbon dioxide and alcohol. After which there is pressing or maceration; then sometimes 'malolactic conversion' to soften the wine and add more taste; then racking of the wine, to decant off the 'lees' or sediment; followed by ageing for months or years, and finally the wine is filtered and bottled. Fining or filtering of the wine to remove the solids that can make the wine go cloudy traditionally used ox-blood, egg white and isinglass, made from the swim bladders of sturgeon. Blending of different types of wine (*coupage*) is common in Bordeaux. A blend is described as a *cuvée*. Some of the finer detail is left out. In any case my visit to the winery was soon over, for I was then sent to the vineyards to learn about all the things that go on there too.

The grapes I saw were 'full to bursting', by which I mean they were ripe. I don't know if you can describe a grape as 'ripe' but apparently the harvest or *vendange* was days away. There were also people I met who had 'oversight' of the vineyards, and the same afternoon I caught sight of a girl, to whom the others in the vineyard deferred. I think it must have been the same girl driving a white car the night before. I trudged back much later to the grand house, dust on my shoes, tired and beginning to ask why my uncle had such an idea to send me to a vineyard in Bordeaux, even if it was one in Margaux, a name of some substance, and readily known in the region.

In the lobby as I passed through on the way to my room, I could smell the sweet scent of roses. Madame Saintoissant caught my arm.

'Do you like roses, Mohammad? I can tell you appreciate them, without even seeing them. Please follow me.' She led me into what I suppose the English would refer to as 'a drawing room'; I have discovered this is a separate room to which guests might comfortably 'withdraw'. Language is such a funny thing. In Persia, or should I say Iran (in use from 1935, or the Islamic Republic of Iran since the 1979 revolution) we just go into one room from another, and we don't have many rooms either. Any room in our house is always open to guests. They come and go entirely as they please. Taking off shoes is customary.

The Comtesse, for such I called her then, led me to a table in a grand room beyond the lobby, to see a small wooden table graced by a large, pale blue jug in which reposed – I can think of no finer word – a stand – or was it a bunch – of fine roses, white with faint pink at the edges. 'In English this rose, do you know it?'

I shook my head.

'This is the maiden's blush,' she said without any embarrassment. 'In France, we know this rose by another name. We call it, "*Cuisse de Nymphe*" or Nymph's Thigh. It is very elegant.'

I coughed, being surprised at the mention of a nymph's thigh. In Iran, if one has been brought up strictly, the contemplation of such things is for the imagination only. Indeed, in Tehran's Museum of Contemporary Art, there is a high-security vault containing priceless masterpieces by great painters, most considered too risqué by the clerics ever to be on public display. This includes Renoir's *Gabrielle with Open Blouse*, valued at $8m. Gabrielle displays her bare breasts, coyly framed by her blouse. Even I was confused by this secrecy, and the attribution of 'morals' to what are the entirely functional attributes of mammals. 'Yes, yes', I agreed readily. 'They are beautiful.'

The Comtesse seemed to appreciate my remark. Her face had immense quality, if that is the right word, a strong face with good structure, a nose that many Iranians would admire, being prominent but also straight, and a brow of discernment and empathy; I believe the French have a word for this – *sympatique*.

'Mohammad,' she said, inviting me to stay a moment, 'tell me, how was your first day in the vineyards?'

'I have never seen so many grapes! Rows upon rows, and all that machinery, it was wonderful.'

'Will you come to dinner tomorrow night, no say the day after, on Friday?'

'*D'accord*,' I blurted out in my enthusiasm. 'Yes, I mean, of course, Madame, thank you.

'*À sept heures*,' the Comtesse said, 'and don't be late!'

I found the prospect of dinner exciting. For my meals, along with a few other staff, I could choose whatever was on offer that day in a communal kitchen adjacent to the main house; anyone could take a plate or bowl and sit on a wooden bench next to a large table on which other staff, I would not call them servants, placed food at breakfast, and dinner. Lunch was not readily available as most of the vineyard workers were expect- ed to take sandwiches or rolls and drink water from outside. I felt it would be some time before I was let anywhere near the accounts; that was for later, after I had proved my ability to 'learn the ropes'. This expression I could understand in Britain with its history of ships but in Bordeaux 'learn the vines' might be more appropriate. If the British change their minds about something, they say they are 'rowing back' from whatever it was being contemplated.

In the staff kitchen that night were some other workers. A large carafe of red wine was passed round, inviting as much attention as our food. This surprised me as appetite increases after a long day working outside.

A young man, who introduced himself as Gilles, 'Geels' in the French way, a fresh-faced lad, indicated with a nod of his head if I would like some wine. Instinctively I refused, as politely as I could. I began to wonder at the 'conditioning' of my upbringing – even allowing for Alice's offerings and my uncle's vodka. In France, children are no doubt introduced to wine when quite young – it does not invoke I am sure the indrawn breaths of silent condemnation as if fit only for the devil. I suppose very few of these reprovers ever read even a stanza of our great Hafez, or going back even further, the Odes of Anacreon, who sang with as much vigour as our beloved poet on the matter of 'the ruby tides' in a bowl of wine, though at that time I was unfamiliar with the Greek lyric poet, who shares the esteem of ancient scholars, along with some other poets, such as Sappho of Lesbos, Alcaeus of Mytilene and Pindar of Thebes. Of course, there is the irony that Anacreon is believed to have died at the age of eighty-five from choking on a grape pip.

From such poetic, even literary musings, I was suddenly 'brought back to earth', jolted to another reality, although 'unreality' is closer to the truth. It was the portly Gregor Samsa again, this time confined to the lobby of the great house, so that no one could leave or enter. If by some other miracle he wasted away enough to break out or his wings worked (if he had any wings), or if not he might, like that Catholic saint, grow them, and escape alive into the vineyards, there he could make havoc among the vines, bumbling from one to the other, flattening all before him so the year's harvest would be destroyed! I must have been in quite a good state of mind, however, as Gregor might have been trapped but I was now *free*, free from worrying about having to teach a class of eager 18-year-olds a string of gruesome lectures on Kafka. I had never felt as free as I felt in the vineyards, so much fresh air, and the gorgeous lushness of the ripening grapes loading the vines with their bounty. Why should anyone dig up and destroy nature so violently as was done in my country at the time of our 'revolution'? There may have been a revolution of sorts but I felt my own people, Iranians, were just prisoners in their own country. Freedom was pretence. The clerics took care of that – even suggesting suitable marriage partners, and telling you what kind of music was 'acceptable'. The strident railing against western values and the Great Satan, *Āmrikā*, and the 'Little Satan', Israel – all of these were by then meaningless to me. I was now in France, a country where the word 'liberty' means so much more than mere sloganizing and pointless political brickbats or shoe throwing.

But I must tell you about the dinner. The day before I achieved very little but gained satisfaction nevertheless. I was given the task of walking round the entire estate, accompanied by Gilles. The land under vines was 25 hectares, about 60 acres, growing mainly Cabernet Sauvignon, Merlot and Cabernet Franc varieties. Gilles said another 20 hectares was woodland and for agriculture. As the Margaux appellation covers an area of about 1060 hectares, or 2600 acres, I guessed that the Saintoissant Margaux holding in the total commune area to be less than one per cent – yet how much wonder and grandeur there were on these few hectares! The estate was about 70 metres above sea level, with a few *jalles* or small streams crossing the vineyards. He told me the *terroir* was a gravelly mixture of sand, limestone and clay. He had fun trying to tell me this. We had to use Google translate most of the time.

We stopped for lunch. We shared our sandwiches like old mates. I think he was about my age but perhaps more knowledgeable about the world. 'You know the girl?' he asked quietly, still munching on a sandwich, and looking away as if he didn't want to say too much.

'*Quelle jeune fille?*' I replied in my best French.

'*La fille de Madame Saintoissant.*'

'*Pas encore,*' I answered truthfully. '*Pourquoi?*'

Gilles didn't reply except for a Gallic grunt. He looked down, kicking the toe of his left shoe into the ground a few times, as if turning over thoughts in his mind. After a moment he let out a long breath through pursed lips but said nothing more. I noticed he slowly shook his head from side to side. After a long pause, he said, '*Ce n'est rien, Mohammad. Vraiment.*'

I felt I had only to wait a little longer and he might tell me. I offered him half of my last sandwich. He shook his head, and only stared deeper into the vineyards. Then he said, very directly, turning to look at me, '*Elle est vraiment canon. Très jolie.*' I looked away. He meant the girl was 'hot' and very pretty. The question of women and their attractiveness I had managed to put to the back of my mind since leaving Oxford. It's true I sometimes remembered Alice with warmth and pleasure but women and drink, that is to say alcohol, are not what one might term a holy alliance in many parts of the Muslim world. Admittedly, I considered myself Iranian first, and a Muslim second, and my prayers to Allah, peace be upon him, seemed to have all but vanished. For some Muslims even tending vines, before squeezing a single drop out of them, would bring displeasure to our great Prophet. To consider a woman licentiously *and* in a vineyard where the grapes were on the point of being harvested – and not praying every day – was rather troubling. Even so, I felt these were challenges I could deal with. They were not to be hidden away but confronted.

I had to tell you this in advance as it will help explain what happened when I attended Madame Saintoissant's dinner the following evening.

Fifteen

THE COMTESSE CALLED TO ME. '*VIENS MOHAMMAD!* WE ARE outside in the courtyard.' My eyes followed her beckoning arms to a sunny terrace surrounded by a stone balustrade, covered with shrub roses intertwined with yellow and pink honeysuckle. As I walked through to the terrace I could smell them. In the distance vines, rows and rows of them, reaching towards the horizon. In the foreground one of Madame Saintoissant's workers tended a brazier, feeding it with bent, crumbling old logs and sticks. Blue smoke and the perfume of smouldering wood mingled with the honeysuckle, the air redolent of a woodsman's sylvan glade.

On the terrace a large wooden table sparsely and simply laid with a pink-lined tablecloth, a bowl of fruit, plates, knives, forks and wine glasses, a bottle of olive oil, and an unopened bottle of red wine.

A moustached older man joined me; I recognised him as the main *vinificateur* or head winemaker from my induction day. His name was Alphonse, Alphonse Daudier, as I remember it now. Quite abrupt and formally polite but a master of vineyard techniques. '*Bonsoir monsieur,*' he said quietly. '*C'est les vendanges bientôt, une bonne vendange!*' I understood it was soon to be harvest time with a good vintage.

Madame La Comtesse shouted something and immediately two girls, not servants but maids from the house, appeared carrying food for our table. Fresh bread, butter, pâté, olives, and a huge bowl of green salad – chopped tomatoes, herbs, and lettuce, all glossy with dressing.

'*Viens Margot, viens!*' the Comtesse shouted again. We sat down to eat, but waiting for Margot. I began with a few salad leaves, bread, and olives. It was too much to expect rice (and crispy *tahdig*), which in Farsi we write as جنرب Are you any the wiser? It must sound 'churlish' to complain about the lack of rice. But it mattered not one bit as, with almost boyish strides, Margot strode towards us. Even Alphonse I noticed perked up a little at the sight.

I was already thinking of Gilles, his premonition – no, not the right word – his foreknowledge, his assessment. When one sees something extraordinary, not just something new, but a sight out of the ordinary, beyond the ordinary, there enters into one's soul a messenger. Such moments I was sure are well documented in the historical past. Take the Annunciation by Gabriel to the Blessed Virgin Mary, whom we revere in the Qur'an. He came (the angel) to an unmarried Galilean peasant girl to announce she would be the mother of Jesus Christ. Likewise many years later Jibreel, the same angel, came to Muhammad, peace be upon him, in the cave at Hira and commanded him to 'Read', that is proclaim some few verses to begin with, which you can find today in our holy Qur'an. Whatever happened at these times never left the person who experienced it. It reached deep into their souls, like blood in the very smallest channels of the human body.

I suppose you must find this ridiculous. Yet to me it was real, just as there is still blood in my veins. Perhaps now is not the time to explain to you the effect on me of the daughter of the Comtesse – as she appeared before us like an apparition – only to sit next to me! She was served a little salad by her mother, and we exchanged names, and I felt my world, the world under my feet, swallow me, when I said 'Mohammad, Mohammad Reza', and with the briefest of acknowledgements buried my fork in the green salad in front of me.

'Mohammad is coming from Paris to help us in the vineyards,' the Comtesse said, addressing her daughter. 'You remember Monsieur Arvani, Mohammad's uncle.'

Margot turned her head slightly to look at me, saying, 'I think that you are the only person from Iran here. It's an honour to meet you.'

I nodded but desperately returned to my salad, poking it with my fork and not managing to pick anything up.

'Mohammad is learning fast,' declared the Comtesse, 'just in time for the harvest! It's when we work the hardest.'

A few moments later Alphonse sighed, as if he had forgotten something, but then in an almost involuntary movement, his right arm swept across the table to clasp the now open bottle of red wine. '*Du vin, Monsieur Mohammad? C'est le meilleur dans toutes la region de Bordeaux!*'

I held out my hand as if to say 'No, thank you', but this was either mistaken or misinterpreted. Alphonse, shrugging off any reluctance on my part, slowly poured a little into my glass. I was suddenly aware of three pairs of eyes looking at me. At the same time, two maids brought a serving plate with several racks of roast lamb, cut into neat quarters, some steamed French beans with new potatoes. I had no option despite this temporary diversion, as the lamb looked so delicious, but to raise my glass, and remembering my French, called out, quite boldly if I can say so, '*A votre santé!*' Of course I was meant to try it first, so I took a small sip, declaring blandly, '*Le vin, c'est bon.*' I thought it best not to remember the imam who said even swallowing one drop would call down curses. '*Trés bon,*'

I said, anxious to put down my glass on the table in front of me, though the taste of the wine was full, deep, and lingered in my mouth.

At this, there seemed to me to be a sudden relaxation on the part of Alphonse, Margot and her mother. They 'toasted' me with their glasses, and I found myself saying, '*Salamati*' in response, the Persian for 'cheers' or 'good health'. Margot heard for she smiled at me, '*Salamati, Monsieur Mohammad Reza. Bonne chance et bonne fortune.*' 'You know Persian?' I asked. 'No,' she replied. 'I just know the words for "*A votre santé*" from a few countries. I have never been to Iran.'

'You must come,' I told her. 'The Flower Garden of Isphahan, and especially Shiraz, you must see once in your life!'

You may remember I mentioned there was something about the dinner. It wasn't really anything to do with the wine, that I had tried my first glass of red wine, and once more escaped curses from the prophets for consuming alcohol. It was more to do with Margot. I tried to avoid her gaze. I was not used to bold, self-confident women who tossed their hair lightly, unbound by any *hijab*, *niqab* or *chador*. I had lived in Iran among so many beautiful young women that I thought none could contest their fiery, matchless good looks but Margot's eyes mesmerised me: dark depths, two pools in which my gaze seemed to drown, willingly, scarcely being able to muster any sensible resistance. She had such fine features, a mixture of strength and sweetness, fair to dark hair, high cheekbones, a thin gold necklace around her neck, impish ears, and a laugh that made my insides quiver with erotic excitement. I had to 'pull myself together', as the English are wont to say, and to my consternation I found myself reaching for another mouthful of wine, to which Alphonse had added more. The second mouthful was calming in its effect. I had drunk so little I felt the prophets, even our great Prophet, must surely have been able to allow me just a spoonful of leniency.

The lamb, something like the lamb *shashlik* we have in Iran, was memorably sweet and so tender. I wondered innocently if the lamb had grazed on vine leaves. Then we had a dessert of strawberry tart and fresh cream. Some local brandy was served, I don't know enough about it but it may have been marc brandy made from the grape pomace, left over from the grape pressings. I had to refuse it, as I felt I had already taken too many chances with alcohol, escaping very lightly from these misdemeanours, although drinking wine was, in my religion, anything but.

A misdemeanour in most countries of the world is not sufficient to condemn a person to *Jahannam*, that fiery pit for sinners where they roast in eternity. There are seven gates leading into this hell, each for a different kind of sinner. Hypocrites end up at the bottom. It's not a nice place. The skins of those who arrive there are scorched black, then given new skins over and over so the torment continues for ever. These wretched souls are not allowed to die. Boiling water is poured over them too, which melts the skin and everything beneath it. If a person tries to escape an iron hook will drag the sinner back. Women suffer in the flames, hanging on hooks, and licked by the ravenous flames for exposing their hair to strangers.

From my studying of our beloved Qur'an and the Hadiths, I could find only one 'crumb' of comfort. It is written that '…no one will enter Hell in whose heart is an atom's weight of faith'. An atom's weight of faith is so small as to be immeasurable – other than with a mass spectrometer or via quantum mechanics, I believe. I had not lost faith in our great Prophet, peace and blessings be upon him, so I doubted I would be condemned 'out of hand', and this gave me a measure of reassurance. Actually, it felt very odd to speculate on these things in a French vineyard.

Margot dragged me back sharply from my reveries. 'Tomorrow, Mohammad, we will begin the *vendange*. You can come with me.' As she leant towards me ever so slightly, I caught sight of the exquisite marble whiteness of her breasts inside her blouse, though her face and arms had browned in the sun. I thought it very strange that the $8m painting locked in a vault in Tehran, *Gabrielle with Open Blouse*, could not be seen by anyone but I had a much more beautiful sight that was entirely free – right next to me, and perfectly priceless. 'Of course,' I told her, 'I would like nothing better.' Later I thought this remark of mine a little arrogant, as really I had no choice. I was only a beginner, a helper, someone learning the ropes, a *stagiaire* so to speak, even though I had been pitched in by my uncle at the level of junior management.

'*Alors, jusqu'à demain,*' she said firmly, her gaze, I was certain, lingering on mine. 'Please be ready in the courtyard early, by eight.' With this, and after drinking a small cup of black coffee, Margot got up to leave, with a toss of her hair. She said goodbye courteously to Alphonse, and kissed her mother, whose name I had discovered in conversations was Madeleine. I decided to leave also, so I excused myself from the table shortly after.

It was still light being summer, so I strolled round by the staff kitchen, trying to make sense of the evening. I felt a hand on my shoulder. I turned round to see Gilles, obviously drunk because he could hardly stand up, and was waving his arms, and muttering to himself although he did acknowledge me with a nod of his head and a brief smile. '*Bonsoir* Gilles,' I said, holding out my hand. Gilles took my hand in his, still swaying on the spot, and suddenly without warning threw a punch at my face but missed, falling on the ground, and bruising his hand so badly that he was bleeding. '*Salaud,*' he said grimly, repeating the word several times. I was sure he wasn't calling me a bastard, just life in general, so I helped him up. *'Tu comprends maintenant?'* he asked me. *'Cette fille, elle me rend fou.'* I understood. Margot had got to him in a bad way. I felt only compassion for Gilles as I walked him back to his room. He had allowed himself to fall so far under her spell that he felt he was going mad!

When I got to my room on the top floor of the chateau unsure of what to think about the episode, I rinsed my mouth and brushed my teeth, as a kind of involuntary act. Of course it made no difference; the wine was already being digested. I thought it time for prayers. I couldn't be bothered to take any ablution, and as for *qiblah*, finding the direction of Mecca, it was only a guess. To my horror I couldn't find my prayer mat anywhere, so I had to kneel on the wooden floor. I chose the same prayer as before, but could not finish it.

In the name of God, Most Gracious, Most Merciful
Say: He is Allah, the One and Only!

I felt sick. Muslims are taught that the whole purpose of our existence is to worship Allah and not praying is disobeying the Creator. Abandoning any formal prayer, I tried to address Allah directly. 'Please forgive my sins, the drinking of wine, and the pleasant feelings I experienced today at the table. May Allah cleanse my mind from all impure thoughts...' I stopped. *Why* should I ask Allah for forgiveness, merely for admiring the young woman Margot as any man might, even the lovelorn Gilles?

I surmised that all humans are misguided but some are less misguided than others. In bed, I sought consolation from my iPhone listening to Persian music. Still, a dilemma, a pointless one in my view, came to mind. Was listening to music *halal* or *haram*? The scholars have written volumes on this single theme, trying to distinguish what is permissible from what is not. Music, singing and dancing at any gathering for entertainment and amusement is *haram*. One can listen to forbidden tunes if the listening is *unintentional*, for example in a café or waiting area. Singing and dancing encourage adultery, lustful urges on sexual matters, and as a matter of 'obligatory precaution', exercise classes accompanied by dance music, women dancing in front of men, men in front of women, women dancing with women, men with men, making and selling musical instruments etc., all are forbidden. In the time it takes for a single scholar to learn about this, Mozart might have composed a symphony or an opera. There are debates about whether it is *halal* or *haram* to listen to your phone's ringtone.

Worshippers in mosques do not raise their voices to sing aloud, like they do in English cathedrals, where not only are there trained choristers and choirs, sometimes accompanied by fine music, but the people sing too. Singing aloud from the heart can be uplifting to the soul. I felt that the rhythmic chanting we do at mosque prayers is so completely different as to amount not just to a cultural divide but a cultural chasm. One real problem I feel in my heart is that the cross-worshippers can pour out their hearts in songs and music but we Muslims cannot express our feelings in this way. One I heard was 'Hallelujah' – a song to the 'Lord of Song'. I would so much prefer it if we Muslims could compose such secret chords to sing in our mosques, in praise of the beloved Prophet, praise be upon him, music so beautiful even the palm trees would walk again, and all creation praise the Messenger of Allah. We could make songs for Allah too but that is often *haram*, although there are diverse regional differences in Muslim countries. Generally, we may not play or entertain in public – even take up a harp like David – a prophet mentioned in the Qur'an.

Three essentials to the human experience, joy and existence in my view are music, dancing and singing. These are elementals to human life. Most Iranians cannot resist dancing and love their music from the bottom of their hearts. Even the reluctant English can be taught (I remember Zorba's Dance). The French philosopher Albert Camus believed in the 'Four Conditions of Happiness: Life in the open air, Love for another being, Freedom from ambition, Creation.'

If, as is commonly known, 'the law is an ass', then Sharia law for the most part is a great big donkey.

Sixteen

PLEASE FORGIVE ME FOR MENTIONING THIS BUT IN THE EARLY morning I served myself coffee and a bread roll in the staff kitchen. Two young Englishmen were at breakfast, I suppose taken on for the harvest. Perhaps as a welcoming treat the chef had cooked some bacon rashers, and I noticed the Englishmen greedily stuffed their rolls with the bacon. I was peculiarly taken with the English saying, 'in for a penny, in for a pound' at that moment, as aptly from my studies the saying was the same as to 'go the whole hog'. I felt I should place my doubts and misgivings aside and eat some. The bacon was smoked rather than 'green'. To tell you the truth, it was most appetising, once I had overcome my initial doubts.

I have always liked animals. A strange thought came to me. How fortune had smiled on pigs when our great prophet Muhammad forbade the eating of them (and likewise the Jews). Tens of millions of extra pigs to feed Muslims and Jews would be needed if this were not the case, so millions of pigs have escaped being bred and slaughtered, because some humans abhor the meat. In imagining these creatures as filthy abominations, so many pigs have been saved from the butcher's knife. Similarly, beef consumption in India per capita per year is among the world's lowest thanks mainly to Hindu reverence for the cow. One animal is revered and not eaten and the other is loathed and not eaten and both are saved.

One can eat 'underground' pork in Iran but if you are caught in the act, with a slice of bacon in your mouth, by the modesty or religious patrols, you can face fines, even a flogging. One must be very careful to avoid the *Basij*, Iran's paramilitary volunteer militia. Muslims believe that God created us with a purpose – to worship him. Of course we live in a dangerous, uncertain world, and this is why he gave us our book of guidance, our most holy Qur'an. We must submit to Allah's commands and we need not question his divine rule, *because Allah knows best*. When God and his messenger decide something, we have no choice but to follow the decision. Of course one can eat pork by mistake or unknowingly, as there is then no sin. So, if you are in a French café, for example, and unintentionally listen to background music, and the waiter serves you a slice of ham hidden inside a sweet potato wrap, Allah will not punish you. The same for tagliatelle carbonara, if you didn't know the little bits of meat are pork belly. And if you were in the northern Italian region of Emilia-Romagna, northwest of Parma in the Bassa Parmense, and find yourself eating some *Culatello di Zibello*, a magnificent slowly cured boneless ham, keep very quiet about it, and don't mention it to Allah.

How strange it is to learn that perhaps a million ethnic Muslims known as Uyghurs, in the western Chinese province of Xinjiang, are detained in internment camps (known as re-education centres). Just being a Muslim means one is considered an enemy of Communist China and a religious extremist. Muslims have a mental illness that must be 'cured'. Mosques are closed and locked up. In the 'vocational training and education centres', internees are beaten, starved and given electric shocks for not singing patriotic songs loudly enough, and are *forced to eat pork* (and drink alcohol) to erase long-standing cultural customs. One shower a month is allowed, and they sleep 30 to 40 in a room.

China is a country where someone can be arrested on the nebulous charge of being 'two-faced', a deliberately vague term chosen by the Chinese authorities to harass those suspected of secretly opposing government policy. I suspect Allah is incensed by the pork enforcers.

Of course, we have political prisoners in Iran too. Many of these are terribly treated, tortured and abused by our present government. Before, during the Pahlavi dynasty, we had the most feared and hated SAVAK secret police who behaved in exactly the same way.

I really don't know how Allah gives out his punishments, or where he finds the time. If he has some sort of 'spirit in the sky' court to administer justice, the waiting lists must be interminably long. In fact, due to human nature, they must go on for ever. It must not be a happy existence, even for God, to have to spend one's time meting out due punishments time after time, as well as keeping watch over *Jannah* – Paradise. Of course, it is entirely possible that paradise runs itself, without the need for divine intervention, every now and then. Actually, to be clear, Iranians don't really talk about *Jannah* very much – we use the Farsi word *behesht*, for paradise. Some of us believe that paradise is a fragrant meadow in an Iranian garden. Imagine a walled, enclosed garden where is found peace among the tiny water channels, or rills; a garden with evergreen trees like cypresses, flowering pomegranates, almond blossoms, and damask roses in spring and summer. In Iran we believe the first paradise included four rivers: rivers of water, wine, milk and honey.

At ten to eight I stood waiting in the courtyard. I suddenly thought of the great Ghorbali Khan with his three hundred men in the snow-barred mountains of Iran. It was not quite the same in a Bordeaux vineyard but I still felt excitement at the future in front of me, and I couldn't wait to see Margot again. Not long after a red tractor and trailer drove into the courtyard but to my dismay it was not driven by her but by Gilles. He stopped and beckoned me to step up into the trailer.

'*Bonjour, mon ami,*' he said somewhat curtly, but he did manage a smile, especially when he saw I was not very agile, trying to clamber into the trailer. We set off leisurely enough, though Gilles revved the tractor round each bend in the road so that occasionally I was forced to hang onto the tailgate. Madame Saintoissant still insisted on hand harvesting rather than machines, so we were going to have to handpick all the grapes. Fortunately, other workers were there, about twenty-five to thirty, to help. The bunches of grapes were to be placed in crates, and the occasional bucket, and then loaded onto Gilles' trailer, so all day long I lifted the crates and Gilles disappeared on his own to take the grapes to the winery for pressing. The vines were all about hip high, and there was much bending and stretching.

By noon I was drenched in sweat, there were grape stains on my clothes and hands, and probably on my face. I had eaten some of the ripe grapes, just to experience the crush of fresh juice in my mouth. By one o'clock I was starving. There was no prospect of leaving the vineyard till nightfall.

When I and a few other workers had loaded one more trailerful of grapes for Gilles, and had watched him drive off to the winery, in the far distance a horse and rider skirted the woods at the far end of the vineyard. I thought nothing of it but when I stood up to stretch my aching back, the horse had moved nearer, going from a canter to a trot, then a walk as it moved between the rows of vines. The rider stopped to speak to a grape picker. The man stood up, looked round, and then pointed in my direction. The bay horse came towards me and I realised it was Margot in the saddle!

'Mohammad, Mohammad Reza. You forgot your lunch! We make an exception during the harvest.' Reaching into a knapsack she pulled out a sandwich box and a small bottle of water.

I found it hard to take my eyes off her. It was miraculous that I caught both bottle and the sandwiches. 'Thank you, Margot,' I spluttered with sweat pouring from me. I must have looked unkempt and dirty but Margot smiled at me like an angel. Angels have a prominent place in Islam but of their actual number only Allah knows. Jibreel was once seen with six hundred wings, and from his wings fell jewels, pearls and rubies. We Muslims have to believe in angels, just as we believe in Allah, his books, his messengers, and the Last Day. If not, we are unbelievers, or *kafirs*.

'Truly you are an angel,' I said to her. 'Don't be silly, Mohammad,' she said, looking at me with disdain. 'My horse may have wings, but I don't!'

'You mean like Jibreel? I said foolishly.

'*Quoi? Comment?*' Margot was perplexed.

'In English he is called Gabriel.'

'*L'ange* Gabriel?

'*Oui*,' I nodded. 'He had wings.'

'*Merde alors! Nom de Dieu! Ce vignoble…*' she began, and then switched to English. 'This vineyard needs no angels, just good weather and hard work!'

'Sorry for the misunderstanding,' I said, deciding to drop any further mention of religions, religious figures, saints or angels. I haven't yet described Margot to you properly, I know. How could I? If love is blind, then for sure I had no eyes left. I discovered Margot's full names later. She was called Margot Camille Hélène Saintoissant; Camille from her grandmother

136

on her mother's side, and Hélène from her great-grandmother, also on her mother's side. I didn't care what names she had, only that Margot was the most beautiful girl I had ever seen, and that is exceptional really, as so many Iranian women with their distinct Persian heritage are great beauties, even more so than the *houris* it is claimed we shall meet in Paradise. From what I had read about these paradisal *houris*, I am not at all certain I would like to spend time with them. It is written that we shall recline on cushions in pavilions with the *houris*, and each man will be given the strength of one hundred men. They will have wide, lovely eyes, and the marrow of their bones will show through their clothing. The idea of so much strength is just to gain the pleasure of eating, drinking, feeling desire and having sexual intercourse, and constantly deflowering virgins who have become our wives. If a man wants a child, pregnancy and birth will happen within the hour.

It is written that their breasts will not be pendulous but, to use an English term, 'pert'. Other sexual parts of them will be 'libidinous' and welcoming and 'appetising'; their only bodily excretion is sweat, and they will be very tall, I don't know the number of cubits for their height, but fifty or sixty feet tall might be about right. The men who enjoy this paradise will also be more or less permanently priapic, that is able to engage in intercourse 24/7. I am sorry to relate this to you in such detail but our beloved Qur'an is so full of detail that our jurists and scholars have been busy interpreting and debating the content for centuries. (By the way, I dislike using the term '24/7', perhaps now it is universal, but it is meant to explain the state of physical readiness of men when they get to *Jannah*.) If this is true, it leaves little time for quiet reflection and meditation.

It made me think that Baudelaire might have liked being a Muslim, as he was so fond of languor, of reclining with ample women, and the sultry perfumes of paradise but, for him, I expect *Jahannam* was waiting.

By the time I had run through these thoughts in my head, Margot was leaving, having first dismounted to adjust the girth on her horse, and generally fiddle with the reins and bridle, as if not sure she wanted to leave. 'One day,' she said quietly, 'you must tell me about your life in Iran. Do you ride?' she asked suddenly.

'Yes, in Iran we have great horsemen.' It was true. Our horsemen and knights were legendary.

'Then take her,' Margot said. 'I will take charge of the grapes for the trailer. You see that small hill with the trees? Ride there and have your lunch. There is a wooden seat. You will see all the vineyards of our estate.'

'Okay,' I answered without hesitation. I love animals, and riding is so much fun. In Iran my grandfathers played polo. Ghorbali Khan was an accomplished horseman. I took the reins from her, the bay taking my weight easily. 'Come back when you have eaten.' Margot smiled at me, once again her gaze lingering on me.

I had not been on a horse for some years so I walked the horse slowly through the vine rows. At the far end I could canter and just as I did so Gilles passed me on his way back to the grapes. He stopped as if to speak, and then revved his tractor a couple of times, which acted like spurs to the horse, so I galloped away leaving Gilles staring blankly after me.

Margot's horse must have known the way to the seat on the hill with the trees. Having tethered the horse, I ate my lunch slowly, thinking about all the workers below me, like coloured dots moving in between the vines. How much I enjoyed the physical work! To sweat and labour all day under the warm sun, I loved to have something to do, to be busy. Once again, while

Margot's horse was munching grass, I thought of the man who wrote *The Story of My Heart* – the quote I gave you earlier. The passage I selected could fit the life of the vine just as well. The soul of the earth, the sun, the air, even the sea breezes blown inland, all touched the growing vines. After pressing and bottling, there was mystery and glory, brilliance and light, depth, colour and sweetness locked in a wine bottle. Over time the wine gained in mysterious complexities, took on more than it started with, an organic process subtler than an alchemist's dream.

For a moment I wanted to see what was behind the hill, so I followed a small path round the wooded hill but there found a wooden post to which was attached a sign that read '*Passage interdit*'. I had no idea who put it there or why I should not follow the path further. After a moment's reflection, I thought the same sign in Oxfordshire would probably have 'No thoroughfare' on it, slightly politer in the old-fashioned English style than letting you know further progress was 'not allowed'. I actually found myself shrugging my shoulders in the French way after this, and then went back to the horse.

I rode back to Margot feeling refreshed, ready for a long afternoon's work. Gilles was still there at the tractor, looking surly, not bothering to acknowledge my return.

'*Bienvenu*,' said Margot. 'You can ride a horse well!'

'What's her name?'

'Most of the time we call her *Jolie*. Her real name is *Châtaigne*, like chestnut, the sweet chestnut.' With this, Margot agilely mounted the mare, and with the slightest push of her heels, rode off down a row of vines. I watched her skirting the vineyards in an easy canter back to the house. When she had gone I felt alone with only the grapes and their mysterious fate for company. By this I mean the sudden change from being connected to a stem to a vine to the earth, being dropped into crates or buckets, then being pressed for their precious essence, only to undergo a transformation, a special kind of metamorphosis into the 'ruby tides'. Of course I know they might be white, rosé or sparkling tides. It's not just red wine that can hit the sublime notes on the palate; think of those delicately floral, 'tasting of Flora and the country-green' lighter triumphs: some of the white wines are up there too, more Bach than Beethoven, more Mozart than Wagner, more Keats than Khayyam if I can mix them so (or even 'jade tides' with Vinho Verde or 'amber tides' with a fine Riesling Spätlese) but red wine, the best red wine, is full of luminously light and dark shades of colour; it *is* 'wine dark' to the eye. It becomes with a swirl a sacred mystery in the glass. It is never just 'coloured water' as the guides tell the pilgrims of Hafez in the Musalla Gardens in Shiraz, where they can also read some of his *ghazals* engraved on a veranda – the *ghazal* originally being an Arab poetic form based on rhyming couplets and a refrain (usually a love poem). But of these mysteries I was still a novice.

I had firmly decided by then that I liked the Margaux countryside. It was by no means a kind of Ovidian exile but more of a sacred place of the heart, as Horace sang of his Bandusian spring, though to be fair the scant *jalles* or streams in the vineyards were not very enticing.

The daily toil in the vineyards lasted almost three weeks. I briefly saw Margot from time to time but she seemed to take little notice of me. Gilles had sunk so far into a state of repressed misery that he no longer threatened me openly, and if he kept a secret grudge against me, he did not show it.

At night in my room on the top floor of my house, I slept peacefully. Every day my strength would be tested so that all my muscles ached but each morning I awoke refreshed and ready again for the vineyards. As I was involved in the making of wine, even at the very beginning of the process, I made up my mind to pray to Allah when I could, or when I remembered. Intellectually and morally, this idea was doomed: that I might placate Allah by offering him *more* prayers rather than fewer, like offering to run errands for one's mother to lessen one's misbehaving.

Louis Pasteur wrote: 'A bottle of wine contains more philosophy than all the books in the world.' If that is true, making wine, being involved in the making of it, should not be seen as sinful but rather welcomed for providing work, paying bills, and so forth. Nevertheless, I would continue to pray in the hope that Allah might forgive me. I had also decided that I would not pray just to be assured of a happy life in paradise. I had no wish to live in eternity being cosseted by *houris* but rather to slip away, go back to star dust, from which we humans are said to have evolved. I had the thought too about all the barren sand around Mecca – it was not grape-growing country – and more's the pity. If vineyards had flourished around that holy spot it could be conjectured that Muhammad, peace and blessings be upon him, might have been ingenuously seduced by the ruby tides – and perhaps taken a less vitriolic stance on alcohol.

As for Adam and Eve in a garden – and Noah counting the animals into the Ark – what wondrously fanciful ideas! However, Adam and Eve appear in the three major Abrahamic religions – Judaism, Christianity and Islam. Belief in one god, monotheism, and in the role of Abraham and his descendants, feature prominently in all three.

The Jewish New Year is known as Rosh Hashanah, the birthday of the universe, that very special day when God created Adam and Eve. You may see the deity written as 'G-d' in some Jewish literature – too sacred to be written or spoken. God is proclaimed as the 'King of the Universe' on this day, and there is much blowing of the *shofar*, a ram's horn. A cantor or choir leader sings *Hineni*, Hebrew for 'Here I am.' This in memory of Abraham speaking to God, about to sacrifice his son Isaac. A singer who is dead now sang about it – songs about imperfections, flaws, cracks in things, but the breaks allow in the light. If everything was perfect it would make no sense, and only Allah can make something that is perfect.

Ten days after Rosh Hashanah is Yom Kippur, the holiest day for Jews, the Day of Atonement. It's a time of fasting and prayer, when God decides whose names will go into 'the book of life' for the coming year. Wicked people who fail this test will be condemned to death.

In Islam, Adam was the very first human who learnt how to plant seeds, harvest crops, and bake them, whether in an oven or not is not specified. He was extraordinarily clever: God told him what foods to eat and not eat, he was made the first prophet by God, who also taught him a number of scrolls (21), so much so that he was able to write them out himself. Of such fables and myths, there are far too many in all religions, so I must soon continue with my story.

The Christian idea of 'original sin' has always seemed to be a good example of original nonsense – the idea that all humans fell from 'divine grace', heaping blame on Adam, that humans inherit Adamic guilt. According to Martin Luther, we are all in a state of sin from the moment of conception. Such an idea, the concept of inherited sin, is absent in Islam and most of Judaism. In Islamic teaching, Adam and Eve were forgiven by god. On the subject of similar religious beliefs, Muslims believe in the second coming of Jesus Christ – definitely not the one envisaged by Yeats, where among the indignant desert birds 'the rough beast', whatever or whoever that might be, 'Slouches towards Bethlehem to be born'. Today, it is not Bethlehem that is the focus. It is, was, and probably always will be, among the Abrahamic religions, Jerusalem.

For Jews it is the place where Abraham nearly sacrificed his son Isaac. Solomon built his temple there. All synagogues face it. For Christians, Christ preached in the temple, and ate his last supper; his tomb is in the Church of the Holy Sepulchre, so the Holy Sepulchre is always associated with Christ's burial and resurrection. For Muslims, it was the original *qiblah*, and the city to which Muhammad made his dramatic night-time journey, and ascension to heaven from Temple Mount (site of the Al-Aqsa mosque) after first engaging in a prayer session with other prophets. In heaven he had an audience with God, who told him about the importance of prayer and not much else. The holy city is often called Al-Quds in Arabic ('the Holy City'). In Iran, one of our elite fighting units is known as the Quds Force, a Special Forces division of the Revolutionary Guards. One of their main motivations is 'the liberation of Jerusalem'. Everyone still fights over the holy city.

Each time I attempted to pray to Allah, I could manage only two lines, as I had done earlier. The last three lines would not form on my lips.

In the name of God, Most Gracious, Most Merciful
Say: He is Allah, the One and Only!

Worse still, when I spoke my prayers, I did not see Allah as some supernatural lord of the universe but the face of another human being. I saw Madame Saintoissant's daughter: Margot, with her pretty face, no not pretty, but a divinely beautiful young woman with the face of a goddess (no particular religion either). High cheekbones, a straight, noble nose, lips more luscious than crimson cherries, flowing hair the same colour as her horse, cascading to frame a vision of loveliness. Her eyes the windows of her soul, yes – her eyes could make an unbeliever believe in souls.

I remembered my uncle then. How he made me bring back the scroll of names, and immediately I imagined Margot herself writing her own name, and I was guiding her fingertips. Well, I suppose, we all have dreams. To tell you the truth, I thought I might as well as have been scattering *tokhmeh* in the vineyards, making idle wishes, as I had done once before on Magdalen Bridge. By good fortune some of us go to *Jannah* and some by misfortune to *Jahannam* and there is no telling which. If only Margot could be my *houri*, my companion, here on earth!

That was too much even for me, so I got out of bed and uttered one more prayer to Allah. Is Allah not there to listen to us? If not, to whom are we praying?

Seventeen

By late September most of the grapes had been picked. My time as a *vendangeur*, a grape picker, was coming to an end. The highlight of this time was the '*bal*' given by the Saintoissant family – a ball in the French village style, like a *bal musette*, in a barn behind the big house. It was a bit like French café music, with two accordionists, a harpist, a fiddler and a French horn player. Do you remember that kind of music, the kind you hear all over France, especially in Paris?

I find the music hypnotic. It may be predictable but it carries you along in a light-hearted way. People are much *happier.* They want to dance. Monsieur Daudier, the winemaker Alphonse, was there with his wife, as were most of the workers from the vineyards, who I think still had aching thighs and backs. Gilles was arm-wrestling. There were people I had not seen before with Madame Saintoissant, grandmothers with grey hair, old men with pipes, and neighbours with their families. There were children of all ages running around, one or two dogs following. There was food everywhere, soft creamy cheeses, pâtés, *saucissons*, canapés and crudités. Thin slices of ham with olives. Large baguettes to fill with whatever you liked. One might avoid the ham out of religious necessity but for those who take an interest in such things, the delicious *saucissons* are likely to contain cured pork.

Of course, there was wine, mostly from the estate. White,

red and rosé, the red from a barrel, and, partly hidden by glasses, several bottles of *eau-de-vie-de-marc*. All of the above, you realise, is only happening because of the sturdy vines with their flowerings of fruit. For the purist a grape is a berry if classed or classified botanically – just as chilli peppers are fruits and not vegetables.

The music stopped for a few moments. Margot had arrived with a group of girlfriends, wearing a white summery dress with thin shoulder straps. I saw she noticed me, and at the same time Gilles dropped his guard in the arm-wrestling and was beaten. Margot came towards me.

'Would you like to dance?'

I am sure you must have experienced something similar – at least once in your life, or perhaps more, the heart-stopping. It is always one of recognition by the self, because you are witness to a beauty that shakes your heart, as it did Sappho, when she remembered how without warning the whirlwind shook an oak. It reaches the heart instantly. Another name for this might be Stendhal's syndrome – being made faint and dizzy at the sight of great art, ineffable beauty. I don't know if Saint Dennis could still have experienced this feeling, after his head was cut off. After carrying it for some six hundred yards, he dropped dead. Perhaps he knew only the text of his sermon, mere words in his head he insisted on preaching with his last steps, even though his head was separated from his body.

'In Iran we are always dancing. We dance to everything!' I took her hand, my heart pumping exuberantly like a drummer boy before battle.

Something of the old dervish dancers, we call them *darvish* in Persian, the whirling dancers, celebrated by the great Sufi poet Rumi, entered my soul. I made twirling movements with my hands with outstretched arms, one palm to the sky, one

146

palm to the earth in circular movements like a cosmic whirl, spinning in unison with the world; my single pair of shoes tapped the floor as if always trying to find my feet; my body an embrace with the space between me and Margot. I felt I was better than Zorba! It was time to abandon my shyness. We Persians are never shy when we dance. Life is to be lived for that very moment, we are without inhibition, and we give back to our ancient history something unique. A Persian in the act of dancing is abandonment to an intricately sensual sequence of self-expression, without artifice, without guile, a form of innocence known only to the dancer, communicated to the other dancers. How pure it is to dance like a Persian!

She had asked me a question with only five words. I did not answer with words but with dancing until there was only me and Margot, or Margot and me, with everyone watching, even Gilles so caught up that he was beaming with good-natured humour and urging us on. For the first time Margot called me Reza, not Mohammad or Mohammad Reza.

'*Mon cher Reza!* You are a very good dancer.'

'To dance is to be alive,' I shouted passionately. 'Life must be lived.' At the same time, although I was elated by dancing with Margot, I felt my words were mere truisms.

'Time to celebrate *la vendange*,' Margot yelled at me. 'Come on!' She grabbed my hand just as I was imagining the *darvish* dancers and trying to be like them, my arms outstretched and hands twirling in small circles. Margot managed to pull me aside. She took hold of a bottle of marc and poured generous measures into two glasses.

'Margot! What are you doing?'

She shrugged her shoulders as if it was nothing. '*C'est la vendange*, Reza! Anything goes!'

Without any hesitation Margot sank her brandy, making her

eyes screw up, then water copiously as if she had been crying. To tell you the truth, I actually considered for a moment Allah and his prophets and angels getting ready to send down their curses if I so much as swallowed a single drop. But, I had '*bal* fever', induced mainly by the merry accordionists, the fiddler, the French horn player and the harpist. There is no doubt that if I were ever to reach *Jannah* in another life, I would cry with happiness at having been saved from the Burning Pit of Fire. And I would want to dance! Not recline on cushions in pavilions, eating my fill to abundance, and being swamped 'to the gunwales' by virgins, as tall as giants.

'Let's go outside,' Margot urged. So we left the noise of revels in the barn and emerged into the cool night air. '*Aah, regarde les étoiles!*'

'It is exactly like this in Iran at night. The sky is always full of stars.' And yes, I did reflect a moment, in memory of that pilot seer who wrote, 'If you love a flower that lives on a star, it is sweet to look at the sky at night.' A lover after all holds all the heavens in his embrace. His passion reaches to the stars. He feels a kinship, an affinity in his deepest soul because he knows the depth of his love is as immense as the night sky above him. Like the starry night above Van Gogh's café terrace, all the vast night sky, every black chink of it, every shining unknown star, shares with him the same secrets.

'Make a wish,' she whispered to me. 'Try, it might come true.'

'I wish for…health and happiness…as there is no happiness without health…and a long life.' We both looked up as if simultaneously making wishes. 'And you? What do you wish for?'

'A good vintage, of course,' she laughed. 'Margaux makes some of the best wines in the world. And my family, I wish for them too.' She adjusted one of her shoulder straps. 'Do you like swimming, Reza?'

'I was swimming in the Caspian Sea, earlier this year, with no clothes.'

Margot looked shocked. 'I didn't think that was possible in Iran?'

'No, it isn't allowed but I didn't care.' I told her the story of the young girl beaten by zealots for swimming in the 'wrong' place, and how the girl had been paralysed, why in support of the girl I tore off my clothes and ran in naked.

'*Comment intrépide*,' she said quietly to herself. '*Bien*, at the weekend we'll go swimming, Reza. The sea is still warm.'

'Is it far?' I asked her, thinking about what I could possibly wear. I still had my rucksack, could borrow a towel from my bedroom but had no swimming costume. I asked Margot about that and she said she would find something that had belonged to her father.

'It's about an hour's drive. We have many fine beaches. There are beaches at Arcachon, Cap Ferret and Dune du Pilat. We can drive west to Lacanau – it has the nearest beach with kilometres of sand and the rolling ocean.'

I don't know why but the mention of dunes set my heart singing. One song I remember from my college days had the line, 'Let's slip off to a sand dune, real soon.' There was another line about singing your camel to bed. Only years later did I find out it's not about crooning the camel to sleep but *sending* it to bed. My god, I just remembered the Battle of the Camel! Aisha, then Prophet Muhammad's widow, led a battle on a camel – the Battle of Jamal. It was fought between Ali, the first Imam of the Shi'as, regarded by Shi'a Muslims as the rightful successor to Prophet Muhammad (and also his cousin and son-in-law), and Aisha (may Allah be pleased with her). Her warriors grouped around her camel, holding its reins to protect her, but one by one they were beheaded. The battle ended when Ali commanded his men to cut the legs off Aisha's camel – so she was dragged from her howdah, and the battle was lost.

This event happened a long time ago in 656 CE but from this date you can trace all the divisions between Sunnis and Shi'as. The majority Sunni population believes that Muhammad, who died in 632 CE, had no rightful heir and they prefer to elect their own religious leaders, whereas Shi'as believe only Allah can choose who are the leaders, hence they must be direct descendants of Muhammad's family, like Ali ibn Abi Talib (Imam Huseyn, a grandson of Muhammed).

As our family were Shi'as, we took little notice of Sunni practices. Our main annual celebration was at Karbala in Iraq, where Imam Huseyn was martyred (captured and beheaded) at the Battle of Karbala in 680 CE. Shi'as observe Ashura on the tenth day of mourning in memory of Imam Huseyn. On the day of Ashura, when I was growing up as a boy in Iran, I can even remember my father, who did allow himself a glass of vodka from time to time, consider the day of Ashura to be so holy that if would immediately rinse his mouth with fresh water if he had allowed himself a small shot of vodka beforehand.

Sometimes people ask me, without warning, what is your most ardent desire, your most fervent wish – as if I had the lamp of Aladdin in my gift. Nearly always I know the answer. It is to heal the rift between Sunni and Shi'a, which is worse than the most odious, disgusting and vile of all poisons. If Allah truly knows best, he did not foresee how hate corrupts these two main branches of Islam. If ever there were to be another prophet, of course not like the greatest of them all, peace be upon him, but some other divinely inspired messenger – that wondrous person must bring the message of mutual acceptance and tolerance of each together in a great act of healing and understanding, such as when an intractable wound somehow manages miraculously to heal itself from within. Sadly, *pacem in terris* – peace on earth – is a long time coming...just like another kind of impossible dream.

Two days later I climbed into Margot's Citroën, a pair of her father's swim trunks in my rucksack. We drove through pretty countryside, with more vineyards leading past small lakes and pine forests. In the pine forests, *les cigales* or cicadas kept up a strident din. I had the silly thought that each one was a miniature Gregor Samsa, in bug form, with noisy wings. We reached Lacanau after an hour or so. Margot went a little to the south until we parked by a huge dune (although compared with the monstrous sand mountain that is the Dune du Pilat, it really wasn't much bigger than a molehill). I ran excitedly to the top with Margot right behind me. I thought of those Greeks in Xenophon's time shouting with joy at the sight of the sea. The ocean was an immensity, and rugged surfers rode the Atlantic rollers with ease.

Margot's bikini was a delicate red colour; imagine wine dark or regal red. Her body seemed so athletic, her legs long and in great shape, like her arms, from working the vineyards. Her father's trunks were a good fit, thankfully. Luckily the sun was still warm – it was about two in the afternoon – but the sea for me only just bearable. We swam a little and splashed about like children. When Margot walked out of the water, my eyes followed. I admired the curve of her hips and their seductive swing. At once I felt Allah might be displeased with me but I also felt sufficiently strong to ignore such an idea. I was not being seduced by some terrible lust but incited by beauty. In fact, later I came to know that the incitement of beauty is something so natural, cleverly worked out by nature, that it is pointless to fight it. The selfish genes wishing to reproduce simply suborn beauty to their aid, commandeering the senses and most of the victim's thoughts, and even dreams under the cover of darkness. I wondered why Gilles had reacted so badly. I supposed he had been similarly mesmerised but for some reason he couldn't handle it.

After our swim we walked along the beach. We'd seen a flag flying above what seemed from a distance to be nothing more than a shack, like another beach explorer on another continent described in the book *Papillon*, if you can believe the story. As we drew nearer, the shack seemed mostly made from driftwood and long planks, rescued from a shipwreck. In fact it was a beach bar or *cabane à huîtres*, an oyster shack.

Sea creatures that are not fish with scales and fins are considered *haram* by many in Iran. An exception is made for shrimps and caviar. Lobsters, crabs, and shellfish are not *halal* and because of this, although I had tasted caviar, I had never eaten an oyster, a cockle, a whelk or a clam.

'How are you feeling?'

'Refreshed,' I answered truthfully.

'People here love oysters but I don't like too many at once. Shall we have *une demi-douzaine* each and a glass of white wine?'

We sat down by a small driftwood table. The oyster menu listed them as *petit, moyen, grand* and *très grand* – from small to medium to large and very large. The idea of drinking white wine reminded me of Alice lying down on the grass in Christ Church Meadow. I quickly realised that a repeat of my previous performance was undesirable. It was not the time to be squeamish; I had to play the man.

'Can't remember the last time I had oysters,' I lied. Squeezing a few drops of lemon on the *moyen* oysters, I picked one up. It slipped down my throat leaving an aftertaste of the sea. I am not too sure how to describe it 'organoleptically', which

I believe is the right word. It contained something of the briny ocean with an ozone freshness. *Why* would anyone wish to declare such fruit of the sea as *haram*? The white wine was perfectly dry and crisp, and cold – the bottle studded with tiny beads of condensation. I saw Margot's face glowing from our swim, flushed a little from the wine.

'Do you like the wine?' Margot asked me.

'It's perfect.' The wine had relaxed me. My muscles, exerted from the swim and the walk up and down the sand dunes, loosened contentedly. The idea of Jahannam seemed very distant, far out of mind, even when Margot poured me another glass. Just then she placed her hand on my thigh, quite innocently, to thank me for the day out. The touch of her hand warmed my heart. 'How strong is this wine in alcohol? We call alcohol '*mashroob*'. I looked carefully at the bottle; it was 12.5%.

'It's not strong,' Margot told me reassuringly. Perhaps she had noted my earlier reluctance to drink at the dinner table. 'One day, you must try some of the wines from Château Margaux, really good ones. We have in our cellars some bottles from 1970, 1985, 2000. Others from 2004 and 2005 are still maturing but are good to drink now. You would be amazed by the experience. Our own Chateau La Comtesse de Margaux is beautiful too. You must try some!'

What most impressed on my mind then was that trying one of these grand wines was going to be 'an experience'. How different from life in Iran! Of course many people drink alcohol in my country – in secret – but if the morality police catch you the punishment is 80 lashes or prison. Once you begin to think about one country, another comes to mind – I mean what are 80 lashes when in Saudi Arabia you can get 1000 lashes as jailed Saudi liberal and blogger Raif Badawi did, although so far he has only had 50 lashes because his health is poor. Just to be clear, he was not drinking alcohol. His crimes included insulting Islam – through his website – and 'promoting liberal thought', apostasy, and 'going beyond the realm of obedience'. If one is unfortunate enough to be detained in Dubai for minor misdemeanours, legal punishments include 80 lashes for insulting a person's honour, alcohol consumption, kissing in public, and 100 lashes for 'illegitimate pregnancy', and for premarital sex. Death by stoning and crucifixion are other punishments, as well as death for apostasy. A woman victim reporting rape is likely to face flogging and a long time in jail. It is illegal for Muslim women to marry non-Muslims. Swearing on Whatsapp can result in a fine exceeding $65,000, imprisonment, and deportation.

Suddenly, the study of Franz Kafka's work did not seem so alien to me; this was the surreal as experienced by some of his characters – punished, but in the absence of any crime being committed. One can see why no criticism of Islam, however minor, is allowed, and is 'stamped on'. As soon as one confronts edifices of constructed beliefs with rational thinking – if one is even allowed to draw out a single brick – the structure is in danger of collapse. Eventually the beams that support the entire construct must be shored up with the corpses of those who disagree or take exception – further reinforced with the disposable bodies of martyrs. Of course, Allah must have taken this into account. Allah knows best.

We did not say much on the drive back through interminable tracts of pine forest, and then miles of vineyards, most without their perfect parcels of pleasure – the grapes. The vine leaves were turning into a fiery riot of autumn colours – yellow, brown, orange, crimson and scarlet. Some of the vine leaves were the same colour as claret, that word so beloved by the British as their name for red Bordeaux wine. Claret can be traced back to the time when King Henry II of England married Eleanor of Aquitaine and acquired through marriage a large tract of France. One of the most popular Bordeaux wines shipped to England was then known as 'Clairet'. The Bordeaux region is home to many famous wine communes including St Estèphe, Pauillac, St Julien, and Margaux; Pessac-Leognan, Graves, Barsac and Sauternes; St Émilion, Pomerol, Fronsac and Côtes de Blaye.

When we got back to the estate, it was dusk. The great house loomed up as we drove in to park in the courtyard behind. Margot walked back with me. 'Thank you for today, Reza. I'll never forget that poor girl in Iran, in the Caspian Sea.'

On the steps just outside the front door, Margot leaned forward and kissed me lightly on the lips, at which I have to say my heart jumped. I was expecting a kiss on both cheeks and perhaps even a third, in the French manner, but not on my lips. For a moment I held her in my arms and it seemed to me as if I were holding a kind of treasured thing to which I had no right. I kept my kiss in return quite brief. Just because the national motto is France is *'Liberté, égalité, fraternité'*, how could I take liberties with her? Suddenly, without warning, a vision of Ghorbali Khan came to me. He was standing so proudly in his fighting uniform, this man who led three hundred fighters, his *'Jangalis'* (from *Jangle*, the 'Jungle Movement') in a bid to end government corruption, foreign interference, and bring about tax and land reform about a century earlier.

He gave me courage. I turned back and caught Margot's hand. I kissed her again a little more fully, and held her head through the curls gently with my hands. To my utter amazement Margot did not rebuff my affections. I could even taste the saltiness of the sea on her cheeks. It was the most magical kiss of my life. 'The most perfect day,' I told her. *'À demain!'* she answered, as if to say we would continue the next day.

155

I did not bother eating anything for dinner. I was simply not hungry although my body was aching for Margot's kiss. I ran up the stairs to my room, not bothering to turn on the light, just standing there in the darkness, holding my head in my hands, crying my happiness to God. It was just unbelievable.

I felt so light-headed, as if I had drunk a potion of spells. My mind was infected as if by a secret philtre, slipped to me on the night air by her lips. Sensing the need to do something, I made an effort to locate the Kaaba (*qiblah*), even roughly, it did not matter. Of course I could have used my phone; Google map data ('Qiblah Finder') would have shown me instantly but I felt inspired to guess, noting where the last light of the sun lit the sky from my room, and taking from that an approximate angle.

This time I thought I should really pray my best, so I began:

Praise belongs to God, Lord of the Worlds,
The Compassionate, the Merciful.
King of the Day of Judgment.
'Tis Thee we worship and Thee we ask for help.
Guide us in the straight path,
The path of those whom Thou hast favoured…

I got stuck as soon as I said '…the straight path, The path of those whom Thou hast favoured.' Did not Allah lead me? When I asked myself that question, I felt like those poor souls who answer polls or surveys in this way: the 'don't knows' who cannot make up their minds, who can't decide which way to turn.

I even wondered if my thinking about it made any difference, since 'Allah is the One who sees all that his slaves do.' It is quite hard for some to find the true path in Islam, the straight path, because life becomes complicated with so many rules and prescriptions. *Fatwas*, or rulings on Islamic law, are non-binding and only advisory but many people take them seriously, especially the scholars. A question (no. 140497) on an Islamic question and answer forum is 'Responding to Greeting of Parrot'. A questioner asked about passing a parrot in his grandfather's house. As he went by, the parrot (*bahgba*) greeted him with the Islamic greeting, '*Al-salāmu 'alaykum*' (peace be upon you) and returning the greeting is usually obligatory. The wise answer given was that the parrot saying 'salaam' was not an act of worship or supplication by the bird; it had no such intention, being without the power of reason, it was merely mindlessly repeating what it had been trained to do, so there was no need to give the parrot a formal reply.

Anyway, none of these important or trivial questions mattered that much. It is not just impending death that focuses the mind. There are many other contenders, and one of these is falling in love.

Eighteen

THE NEXT MORNING DELIVERED ME TWO PECULIAR 'BLOWS'; one mental and the other physical.

Being brought up in an Iranian household, where the Islamic way of doing things was not constantly rammed down my throat or forced upon me, had given me a fair degree of latitude in my thoughts. But, that morning, as I was shaving, I thought perhaps I should acquaint myself more fully with the requirements of what the Americans call 'the rest room'.

Answering the call of nature, if you are a devout Muslim, would provide plenty of reading material when sitting down to read the detail *but* reading a newspaper, any verse from the Qur'an, chewing gum, smoking or singing on the toilet are all frowned on. 'In the name of God, most Gracious, most Compassionate (*Bismallah ir-Rahman ir-Rahim*)', so what? Does it matter that I am supposed to enter with my left foot and leave with my right foot first? It is surely most wise that anything like an amulet with the name of Allah on it should be hidden from view. Likewise, strict Muslims will utter a prayer or two on entry to the 'bathroom', including a verse which asks for protection from male and female devils, because djinn and devils people such places. Private parts must only be 'revealed' at the very last moment, the closer to the ground the better and quickly covered up after. Indeed, the Qur'an says (2.222) that 'Allah loves those who keep themselves clean', which is very solicitous of him.

Please never squat on a toilet facing in the direction of Mecca, and certainly don't keep your back and behind facing the *qiblah* either. Always use the left hand and three middle fingers to clear away 'the filth', never use your right hand. Use water to clear away the 'filth' or the help of three or more stones; if there is no cloth for wiping; one can use toilet paper if provided, since toilet paper is made for that purpose, but not any other kind of paper. Never urinate standing up, or hold your penis with your right hand. Urinating standing up is a sure way to go the Burning Pit of Fire when you die. One must be very careful to wipe in the correct direction, to avoid exciting the sexual organs, and naturally when our sisters wash themselves, they should not open their legs too wide. A person should not spend too long sitting on the toilet as this encourages piles.

Never get any drops of urine on your clothes or your hands or there will be more punishment in hell. If there is just a mere drop of urine left after shaking, the devout should find a piece of cotton wick about the size of a barley seed and insert that into the very tip of the opening to prevent the last drop from spilling out and soiling one's clothes.

One should never look at one's private parts unless out of absolute necessity (if one does it may weaken the memory); armpit hair should be removed regardless of gender, cover the head when entering the bathroom and leave it covered until one exits; say a prayer or two just before leaving (asking for pardon and praising Allah (the Exalted One) for granting relief from discomfort); preferably wear separate clothes solely for use in the bathroom; always wash one's hands afterwards; and exit the bathroom with the right foot first. Do not talk to anyone in the toilet as Allah is displeased if two people who are uncovered talk to each other. It is better to cough three times as an indication that one is also in the toilet. The various prayers and supplications are intended to help the *Ummah*, which is the Islamic world and its people as a community, to avoid the influence of *Shaytân*.

I don't have any objections to these rules because it is known that Allah knows best. I merely question their practicality.

The second blow that morning happened like this. As the harvest was virtually over, I had been given access to the office containing the various files of expenses, profit and loss, wages, etc. I could see on a computer what stocks of wine were held, and the various orders and estimates of total production and sales. Being a novice, my role was simply that of becoming acquainted with their accounting and payroll systems.

I had my lunch in the canteen. It was there I saw Gilles skulking, or so it seemed to me, in the back of the courtyard. He was pacing up and down like an imprisoned Amur tiger – perhaps I should say like a Caspian tiger. His way of walking gave the impression that he was trying hard to contain himself, a kind of premeditated foreboding of a sudden rush, to strike at some unseen assailant he knew was nearby. I had to leave by the courtyard, so I hoped he might give up by the end of the afternoon, having expended all his energy by then.

At six I closed the office. There was no one in the courtyard. Perhaps Gilles had gone. I didn't have to walk far. He was there, waiting for me behind a stone wall. Gilles was staring hard at me as I approached.

'I saw you were out with her yesterday. I am not happy with that!'

If there is one thing I dislike intensely, it is someone telling me they are 'not happy' about something, something of minuscule importance I have allegedly done to them, as if I am totally responsible for their happiness or lack of it. Thugs use this kind of behaviour. They are upset, so the thug thinks (if they ever do

161

actually *think*) that you must 'pay' for their being upset. People get upset about so many small things. Have you taken their parking space? Have you put the wrong rubbish in the bins? Have you parked carelessly? Are you looking at them? Have you upset the Prophet (peace and blessings be upon him) by drawing a cartoon? Have you blasphemed? Are you an idiot? Imagine eight billion people with 'gripes' about this or that. There is so much pain in the world with hunger, disease, finding somewhere to live, being attacked by strangers, being raped, knifed, and shot, or maimed by bombs or mines. What a mess!

'You went out with her!' He was squaring up to me ready to fight. I told him it was nothing, not important, and tried to reason with him.

'*Salaud! Fils de pute! Putain de merde!*' I was a bastard and the son of a whore, and worse still. Still I contained myself. I had no argument with him. I even sympathised with his plight. Persians are not cowards, I told myself, even though King Darius III, the last king of the Achaemenid Empire of Persia, fled from Alexander the Great but, if one loses a battle, discretion, as the English say, is always the better part of valour.

Gilles lunged at me with a right hook. I neatly sidestepped it. His face grew even more contorted, a bit like those grinning gargoyles one sees above the guttering on English cathedrals. He threw more punches and most of them missed. I only felt the last one because it hit me square in the face. '*Ay voy!*' I said to myself, an expression we Persians use when surprised or scared. Then, '*zahré mār*', which means, literally, 'the poison of a snake'.

My mother would have yelled, '*Pedar sag!*' at him, telling him his father was a dog. By then I could taste blood in my mouth. I got my right arm round his neck and with my left tried to restrain his arms. Gilles kicked at my shins, catching me off balance so that I fell over. He stood over me, grimacing with the relish of someone who thinks he has won the fight. I was winded by the fall, lying flat on my back. My *khahar kuchulu*, my little sister Bahar, often played a game with me when we were growing up. I lay on the ground with my legs in the air; she got them under her arms, and I lifted her up. As Gilles launched himself at me, I tried the same trick. My feet touched his chest, and then I lifted his weight, thrusting my legs as far back as I could. Gilles went right over and landed in a heap behind me.

He tried to get up and did. I shouted to him to stop but he wouldn't listen. With a choked roar of suppressed rage he came straight at me. This time he walked into my right fist, the punch aimed to the side of his jaw. He dropped like a stone.

Some workers from the canteen had gathered to watch. Fearing for my job in case Madame Saintoissant heard the commotion, and having no bad thoughts about Gilles, I helped him up. He brushed away a few bits of gravel from his clothes, and felt his jaw, but I could tell he had not come to any harm.

'*Merde alors*,' he said. '*C'est la vie!*' He shrugged. Then his face opened into a wide smile. '*Tu es vraiment formidable.*' It was evident, unless I was utterly mistaken, that Gilles wanted to be my friend. 'It's over,' he said, speaking in his accented English. 'No more fighting over a woman!'

From that day on, it seemed there was nothing Gilles wouldn't do to help me on the estate.

I met Margot in the lobby of the house the same evening. She suggested going for a walk at the weekend, while the weather was fine. Of course, she already knew about my altercation with Gilles, aptly enough 'through the grapevine'. Margot said we could pick some 'prunes' on the estate, a remark which baffled me until I found out she meant plums or damsons.

'We call them "*alou*",' I told her, a favourite of mine too in

Iran. The taste of an *alou* is tart and refreshing. As well as the *alou*, I remember big golden globes hanging on trees in Iran – these were yellow plums. Persians have a name for these big yellow plums – 'drops of gold' – because that is what they look like, in orchards in the slanting sunlight of evening. My mother had also sent me a parcel from Iran with small packets of *tokhmeh*, *tut*, and raisins, ingeniously wrapped in foil inside two new pairs of socks. I thought I could share the *tokhmeh* and *tut* with Margot on our walk. I transferred them to my jacket pocket. Our raisins are not like the small brown ones usually found in Britain, only good for cakes. Our favourite are the long, sweet raisins from green grapes. Dates we like too – especially the light brown, dry ones not thickly coated in syrup.

I could certainly do with the socks, I thought. My clothes 'wardrobe' was sparse, to say the least. If clothes make the man I might soon be found wanting. Luckily, Margot seemed very unaware of material things, with that young innocence that does not question certitudes and fashions as essential to daily living. That evening we made plans. On the first free day we would hike through the vineyards, look for the *alou*, find a pleasant spot to rest, and then have a *picque-nique*.

Several days later, with a goodbye and blessings from Madame Saintoissant, we set off to the vineyards. Margot had filled my rucksack but I didn't know what she had packed in it. It was quite heavy. Once I made an attempt to open it but Margot abruptly stopped me.

We went through rows and rows of vines with their bright-coloured, fiery vine leaves. At the far end of the estate, towards the west, Margot showed me a small orchard. The apples had all gone apart from some red ones on the ground. But a single small tree with spreading, thin branches had damsons. It was I admit late in the year for damsons yet there they were on the tree in front of me!

'*Alou! Alou!*' I cried with joy. I had not seen any since leaving home.

'Pick some for me, Reza,' Margot said. I gave her two handfuls. We both ate a few. The taste was sharp. The rest she put in the rucksack.

For a while we continued, walking in silence, only the odd remark about a bird seen, or trees in the distance, or the afternoon light. It gave me pause to think a little, what to say, for example, if Margot asked me what I liked about my religion. It would be difficult to express my love for Allah in a meaningful way that another person might understand. I think it was Jesus who said, 'I am that I am.' There is no arguing with that. In the same way, most Muslims, nearly all Muslims, never need to question their absolute love for Allah and his messenger (peace and blessings be upon him).

I think the fresh French air had made me lightheaded. I had only two immediate thoughts, both of which I could not sensibly mention to Margot. Firstly, I was quite pleased that if a person breaks wind (farts) during a minor ablution before prayers, he or she must start again. In Iran we call this gross but necessary act a '*gooz*'. I dislike those people who openly fart in front of you when they hardly know you, especially when they momentarily pause in the conversation, and then self-satisfyingly inform you, after a hideous noise and slight shift in their chair, 'Aah, that's better!' People should keep their *gooz* to themselves, and only broach the air in absolute necessity or urgency.

My second banal thought for the day concerned the phrase, '*Allahu akbar*', translated in the West as 'God is greatest' or 'God is greater'. I had begun to think that it was becoming like a mantra out of control. For many it had become the last words before martyrdom. To be sure, when the end of the world comes, there will be large groups of people yelling something or other, whether it be 'I am Adam, Je suis Charlie, Allah knows best, My god is better than your god, God lives forever, The Earth is not flat, The Sun still shines, The end of the world is nigh, The medium is the message, Jesus Saves!' Anything you care to name. Of course, as Muslims we know that God *is* the greatest, and there is no god but Allah but why repeat it so much that it eventually loses its meaning, and in some cases excuses the most wretched of acts? I doubted if suicide bombers went to *Jannah* as martyrs; instead the moment they blow themselves (and others) into bloody little pieces, they go instead to a Burning Pit of Fire on earth.

Many English people, I know, think that god is an Englishman. Of course they will never mention this to your face but under the surface, this thought has some currency amongst the most stalwart of the English race. They never mention it, being masters of diplomacy. The English way of doing things is very subtle, having acquired a medley of racial characteristics from the canny Celts to the treacherously cunning and adaptable Normans, who still retained the barbarously courageous traits of pirates from their Viking ancestry. If an Englishman went about shouting 'God is an Englishman', before committing some vile deed, he would have no supporters. That, it seems to me, is the trouble with mantras. They become mindless and for the mindless. I suppose saying *Allahu akbar* (not actually found in the Qur'an), known in Arabic as the 'Takbir', and with a finger pointing up, is making a point.

After having run through these thoughts in my mind, I wondered if I had displeased Allah. In which case, should I offer a supererogatory prayer, not one of the obligatory ones but one made up 'on the spur of the moment'? The best I could do was 'Oh God!' Closely followed by *'Khodaier bozorg'*. I tried again. *'Bismillahir Rahmanir Raheem* – in the name of Allah, the Gracious, the Merciful, God with ninety-nine names. I seek refuge with Allah from Satan, the accursed.' Anyway, it was too late for me to learn *all* the Qur'an by heart as that can take six to nine years – unlike the great Hafez, 'the memoriser', who learnt the entirety of the Qur'an when very young.

I was so happy in my contemplative mood that all these thoughts passed unnoticed by Margot, although she had looked at me with concern from time to time. How could I possibly explain that I had just uttered a short prayer seeking 'refuge from Satan', when Margot's family had provided me with a refuge of sorts, as initiated by my uncle?

I began then to consider god in person, surely a mistake. My thought was how patient he must be, having to listen to the wailings, entreaties, supplications, prayers and the like, *round the clock*, so to speak from planet Earth. If we humans, as the Christians say, are made in the image of god, then god must be a little like us in some ways. Did he never get short-tempered? Many, countless numbers, swear their prayers are answered. What about god? Does god not say, if only in fits of remiss, 'Now listen, Mohammad, I have heard your prayers for forgiveness 500 times already, and I can't stomach any more.' Forgetting whether the Holy of Holies actually has (unlikely) an alimentary canal, from mouth to anus.

'Are you ready to eat, Reza?'

'Yes,' I replied unwittingly, thinking only of my mother's *tokhmeh* and *tut*, not what Margot had packed in my rucksack. I pulled out from my pockets the *tut* and *tokhmeh*, inside their parcels of tin foil. Margot seemed highly amused. She tried a few *tokhmeh* after I had shown her how to eat them by exerting gentle pressure between the front teeth. They were not very successfully eaten, and bits got stuck in her teeth but the *tut* she liked. I explained they were dried white mulberries from my mother's garden.

At the far end of the field we were in, a kind of open copse, we found a sturdy wooden bench and table, like ones I have seen outside English pubs – I think they are called picnic tables. Margot reached into my rucksack and pulled out a plastic sandwich box. Inside were four cheese sandwiches with a kind of chutney relish, a handful of white grapes, a *saucisson* cut into several pieces, and some ripe vine tomatoes.

'Voila! Just a moment…'. She reached into the rucksack once more and produced a bottle of estate wine – Chateau La Comtesse de Margaux 2004. It was an '*Appellation Margaux Contrôlée*' wine, bottled on the estate, '*Mis en bouteille au chateau*'. Two wine glasses followed, roughly wrapped in paper. From a side pocket of the rucksack, she took a corkscrew, I think the type is called the 'waiter's friend', easy to carry and open wine with. She extracted the cork, which came into this world, from the confines of the bottle, with a satisfying pop.

Because of the late warmth of the sun, and my general state of happiness, a kind of contemplative harmony flowed through me so that I felt not the least apprehension at the sight of the wine. If only Hafez or that old bibber Khayyam could see this, I told myself teasingly.

'First,' Margot announced as if conducting some sort of ceremony, 'we let the wine breathe. This is a good wine. And before you taste it, you must smell the wine, not once but several times.' So the bottle sat on the table, open to the air. Then there was silence. I looked at Margot, she at me. What she saw in me, heaven only knows. What I saw in her was that which moves the deepest slumber in the soul to awake, from nothingness to the delight of being, to knowing, to an awareness of the most profound beauty. Her face was a moving trance. I mean to say each gesture, each trivial movement of her face, every twitch of an eyelash or cheek muscle, every glance of her eyes, the invisibly slight, fair hair on her upper lip, the playful curl of her lips, the purposeful thrust of her chin, the delicacy of her ears, the perfection of her nose, all conspired in the moving trance.

I suppose you might say I am only sentimentally remembering this, like the madeleine man with his yellow cakes, but this is not so. I really felt as if I were looking at an ideal of perfection, of stupendous beauty, as conceived in the imagination of an Athenian sculptor. If I had to choose only one such great sculptor, it would be Praxiteles, as one might choose Lucretius as the master on the nature of things in the universe – without reference to any 'Supreme Being'. A later sculptor has to be Michelangelo, whose famous Pietà arguably depicts the young face of Mary Magdalene, the lover of Isa, and not his mother. I suppose no doubt this 'attractiveness' is a trick organised by nature. One could not hang 'a mating hat' on ugliness. So let the players be entranced, and apart from pheromones, hormones, and the like, beauty as an attractant serves the purpose well. The web must be spun first before the prey is caught. Of course, this is only on the surface. A new study has shown that the allure of a woman is detectable in her armpits – the aroma is more seductively attractive to men when the woman is ovulating – at her most fertile time of the month.

At that time, I felt like a spectator. I knew Margot would pour the wine, if I did not. In a hopeless move to avoid the inevitable, I suddenly moved on the bottle. 'Shall we try it?' I asked, holding the bottle just above her glass.

'Pour me some, Reza.'

I poured, saw the swirling in the glass, the numerous bubble-beads at the edges, supposed to be a sign the wine is good. Not too many bubbles but more than just a few, or none. I filled her glass one third full, and the same for myself, if slightly

less. I caught her gaze, which met mine, and we were both in
the net, spun I am guessing by circumstance, and the day as it
was that fine afternoon, with the trees waving and rustling their
branches in the slight breeze of a very late summer, and not
a corncrake in sight, which I am supposing was unsurprising
since the grain fields, if any, had already been harvested.

I had only time for a glimpse. In my glass I saw them. The
ruby tides.

'*Santé*, Reza.'

'*Salamati*,' I said.

It was the bite that first caught me, after the heady perfume
of the bouquet. The nose of the wine *must* come first in appreciation, before the palate. The flinty bite of Bordeaux followed. I
did not recognise it to begin with, being like a swimmer under-
water, coming up for air. There was no mistaking it. It spread
around my mouth, the flinty bite, more in the lower parts than
the upper. On the tongue and just under it. Mainly in a region
on the front half of the tongue, and at the sides. I hardly had
to move my glass at all, and looking down, the tides swayed
as if bodily. It was the ruby that entranced me, not the white
diamonds, the pink diamonds, the emeralds, sapphires – none
matched in my imagination this pure ruby, wine dark and regal
red, the 'blood' of the grapes. Nothing of this I really knew
then; it was like a supposition, an inkling, a foretaste, a prophet
of an experience to come, with more knowledge, more understanding that would only follow much later.

Even so I was not prepared. I sipped the wine slowly but
no sooner had I done so than I wanted to discover more. Not
to drink more but to delve into its teasing brilliance, to try to
understand the mystery within it, to know the magic of Margaux! If I waited just a few minutes and tried another sip, not
even a beakerful, even a bib of a tipple, a tipple of a bib (or a

jot of a tittle in the writing of it), my senses responded to further depths and nuances, a sip becoming a sensual mouthful of exquisitely flavourful aromas; of cedars and cigar boxes, blackcurrants and spice, smoky-dark fruits with a touch of graphite and pepper in the long finish, the tannins softened by careful ageing; and also a lightness of touch, a taste that was almost feminine, silky and hugely seductive. Then add floral notes of violets and lilac; and plum and tobacco; truffle and earth. It just had to be savoured, and as the wine 'developed' in my glass, it gave me more, teased me more, to possess it, to understand its beauty, its magnificence. The 'body' of the wine reminded me of a female athlete, sinuous and silky, lithe and supple-strong, except 'strong' is the wrong word, more like subtle depth; the 'finish' long and lingering like the memory of a lover's kiss. And it was not even a second or third growth! Certainly not a *first* growth, of which there are in Bordeaux reds just five – in the whole world! The premier grand crus, originally classified in 1855 on the orders of Napoleon III, including Chateau Latour, Chateau Margaux and Chateau Lafite-Rothschild.

A good Margaux does not shout at you to declare its brilliance. It reveals itself to you, discreetly accompanied by superb harmony. The greatest Chateaux Margaux are works of art; harmonious, sublime and magical.

I think it is the gravel in Margaux, the deep gravel in the stony subsoil of the left bank of the Garonne that lends itself to the magic of the grapes, principally Cabernet Sauvignon, then some Merlot, and perhaps a little Malbec, Petit Verdot, or Cabernet Franc. Vines like poor soil as long as they can reach down to the rocks and stones below for minerals. The 'gravel' is an abundance of 'siliceous pebbles', which also ensures good draining of the soil. Vine roots do not appreciate being waterlogged. But the Cabernet Sauvignon is the prince, the greatest of the red wine grapes in Bordeaux.

'*Santé*, Reza!' Margot cried at me, as if to dislodge my attention from the Margaux. 'You like it?'

'I love…it!'

Margot poured me some more, and then slowly added to her glass. 'You know, this wine *is* my family, part of my family. My father tried for so many years to make the best wine. He gave the world La Comtesse, the noble Chateau La Comtesse de Margaux. *C'est vrai. C'est la vérité.*'

'Aah, the truth!' I said, thinking, I am ashamed to say, only briefly of her father who had tended the vines on the estate, his domaine, and gave his life to the vineyards. 'The truth. It's in wine, is it not? In Persian it is different. We say, "مستی و راستی" – "With drunkenness comes the truth", but that's wrong! A sober Persian is just as likely to tell the truth.'

Margot smiled. 'Reza, I believe Persians are great thinkers, to judge them by you.'

'Sometimes we think too much. This wine is so lovely. It makes me consider very carefully, even imagine, but that's not all. It makes me contemplate. It's better than yoga. It feels like it's taking me on a journey in my mind, by drinking it.'

Things got 'out of hand' quite suddenly. We finished the bottle, wanting more of the red fiend (only later did I learn to treat it with the respect of moderation) but there was none. We had hardly touched the sandwiches. I began to pack the rucksack, thinking it was time to go. I nearly knocked over a glass in my hurry but Margot caught it. Then, quite by chance, I tripped over Margot and knocked her down. She fell on the grass and, having completely lost my balance, I followed until I was on top of her, just like that Iranian imam who said if you fell on a woman because of an earthquake, you would not commit any sin…

There had been no earthquake but that hardly mattered.

'You can kiss me if you like, Reza.' I didn't wait. I found

her mouth next to mine. To kiss seemed the most natural of things. 'Why are you waiting?' she said. 'I…I' Before I knew, I was kissing Margot again, like before, but this time deeper. I saw her brown eyes close over, as if acquiescing. This time, *I am tasting Margot*, I thought, not Margaux but Margot. The conjunction of tongues, if you think about it, is such a strange affair yet the participants yearn for the touch of the other, an entanglement of tongues, an act of sharing, no words necessary, nothing but the togetherness of wet tongues, caressing lips on the sidelines.

A sense of oneness overcame me. I felt one with the earth, its soil, its wine, and with Margot I felt as if I had reached a harbour of contentment, all the bad things in my life were falling away, and the good was gaining ground. We lay together on the grass for some little time, our breathing in time, measured, so calm. The ghost of poor Gregor Samsa had been put to rest, I was sure for ever.

'What are you thinking? Margot whispered but I remained silent.

I wanted to tell her I had been thinking about Allah, not to beg forgiveness for kissing a girl in the open air, or for drinking *mashroob*, which the Arabs call *al-kuhl* from eye paint or shadow made from powdered antimony, and some say *al-khul* meaning 'body-eating spirit' – no, none of these – but instead *to thank* God for that day in my life, the day when everything seemed complete, when the future no longer belonged to ghosts from the past. Instead it lay down a road to a vineyard in Bordeaux, with this wonderful human being next to me.

Nineteen

AFTER THE HARVEST THE CULTIVATION OF THE VINES CONTIN-
ues. In the vineyards it is all-year-round work: pruning to limit
crops and improve grape quality; turning soil over beneath the
vines to aerate the soil and kill weeds; shoots to thin and tie to
wires, suckers to remove, vines to spray with fungicide; long
shoots to trim, more weeding; more spraying of the vines, and
further trimming; after the harvest the ground is fertilised; long
shoots are cut and burnt, usually in November or December;
soil is ploughed over the vine roots to protect from the real danger of frost; any soil washed down on vineyard slopes over the
year is carried back to the top; and at Christmas, or thereabouts,
pruning begins again.

Good vintages are very reliant on the whims of the weather.
Extreme heat punishes the vines. Frost can be catastrophic. Poor
summers with heavy rain often lead to mildew and rot. With the
right factors in balance the better the growing season. When
the ripening is optimal a superb wine of great power balanced
by acidity and tannin may emerge. The *vigneron* in his modest
domaine can produce a marvellous *millésime*, or vintage.

Bad weather, especially frost, in vineyards amounts on
occasion to *force majeure* that will cripple the year's wine production. Very occasionally winter frost is good because frost
hardens the wood and kills pests or spores hiding in the bark.
Frost when buds break and flower is the worst. (I know the

175

weather is important to the English, they talk about it enough. I remember from the TV I saw as a student in Oxford that weather reports appeared regularly like adverts.)

While I was learning these annual routines, it occurred to me more than once that believers in those religions relating to reincarnation, as found in Hinduism and Buddhism, might happily re-visit the vineyards in another life. The perduring self, that part of the soul that remains in existence, even in another body, would find much work to do among the vines, and enjoy the fruits of this hard labour, ageing nicely in cellars, for many years to come.

I have heard it said that for a forest monk in the Zen Buddhist tradition, 'the Kingdom of Heaven is truly at hand'; we don't need to 'go' anywhere or wait until physical death, for when the mind is totally, cosmically tranquil, 'the dewdrop slips into the shining sea'.

At that time I remember Margot was blooming. I dare not think this was because of her recent association with me, but it was very possible. The point about any good relationship is the sharing – a team of two, each contributing to the happiness and well-being of the other, openly, wholeheartedly, honestly. Each time I saw her, whether inside the great house, or out in the fields, in various winery buildings, my spirits lifted. We had little time to spend together because what mattered most was the vineyard, the estate, the renowned 'Chateau La Comtesse de Margaux'.

One day I was sent out to walk round the estate, to check boundaries, locks on gates, incursions or litter, and when I had finished that to patrol the vineyards looking for early signs of infestation of the vines by insects or fungi. On my way, close to the wood where I had ridden Margot's horse, *Châtaigne*, I found two hazelnut trees loaded with plump, ripe shells. The nuts inside were so fresh as to be almost milky. I picked several handfuls, thinking to share them with Margot.

In Iran we have so many treats of nuts and seeds, which we are always ready to offer to our guests or visitors. We call the various nuts '*ajil*'. Then there are the all important sunflower seeds, watermelon, and pumpkin seeds. We also love to eat chocolate (*shookoolāt*), and if there is no chocolate we will chew happily on *lavashak* – tart-flavoured Persian fruit rolls, sometimes known as fruit leather. Perhaps you would like a glass of *sharbat*, a sweet and refreshing cordial or fruit-flavoured drink? You'll find all of these in the Grand Bazaar of Tehran, the *Bāzār e Bozorg*, an old historical market with covered corridors extending over ten kilometres.

'Mohammad?' I don't know how to describe the emotion of cringing and being elated. I had firmly decided on Reza as my name but still if Mohammad came from Margot's lips, it wasn't so bad. She must have walked over from the house to find me.

'Margot!' I exclaimed. 'I was just thinking of you. Look, I have something for you.' I hurriedly brought out some hazelnuts from my jacket pockets.

'Aah, *noisettes*,' Margot cried. 'Let's eat them now.' We need some *galets*.' I had no idea what she meant.

'*Galets* are pebbles, you know, small round stones.' So we found some, crushed the nuts lightly, and enjoyed a late autumn feast.

'Reza?'

'Yes,' I replied expectantly.

'Your uncle is coming to visit.'

'Oh. When?' I wondered why.

'At the weekend.'

All at once thoughts raced through my mind. What was my uncle planning this time? Did he want to send me on another 'mission'? I could not bear the thought of leaving the estate, or having to say goodbye to Margot. Life until my arrival on the estate had always seemed to be a series of beginnings that never got far: I began this, I began that, but more lasting accomplishments eluded me. True, I had mastered some of the intricacies and habits of the English when at university, and I had passed my degree well enough. But as for 'getting to grips' with life, I seemed to have done little.

The doctor I visited in Oxford wanted to send me to hospital; the imam I met had misgivings about me; I could not even manage to seduce an English girl who liked white wine and lying down in a meadow, with the sun shining, and the various birds calling out their encouragement from tree and shrub.

On the other hand I had managed to eat a few *haram* oysters, had discovered I had not forgotten how to ride a horse, had swum in the Caspian and Atlantic, and I had begun to fit in with all the people on Madame Saintoissant's estate, even with Gilles, who now counted me among his best friends. I had learned much about the mysterious qualities of winemaking on a Bordeaux estate, and a little about fine wines. And had contrived, by what means I did not know, to ignite a spark in the soul of Margot. Had she not kissed me four times, or even six times? Had she not clung to me just as a vine stem is attached to a wire? Not overly constrained but happy to be held in an embrace of sorts?

For one fleeting moment, and there are many in my life, I considered disappearing later to my room in the big house. I could close the door and consider, try to think what were Uncle's next plans. If completely stuck, I could pull from 'thin air' some of the ninety-nine names of Allah and start praying. If he had been given so many names, were all of them true? (It's not such a big deal having ninety-nine names. Ahura Mazda had one hundred and one.)

Al-Muhsi (The Appraiser) might be a good one to start with; or *Al-Ghafur* (The Forgiver and Hider of Faults); or *Al-Basir* (The Seer of All).

I must have been daydreaming because then Margot shook my shoulders as if to awaken me from a dream. 'Reza, *ça va? Tout va bien pour toi?*'

'*Ça va bien,*' I answered, trying to sound carefree. I dare not tell her that I was so concerned about my uncle visiting that I had just imagined calling on a few of the ninety-nine names of Allah for guidance.

We began walking back to the house. 'Are you Catholic?' I asked Margot.

'Yes. I was brought up Catholic but you know in France there is a big division between church and state. I suppose I am Catholic but, *vraiment*, in name only.' Margot sometimes reverted to French in the middle of a conversation.

We continued in silence. I had suddenly thought my putative prayers to Allah of no account. I was immensely glad that my mind was not crammed with Catholic prayers: 'O Mother of Perpetual Help, grant me ever to be able to call upon thy powerful name, since thy name is the help of the living and the salvation of the dying...Thou art the advocate of the most wretched and abandoned sinners, if they but come unto thee...'.

Oh, the spectre of Marian apparitions, the Joyful, Sorrowful and Glorious Mysteries of the Rosary prayer; the Glory Be prayer, the Our Father prayer, the recitation of the angelus. The Hail Mary prayer is based on Jibreel's (Gabriel) greeting to Mary. Prayers to the 'God-bearing maid' are extraordinarily numerous. Once I heard the Magnificat, the hymn of the Virgin Mary, sung in King's College Chapel in Cambridge. After that, even with my doubts, the Hail Mary was quite a beautiful prayer, it seemed to me.

'Do you think your uncle will mind that your girlfriend is Catholic?' Margot asked as we walked together.

'*Zahre mar*,' I whispered sotto voce. It's a Persian way of saying 'shut up', like '*tais-toi*' in French, but an expression not to be taken literally, as the translation is 'the poison of a snake'.

'What did you say?' Margot asked.

'It's nothing. My uncle would be too polite to object, too much the gentleman. Besides, Muslims think it's okay to have girlfriends who are "people of the book", like Christians and Jews. Funny thing is a Muslim man can marry a non-Muslim but a Muslim woman has no such right. Marrying a "*kafir*" (non-Muslim) is not permissible. Islam is "to prevail and is not to be prevailed over" is a familiar saying of the Prophet – blessings and the peace of Allah be upon him, naturally.'

'Then we should be okay then,' Margot joked.

'We should be fine!' I laughed. 'But who is talking about marriage? Not me.' I tried to look serious. 'You have to be sure,' I said, 'sure about finding the right person.' I felt such a liar. Inside, my heart had jumped into my throat. I don't really know why this expression is so apt because as everyone knows, the heart is firmly anchored in the chest. It jumped anyway because the prospect of Margot being my bride, my eternal *houri*, was to me a road leading to *Jannah* on earth! Actually, talking of body parts, one of the Hadiths (all the ancillary reports, traditions and commentaries gathered from various sources separate from the Qur'an) notes that 'half of a man's wisdom is lost between the legs of a woman'. As a matter of respect, much as I would have liked to mention this to Margot, I thought it inappropriate. Just as I thought so, I immediately remembered my days at Oxford. I thought of those young men and women prepared to stand up and defend what they believed in, and to say so without fear and with courage made them like Titans of the intellect – I suppose in the same way that I admired Voltaire for being so bravely outspoken. (Monsieur François-Marie Arouet, to be precise, as 'Voltaire' was a pen-name invention.)

From my studies at Oxford I had become acquainted with 'The Age of Enlightenment', and the phrase *Sapere aude*. Dare to think, dare to think for oneself! Have the courage to know! From Horace to the philosopher Kant, others had seen its merit, and the saying was widely used. Finding a path through the various entrenched suppositions on faith, superstitions, revelation, mythology and fear is still a difficult task in the world. Natural, if rare, events like tsunamis and the destruction they bring are often blamed on God because the deity is 'unhappy' about something or other – rubbing it in with celestial vengeance. 'Think for yourself. Learn to think for yourself,' said a voice inside my head.

'Reza, please, stop being so serious,' Margot said. 'I can see you can't stop yourself from thinking about things.'

'I was wondering,' I said, 'why my uncle is coming, if there is any particular reason. Perhaps your mother invited him?'

'We must wait until the weekend,' Margot said. Finally we reached the house. 'Promise me something.'

'Promise what?' I said.

'To go to bed and sleep and not to think into the night, about these things that worry you.'

'I promise,' meaning to mean what I said.

On the steps of the house, away from anyone's eyes, I held Margot in my arms once more, savouring the fragrant odour of her hair, the fiery beauty in her eyes, her mysterious perfume, though faint from dilution by the open air and the fresh fields and vines we had walked through, still what remained reminded me of harems, or seraglios with eunuchs as guardians in ancient Persia, exotic visions of *darvish* dancers seen through clouds of hashish and opium smoke. Say in the time of Esther, who was Jewish, and the Persian King Xerxes, a Zoroastrian by religion, about 480 BCE, when women used pomegranate juice as blusher. Each girl to be presented to the king had, with various beauty treatments, to prepare herself for *twelve months*; six months with myrrh oil for her skin, followed by another six being massaged with olive, cassis and myrrh oils, and honey. The most beautiful of all became his queen.

I had no doubt that Margot needed none of these. She was perfection just as it was, just as she was. Again Margot kissed me, and her kiss lingered. Inside, I melted. There is so much talk about women surrendering to men but in truth it was I who was surrendering. Perhaps in the best unions, both yield equally to the other, without terms and conditions. To give is perhaps the most gifted of love's surrendering.

I gave Margot another kiss.

'You will promise, won't you?' she asked with the softest of feminine voices that men fall for, always fall for.

'I promise of course.' And as if to seal the bargain, I stole another.

'*À bientôt. Dors bien*,' she smiled. I was alone in the hall of the great house, where every hour a gilded ormolu clock chimed the hours and halves. I loved the curtains, if you can call them that. Long spectacular draperies, such high ceilings, a grand staircase with wood panelling all giving a sense of time, of history.

By the time I reached my room, instead of being sleepy from the walk, I was wide awake. As for the obligatory prayers, I was by the mirror in my room, looking at my lips for traces of Margot but there were none. Into my mind came two thoughts that evening, both gleaned from my time in Oxford. They seemed more important than offering a prayer to the greatest God. Of course I don't know if Allah *is* the greatest god, but the phrase *Allahu akbar* seems to imply it.

First, I considered an obscure French-German author and philosopher, Baron d'Holbach, who published a work, entitled *The System of Nature* in 1770. At the time of discovery, I thought to myself that this was only the scurrilous work of an atheist. Even so, one line he wrote has always stayed with me. When describing the average human who believes in *Jannah*, or the equivalent paradise and afterlife, he writes: 'He pretends to know his fate in the indistinct abodes of another life, before he has considered the means by which he is to render himself happy in the world he inhabits.'

Secondly, I could understand giving thanks to the greatest of gods, and asking for forgiveness and direction in life, petitioning for his protection, and so on but did I absolutely need *all* the Five Pillars of Islam, summarised as it happens in a Hadith of Jibreel but open to many different interpretations, for example between Shi'a and Sunni Islam? Perhaps I should briefly explain the Five Pillars of Islam: faith, prayer, charity, fasting and making the *hajj*, the pilgrimage to Mecca. Some say there is even a sixth pillar, *jihad*. Among Muslims jihad is otherwise known as war, or the struggle against unbelievers (*kafirs*). I don't understand why unbelievers are treated so badly. Obviously I love my religion but if the threatened *Ummah* took over the world, even I can see it would not be a happy place.

During the holy month of Ramadan, the ninth month of the Muslim calendar, when fasting is obligatory (to celebrate the first revelation of the Qur'an to Muhammad) a Muslim must abstain from food, liquids, and intimacy from sunrise to sunset. Women having their period cannot fast, read the Qur'an or enter a mosque; they are not allowed to fast as they are not 'pure enough'. *'Zahré mār!'* I thought to myself. If nature had made men menstruate instead, the men would have declared long ago that this was Allah's sign of their special status or even their holiness and it would be completely disregarded. For contrast, Hasidic Jews have customs relating to 'the bleeding' – these decide when intimacy between husband and wife is permitted. A woman must carry small white cloth squares; these have to be inserted vaginally, each one for a few hours, to see if the cloth remains clean. If there is any sort of stain, the wife must take the cloth to show the rabbi; he will take it to a window and, examining it carefully, will decide whether the stain is kosher or not. Some ultra orthodox Jewish practices are even more restrictive than one finds in my country, the Islamic Republic of Iran.

At the end of Ramadan, we have the Eid celebration (*Eid al-Fitr*) involving presents, food, and social gatherings, and greeting others with the phrase, '*Eid Mubarak*' (holy or blessed celebration); the exact date when Eid begins is decided by the appearance of the new moon. In Iran some experts go out to different areas of the country and look for the new moon's crescent, and once seen this confirms the start of the lunar month for our Islamic calendar.

Internally, I was also having a battle with Voltaire, since I discovered that he wrote a scandalous play about our great Prophet: *Le fanatisme, ou Mahomet le Prophète*, or *Fanaticism, or Mahomet the Prophet*. He described Muhammad as 'the founder of a false and barbarous sect'. My blood was boiling or at least roiling when I read this, even more so when I learnt that he described our great Prophet, peace be upon him, as a 'camel-merchant' and that 'To pray to God is to flatter oneself that with words one can alter nature.' My main agreements with him, which are rare, are when he wrote that 'Love is of all the passions the strongest, for it attacks simultaneously the head, the heart, and the body'. Likewise for 'Wherever my travels may lead, paradise is where I am.' And 'We never live; we are always in the expectation of living.'

I believe he wrote disreputable things about Christianity too, describing it as 'assuredly the most ridiculous, the most absurd and most bloody religion which has ever infected this world'.

To return to my beloved Islam. Voltaire I believe later regretted some of his criticisms of our Prophet, peace be upon him, and in later life actually admired him. In a letter to Frederick II of Prussia in 1740, Voltaire wrote: 'But that a camel-merchant should stir up insurrection in his village; that in league with some miserable followers he pretended to them that he talks with the angel Gabriel, that he boasts of being carried to heaven, where he received in part this unintelligible book, each page of which makes common sense shudder...'.

Oh God!

I never ceased to be surprised at Jibreel's various appearances – paying visits to Jews, Christians and Muslims alike. Tolerance of other religions is undoubtedly a virtue. It was King Cyrus, Kourosh Kabir, who wrote: 'Today, I announce that everyone is free to choose a religion. People are free to live in all regions and take up a job provided that they never violate other's rights.'

I threw myself on my bed, and slept deeply, even without resolving the matter of the night prayer. In my sleep I remember I had a dream. A beautiful young girl, perhaps she was a *houri* in disguise, asked me for directions to a certain place. I knew where it was but could not remember how to get there. I jumped in her car, and we drove for some while, but still we could not find the exact place she wanted to visit. After a time, I noticed she relaxed in my company, and trusted me. This feeling of trust was mutual. I adored her for it – but not long after

I found myself on the floor with her, heaven knows where. She had somehow shrunk in size to about four feet, and moving my hand to hold her, noticed she had no clothes on, which I thought strange. I did notice that my body was pressed up against hers with a certain urgency, as if I could not bear to be separated from her by even a tenth of a millimetre.

Then I woke up. Sometimes dreams are remembered but one must be quick, before they depart from the memory. One strange thing I recall is that when my right hand slipped down over her back in the dream, I found myself cupping her buttocks, I hasten to add not in any sexual way. They were so small as to fit in the palm of one hand. The question of size alarmed me. Hurriedly, I looked round my room to see that all was in proportion. The window was the same size, my feet and arms likewise. Nothing around me was either larger or smaller. I had not lost my senses. As for losing my senses, not long after I had another dream. I was lying side by side, myself in the middle, with two young girls, both friends, and to one of them I was more drawn than the other. Much of that night we chatted about things of no matter and then we slept. During the night I was horrified, on being momentarily awake, to find that both my hands had found their way into the most delicately private parts of their bodies. I was reluctant to withdraw my hands from the safety, the moist warmth, even security and unique haven, of such resting places. I wondered if either of the two girls might awaken; my hands were motionless, as I was, supine on the bed, and almost holding my breath. As I drifted off to sleep I was comforted because I realised it was anatomically impossible for me to lie in that position with my hands in their separate entrances, unless I had been double jointed, which assuredly I was not. So presuming it was only a dream I slept deeply, to awake alone in my bed, wondering what had happened to my two companions.

Perhaps Voltaire could enlighten me, or I suppose, more appropriately, Freud. As it happened I had no time for Freud since, when one delves into the subconscious mind, there is no end to the matter, and no telling what might be discovered. It occurred to me that Google was, to all intents and purposes, a modern oracle, with none of the noxious gases emanating from beneath the tripod at Delphi. I had only to input a few words, such as, 'But that a camel-merchant…' and the answer would be forthcoming, dependent only on the reception of a signal. I had lost my sense of earlier outrage, since discovering that Voltaire's 'barbs' were not just directed at our dear Muslim faith but many other faiths. I continued my search and read, '…that, to pay homage to this book, he delivers his country to iron and flame; that he cuts the throats of fathers and kidnaps daughters; that he gives the defeated the choice of religion or death: this is assuredly nothing any man can excuse, at least if he was not born a Turk, or if superstition has not extinguished all natural light in him'.

'Remarkably prescient, my dear Watson,' I found myself saying out loud after the manner of that famous sleuth who seems so deeply embedded in the imagination of the English. A foreboding of the devilry of ISIS/ISIL, the darkest flower of fundamentalist corruption ever to emerge from the repulsive rebarbative depths, paid as 'homage to this book'. When the so-called caliphate was crumbling into dust, during the final siege of Baghouz in Syria, jihadist fighters remained defiant to the end, releasing a propaganda video with a man yelling, 'Tomorrow, God willing, we will be in paradise and they will be burning in hell!' With bombs and mortars from the Syrian Democratic Forces exploding all around them, the civilian remnants still alive were urged to 'go to prayers'. Internally, I found myself responding with that very English expression, 'A fat lot of good that will do.' Other militant Islamist groups include Al-Shabaab in Somalia, Al-Qaeda, and Boko Haram in West Africa – meaning all books, especially Western ones, excepting the Qur'an are haram. *Boko Halal is my answer to them.*

Even so, I thought, from the monstrous crimes of Salafi-jihadism, the ashes of genocide, and the barbarous chains of enforced slavery very occasionally survivors appear, phoenix-like, to rise on the world's stage as heroes or heroines, as with Nobel laureates Malala Yousafzai and Nadia Murad. I remember Nadia Murad, whilst sitting next to co-laureate the most noble and good doctor Denis Mukwege, saying, '…the only prize in the world that can restore our dignity is justice and the prosecution of criminals'. Indifference to suffering, torture, and 'violence against the person' should be *haram* too.

Just then came a knock on my door. I have a thing about 'knocks on doors'. Knocks usually foretell something or other. The severity of the knocking counts for much. They may be loud, threatening, and fearful. Knocks from 'arms of the state', like secret police, come as assault announcing more assaults, when the door is opened. This one was soft, almost polite.

'Good morning, Reza. Can I come in?' Hesitating a little at the door, it was Margot, looking stunning, her hair shining, and her eyes more so. 'I have to go away this weekend,' she said. 'Monsieur Daudier, Alphonse, has asked me to source two new oak barrels that need replacing.'

'Where are you going?' I asked anxiously.

'Only to Bordeaux. Alphonse is after fine grain French oak, 225 litre barrels, *environ*. We call the size "*barrique*". If I am back in time, I will meet your uncle.'

'Thank you. I really hope you can see him,' I said.

'I have heard much about him from my mother. Is it true he was a professor at the Sorbonne?'

'Yes. He also knows everything about fish, sturgeon to be exact, from the Caspian Sea.'

'I will be honoured,' Margot said, smiling graciously. In fact, I found her smile irresistible. So much so that I pushed her gently forwards a little and with one swift pull, she was lying on my bed. It seemed just the right time to show Margot some photos of Iran, of my mother and family. The one of Ghorbali Khan I kept till last.

'He looks a bit like you, Reza,' Margot said. I sensed a hint of pride in her voice. 'He's a good-looking man but he looks a bit fierce too, I mean stern, like we say in French, *arrière*.'

I had to agree. There was a certain austere quality about him. I suppose you had to be tough to live in the mountains and lead three hundred armed men. There was always a rifle at your side and a horse tethered nearby for a quick escape. I'm not even sure who he was fighting against. 'His full title was Ghorbali Khan e-Jangali.' If you hear an Iranian say these words, it sounds most rich to the ears, a rolling cadence of impressive sounds.

'What happened to him, this Ghorbali Khan?' Margot asked.

'Honestly, I don't know but I regret to say that most of his *Jangalis* were defeated by Reza Khan, the father of the last Shah of Iran, Mohammad Reza Pahlavi. Their main leader, Mirza Kuchik Khan and the *Jangalis* froze to death in wintry northern Iran, trying to escape from the Khan's soldiers.'

'Hold me,' Margot said suddenly. 'I don't want you *ever* to freeze to death in Iran. Stay here in France with me!' I kissed her warm lips, and for a few minutes we snuggled closely together, letting the world (and the wine) go on without us. I had never felt so happy. I felt Ghorbali Khan would have been proud of me, if he was there in the afterlife. He would assuredly have escaped from *Jahannam*!

Then I imagined how dear Ghorbali Khan might have died. I hoped it was in his bed, raised up, covered with a light Persian blanket, with all his family at his side. The other Jangal leader paradoxically froze to death in the mountains of north Iran and, if he had been a bad man, that is if he had not followed our Prophet faithfully, when the ice finally crushed his spirit, his will to live, instantly he might have been warmed up in the Blazing Pit of Fire. Imagine that! Unfrozen, only to be burn for ever. I suppose they must be 'spirits' in this blazing fire, since the bones and flesh would turn to cinders in no time.

I felt done with the teachings. I knew only the warmth of Margot next to me. When you are dead you are dead, a truism of course, but it's true! Why should human beings be so endlessly worried about life, as Baron d'Holbach said, in the 'indistinct abodes'? The French philosopher Simone Weil went so far as to suggest that we should prefer a real hell to an imaginary paradise. Why be fearful of perpetual punishment in eternity *when you are in the glorious now?* Even allowing for the fact that some physicists believe the present – now – is merely an illusion. Whether the person who calls it is the Buddha or that man of the road Jack Kerouac, it's all the same.

III

Twenty

IT WAS NOT LONG AFTER THIS ENCOUNTER WITH MARGOT ON
my bed that I began to have doubts about 'original sin', the sin
of disobedience by Adam and Eve in the Garden of Eden, the
act of eating the forbidden fruit, the knowledge of good and
evil, so all humanity is cursed ever after. Yes, there is sin, lots of
it but how did it become humanly acceptable that humans kill
millions of other humans in each century, yet humanity considers this as just about normal? On reflection, I decided I had
nothing against the idea of 'original sin'. Of course, man being
the most accomplished human killer ape of all, it must be a
natural gift. It was only the attribution of sin I objected to; that it
fell on the shoulders of Adam and perpetuated itself via clerics,
along with fig leaves to hide 'shameful' nakedness, and the guilt
of ages. Still, if I were a woman in Saudi Arabia or Afghanistan,
I should prefer not to hide behind even the finest silk burqa. And
sometimes, if a dry and dusty desert wind blew, I would like to
unloosen my hair and let the cooling breezes caress it. In some
Muslim countries women seen with their hair uncovered on
social media have to make grovelling apologies to their fans for
'disappointing and upsetting' them by not wearing a headscarf
– it's like having to say 'sorry' they have head hair, a common
enough attribute of nearly every human being.

I suppose this is wishful thinking – wanting to let the desert
wind play freely through your hair – if you are a woman in

a strict Muslim country. In Saudi Arabia female activists are jailed, tortured, electrocuted and flogged, sometimes left unable to stand or walk, just for demanding the most basic rights for women. The list of female detainees includes all those who simply protested on street corners for the right to drive. The law was changed to allow women to drive but those who had publicly asked for this basic right were subsequently thrown in jail. On the list was Samar Badawi, sister of Raif Badawi – the writer and 'apostate' punished for thinking clearly for himself, beyond the confines of destructive, religious dogma. One of the Orwellian charges against him was 'insulting Islam through electronic channels'. I just don't think Allah takes cognisance of electronic channels – today, tomorrow or on the Day of Judgement. When artificial intelligence (AI) and Allah clash, I wonder which will blink first. Allah knows us in the channels of our hearts. Is that not enough?

Despite leaked news of prisoner torture and abuse by human rights organisations, the Saudi authorities claim all prisoners get 'top treatment'. The cynical would say this sounds not unlike Dubai's official claim that Princess Latifa, having been forcibly returned home, is 'doing excellent', which likely means that doctors who should know better are controlling her mind with drugs. There is just no way of finding out.

Dhahban Prison in Saudi Arabia holds a number of female activists including Loujain al-Hathloul, who has alleged waterboarding and threats of rape in prison just for calling for women's right to drive. A lucky few manage to flee the kingdom. The young Saudi teenager Rahaf Mohammed became a new champion for women's rights when she successfully claimed asylum in Canada, having barricaded herself in a hotel room in Bangkok. I prefer not to enter into any discussion about her statement that she had renounced Islam. Perhaps the main reason was her abusive parents. Who would like to be locked in a room for six months merely for cutting your hair or being beaten up for not praying?

I reflected that in Islam we do not have any concept of original or inherited sin. Adam and Eve sinned but then asked God for forgiveness, and God forgave them. I just wish so many things that can be considered as enjoyable were *not* haram. Games of chance, games involving 'guessing' – especially using those horrible two cubes with dots – these are forbidden. It is written, *'...whoever plays with dice, it is as if he were dipping his hand in the flesh and blood of a pig'*. Board games like chess, draughts, or snakes and ladders are in the main haram also. One cannot play around with luck or chance, as Allah predetermines our fate, and Allah knows best...

Forgive me for these reflections. I must return to my story without delay. Allah likes those who spend their time profitably, and you will want to learn what happened next. The weekend came quickly. My uncle arrived by car on Saturday afternoon, with a passenger. I could not make out who it was at first but then I realised it could only be my dearest sister, Bahar, my *khahar kuchulu*. I ran downstairs to greet them. My uncle was dressed very sombrely in dark suit and black tie; my sister seemed not in her usual gay mood.

'*Amujan, Baharjan,*' I cried out. '*Haleh troubeh?*'

'*Mohammadjan,*' my uncle began sadly, 'I am sorry.' That's all he said. He put both his arms around me. My sister Bahar just stood there tearfully, her face screwed up as if in repressed pain. I knew then, in my heart, that something every child dreads had happened. As my father had died, it must be my dear mother. '*Mama!*' I shouted. Then again, but more softly, as the pain sank in, '*Mama, Mama, Mama...*' By then my voice had turned to a hoarse whisper, and I felt as if someone had clutched my throat, and squeezed the breath from me. My heart beat dully in my chest, as if it had guessed the news too. '*What happened?*' I spat out the words as if cursing the earth beneath my feet.

My uncle's normally taciturn features had softened so that I saw another side of his character. No more the strict disciplinarian but possessed of a kind of benign empathy for the world's misfortunes.

'It was sudden,' he said, 'so sudden. We could not call you to the funeral, there was no time. So we buried your mother in Bandar-e Anzali. Most of her village was there. Bahar made a video for you to see.' I had sunk to my knees. The grief overcame me. My voice trailed away into the Margaux gloom. '*Mama!* O Mama my beloved Mama!'

Now I write this, there was no real gloom in Margaux but it was the time of year, between seasons, when everything dies coming into winter only to be born again in the New Year, the brazier behind the house smouldering with logs and old vine stems, the air heavy with wood smoke, and all the birds silent.

Like a bird myself, I made the most melodious noises in my throat, somewhere between the grief and the gladness, the gladness that my mother had given me so selflessly. I was like a mistle thrush, pouring out my song, at once melodiously beautiful yet ultimately wistful, a lament, forlorn, abandoned hope – all hope abandoned.

My uncle dragged me to my feet. 'Come Reza,' he said, unusually reverting to my favoured name. 'Now you must be strong. We remember your mother's life, and it was good.'

Bahar stepped forward to hug me again, and whispered in my ear. 'She went so peacefully.' I saw her fumbling in her coat pocket, as if to find something. My sister pulled out a small box, a Persian inlaid wooden box fashioned by a marquetry technique we call *Khātam*. 'Mama wanted you to have this,' she said. It was a pretty box in bas-relief with four turbaned men on horseback hunting deer. When I opened the box it had inside a curious mixture – some strands of sheep wool, a few pins, and a fossil. Underneath was a blue silk purse. I wondered what my mother had left me. I knew she kept jewellery, mostly gold, but I thought all of these she would leave to Bahar.

'Open it,' said Bahar excitedly.

'I am trying,' I said. In truth, I dare not open the purse. 'Our mother was always one for surprises,' I uttered weakly.

'You will love it, Reza. I promise you!' Bahar insisted. First, I drew out a gold bangle, heavy and lovely, fit for a queen or a princess to wear. It gleamed in the solemn half-light like a lustrous band of eternal hope, brighter than the soft-dying day, incapable of ever being tarnished even by the dimming twilight. Then my fingers felt inside the silk purse because there was something else too, smaller and lighter. On a thin gold necklace hung something I had never seen my mother wearing, ever: a cluster of diamonds, the back or reverse encased in gold, the diamonds in the shape of a small cluster of grapes. How they gleamed in the half-light! Suddenly my mother's face appeared right there before me. I saw the loving kindness in her eyes, as well as the long, quiet suffering of mothers when their children leave home. 'See,' my sister said excitedly, 'how your mother loved you, to give such treasures!'

I hung my head in sorrow. Even so, the two gifts from my mother changed everything, especially the grapes with their small cluster of scintillating diamonds. I saw my uncle looking at me. His face was drawn yet firm with resolve. I resolved too, to accept the blow of my mother's death. I would not be the first or the last. Suffering and joy come to us. We move on. (It occurred to me at that very moment to address a prayer to Allah, secretly in my heart. It is right to pray since it makes us feel better, as well of course being one of the first duties of a Muslim. I began in my mind with: 'To God we belong, and to Him is our return.' Then I considered it fruitless. Should I thank God for my mother's life or my mother for my mother's life – and my own? I did not know.)

I think we pray for succour, to have 'someone to speak to' if there is no one else especially, as the English are fond of saying when 'the chips are down'. Not as it happens the chips the English, I should say British, consume in vast quantities, their plates overflowing with them. Life is a bit like a game of poker in many ways. When 'the chips' go down on the table, there's no going back, the outcome will happen one way or the other, and it matters not one jot how many prayers for success or love or anything else we proffer to Allah. I have come to believe it is natural to offer prayers to God for two main reasons: to ask forgiveness and to offer thanks. A third would be for the care of loved ones, and a fourth for 'blessings' received. A fifth, even, would be to be kept safe. The sixth to thank Allah for the food we eat and the water we drink. If there are five or six main reasons, it means there must be hundreds more whispered appreciations for smaller gifts, as well as countless thanks, for blessings unknown or unseen. One thinks of praying for succour, strength and aid in the daily travail of life, and more importantly, good health. Just being alive is another reason to pray although of course there is no empirical validity to say being alive is directly related to any deity. A believer can place his or her trust in God without the luxury of ever seeing the deity, and if a prayer is not answered, that is just bad luck or 'hard cheese'. (As a matter of fact, we eat quite a lot of cheese in Iran, and make one very hard cheese called *kašk*, which keeps for many years, and when eaten, it must first be crushed and then dissolved in water.) And – when things go well – we say, 'Allah is merciful.'

We also pray to ask forgiveness for our sins and unworthy deeds and thoughts, our inhumanity to others, our greed, lust, and our conceits – for in truth there are as many bad things in life as there are good. And there is no one else to pray to when we are helpless. I think this is the reason for Voltaire's quote that 'If God did not exist, it would be necessary to invent him.'

'Come now Reza,' my uncle said looking deep into my eyes. 'Let us go inside and see what awaits us.' I had not seen my uncle in this mood before, caring as a father should, helping to shoulder the burden of my mother's passing. As we walked together, with Bahar following, towards the grand entrance in my mind (I remember this well) ran a sudden line from my literature studies: 'And one man in his time plays many parts.' You know, the exits and the entrances.

Inside, Madame Madeleine Saintoissant, standing in the hallway with Monsieur Alphonse Daudier supporting her, his hands resting lightly on her shoulders. Suddenly she moved towards us, her arms in a widening embrace. 'Dr Amin, Reza,' she cried, 'Welcome at this sad time.' Monsieur Daudier, taciturn and strong faced, the master of the wines, possessed that classic French demeanour like the haughty indifference of a courtier. Yet behind the façade there was bonhomie, wisdom and a gentle kindness.

While Madame Saintoissant talked with my uncle and Bahar, Monsieur Daudier took my arm. 'We knew only yesterday of the sad news of your mother. Your uncle rang and informed Madame La Comtesse but he wanted to tell you himself.'

It was turning out to be an eventful day. I thanked the wine master gratefully for this information. He turned to me once more, in a low voice saying, 'At dinner this evening we will have one of the noblest wines of all Bordeaux, in memory of your dear mother. I will bring it myself.' With this he squeezed my arm as if suggesting the bringing of the wine was sealed.

Madame Saintoissant called for some tea, which we enjoyed a little later in the drawing room. After some family discussions, I took Bahar upstairs to see my room.

'*Negah kon!*' I said, showing her the view from the window. 'Look!'

'*Ah! Khoob ast, kheili khoob.*' She liked it. In fact, there was not too much to see in the dark except for lights below in the courtyard reflecting on the yellow stonework of the house but beyond that, in the 'Margaux darkling' as I called it, there was only vivid starlight above the dark shapes of trees at the end of the drive.

'Am I not lucky?' I said aloud, even with this sadness. 'And my dear Muma left me these beautiful things!' I reached inside my jacket pocket for the blue silk purse. Carefully I pulled out first the gold bangle, and then the cluster of grape diamonds. 'Would you like these?' I asked Bahar, feeling unworthy of such fine jewellery.

'No! Of course not. They are yours.'

'Are you sure?'

'Certain.'

'Then I know what I will do with them.'

'You want to give them away…to someone?'

I could feel myself blushing red. 'Yes, there is someone. You haven't met her yet. Her name is Margot, the daughter of the Comtesse, Madame Saintoissant…she is away in Bordeaux this weekend, buying wine barrels.'

'Will I see her?' Bahar asked expectantly.

'She is quite special, and she rides like the wind, as our ancestors did in Iran. If she gets back in time, I so much hope you will meet her.'

'Has she captured your heart?' Bahar asked innocently.

'Sister, she has stolen it! Since I met her I have given up addressing Allah with prayers. Look, in my room, out of this window, is the *qiblah* but I have changed, Bahar. Now I say to myself, "Screw the *qiblah*!"'

'What?' Bahar cried. 'I don't pray much too but that sounds a bit extreme.'

'Do you think it makes any difference? You might as well face the North Pole, stars, black holes. The god of everything must also be the god of matter – without it we could not exist. In the scheme of the universe the Kaaba is less than an angel on a pinhead. It might as well not exist. Wherever or whichever way you turn, *Allah is*. So that's why I say, "Screw the *qiblah*!"'

Bahar sat down on my bed, unsure of what I would say next. 'Have you converted?' she asked me quietly, as if this was some dark thing, best kept away from the light. 'Perhaps you and your new girlfriend have become Christians.'

At this I burst out laughing. 'No, sister, I am not a Christian. I don't really know what I am or what I will become.' I paused, thinking why I was letting the joy of seeing my sister, and uncle, be interrupted by pointless religious musings. After a while, I continued. 'There is much to like about the Christians, just as there is with other beliefs. I remember when I was in Oxford there was a Methodist chapel in a side road somewhere or other, with a blue painted sign on the front wall of the building. I remember it because the person who painted the sign had underlined a single word. I stopped in my wanderings round the city, thinking *why* underline that single word?'

Bahar had gone to the window, sighing at the night, as if she didn't want to hear me.

'I know it's silly to say but do you know what was on the sign? It had caught my eye because then I was always thinking about *Jannah* and *Jahannam*. You know how we hate unbelievers in Islam, *kafirs*? Well this sign was also about belief too.'

Bahar raised her eyebrows and pulled a face in mock boredom. 'I am not really interested, you know.'

'Me too but I'll tell you. It had capital letters in places. "For God so loved the world that He gave his only begotten Son, that whoever *believes* in Him should not perish but have everlasting life." The word "believes" was underlined. I mean that is some claim – everlasting life. In which case there is no need for Christians to wait for the second coming of Isa, I mean Jesus, as in some kind of Jesus 2.0, is there? You need only believe. Believe in Jesus and have everlasting life; believe in Allah and have eternity in *Jannah*; believe in the Buddha, and keep coming back in another life again and again until finally you reach nirvana – when there is no need at all ever to be reborn!'

Bahar shook her head. 'We cannot know these things,' she said almost dolefully. 'Almost 99.9 per cent of people seeking nirvana never find it. They try to find it so they won't have to keep coming back, again and again. Why not? I would like to come back, even if there was more suffering. We can't know. We can never know.'

'I am sure of some things nevertheless,' I replied. 'What god is going to interfere in the march of evolution? The ape who became man must have his day. The story would be interrupted if god or prophet came back for a second time to foreclose on earth, and man's, fate.' I did not say these things with too much conviction, but strangely I knew that Persians, well, that is Iranians, many have an innate sense of wisdom, perception, and our minds – though closed in some directions – in others we are natural philosophers and thinkers.

Just then there was a knock at the door. It was one of Madame Saintoissant's maids. She announced politely, '*Monsieur*

Mohammad Reza, voulez-vous descendre en bas? Madame La Comtesse a demandé à vous voir.'

'*Bien sur,*' I replied, amazed that she had used *both* my fore-names. I was also secretly glad to have ended my idle religious speculations. They had to go back in the box, along with Gregor Samsa and the libertine debaucheries of Baudelaire, even though some of his poems evoked unforgettable and tender beauty. Also staying in boxes ought to be the relics of saints – ankle bones, fingers, hair, skulls, the assorted foreskins of Jesus, along with thousands of rusty nails and assorted bits of wood said to be from the One True Cross on the hill of Calvary. There are other objects of wonder – stones, plain and precious – said to have been walked over by John the Baptist or touched by a holy saint as he wandered by. In reality these are but icons in disguise, fawned on by believers; all should be consigned to a grand collection of reliquaries in a single location. Thus, all fifty-five fingers or more of St Peter and the hundred and one toe-nail clippings of Saint Gullible could be neatly shown side by side...

In the hallway when I got downstairs, accompanied by Bahar, Madame Saintoissant was waiting, her hands clasped together as if she wished to impart some news to me, what I could not guess. '*Bien,*' she said to my sister. 'Come with me to help prepare the dinner for this evening. Reza, please go to see Monsieur Alphonse. He is asking for you.'

She did not tell me where I could find him – that was the way things worked on the estate. Mostly, one knew where to look and in this case, not having been given any contrary instructions, I made my way across the courtyard at the side of the house to his office. Alphonse greeted me warmly. '*Bonsoir Monsieur Mohammad! Viens avec moi. J'ai quelque chose à te montrer, quelque chose de bon pour toi!*'

I understood he had something, something good, to show me. Pushing to the back of my mind the anguish and loss I felt for my mother, I followed him through a door down to the cellars. He paused a moment to flick a light switch. I had briefly been inside a few times but the cavernous interior I had left largely unexplored, since it was not my business to ferret on my own through the long (and high) rows of racked, dusty wine bottles or the serried lanes of wine barrels in an adjacent cellar, where the three main factors of good husbandry of the wine were always followed: light (almost none), a stable level of humidity (about 75%) and constant temperature (ideally 52° F or 11° C – certainly between 50 and 59° F).

We reached the end of one particular section. Alphonse Daudier stopped and I was sure I saw him briefly bowing. 'I will show you these,' he said, his English slow, articulated but correct. 'Here are the beauties of the estate.' The bottles were laid at a slight upward angle. 'Let me say we admire *these* most of all – but we prefer to drink '*nos belles cuvées*' – our own lovely vintages. These wines sit here; they will be good until 2035 or 40, even longer. Do you want to look?'

He gestured with his right arm, indicating I should examine one. I picked out the nearest. I saw a white label on which was printed gold-coloured lettering, and in the centre a very grand chateau with four columns in neo-Palladian style. The date on the bottle showed 2005, and underneath the picture of a chateau in the middle, simply read: GRAND VIN, and underneath that, 'PREMIER GRAND CRU CLASSÉ'. I read the producer's name but for some strange reason I did not say it aloud, as if by the very looking at the name its reverential power had been so vouchsafed that I instantly became a silent devotee.

Monsieur Alphonse looked at me, then drew his fingers together and pressed them to his lips, before opening his hand and kissing the air with a loud sucking noise. It was his way of expressing his admiration for the wine. 'We also have some from 1985, 1990, 1995 and 2000 but not a single bottle from 2015, which one day may be the most perfect of all the vintages.'

I shook my head at the thought, the wonder of it.

'I expect they will have some in their *"Nouveau Chai"*.' I didn't know what he meant until I discovered later that it was a new wine cellar built at Chateau Margaux, and an undoubted architectural master work, making it the finest new wine shed in the world. The bottle was replaced in the rack as carefully as one might handle an explosive. By some strange process of the imagination, I happened to remember reading an online Muslim advice forum dealing with the dangerous sin of alcohol consumption; as a subtext the forum had quickly moved on to the dangers of *zina*, unlawful sexual acts such as fornication – especially sex between unmarried people.

'Victims of these shameful relations' had to be watchful in their relations with the opposite sex. 'It should be remembered that the sexual instinct of youth is so powerful that negligence and carelessness about it may result in *any sort of explosion*.' Obviously 'two bombs in one' would be sex outside of marriage, with a glass of wine for further (some might add more complete) consummation.

'*Tu vas bien?*' asked Alphonse, as I was still figuratively scratching my head at the 'two bombs in one', as a kind of double-barrelled sin.

'*Ce n'est vraiment rien,*' I assured him. It's nothing at all.

'Well,' he continued, walking further along the rows of wine bottles, 'for your mother, in memory of your dear mother, I propose one of our very best vintages from the estate. He stopped a little way further. 'These are appropriate.' I followed his gaze. 'Château La Comtesse de Margaux 2000. *C'est absolument sublime!'*

I had no doubt that my friend from college days, Alice, who had introduced me to the medicinal effects of a large double whisky, when at one of life's crossroads, as I had been, in the days when Gregor Samsa and the Muslim cleric in his mosque conspired to deal out nightmares of the sinning flesh, while Baudelaire leered at me from his comfortable, sensual mansions of excess, and those full wine glasses in the college dining hall taunted me, and the gargoyles by turns laughed or sneered at my feeble jaunts through the city, to the doctor who advised my immediate hospitalisation – how I had survived all these – Alice would have cheered me on!

'It would be an honour to try this beautiful wine,' I told Alphonse quite firmly, my spirits lifting. *'Un choix parfait!'*

'Alors,' Alphonse answered, 'Let us take two bottles.' He took two in his hands, giving me one to hold for him. I followed the wine master out of the cellar into his office. 'Wine is many things,' he said, sitting down in his office chair. 'We remember with wine. Sometimes it brings hope, at times joy but rarely sadness, and that is often when we drink too much. Wine comforts the soul of those with good hearts.'

I was quite moved by his sudden soliloquy. If love was 'a loosener of limbs,' wine was a loosener of thoughts, away from rigidity of thinking, bringing polychrome to monochrome and, as long as the sips were measured, no harm was done. I thought how many were the 'cups' shared by civilisations recent and past – liaisons and truces, plights and troths, peace treaties and bargains, lovers' knots and lovers' pledges, true and untrue – the witness to many of these being the cup of red wine. Of course the most extraordinary and wondrous of all cups ever to hold red wine must be what is to many the nonpareil of all such vessels – the Holy Grail, the chalice used by Isa, or Jesus, at the Last Supper. Notable it might be that on that very night Isa declared that he would 'not drink again of the fruit of the vine until that day when I drink it new with you in my Father's kingdom'. Is it not claimed that all the words in all the holy books are true, divinely inspired? Then I guessed the gentle ruby tide has a place in heaven too. But to prove this one must first arrive there, and as far as I know, or can know, no human or animal or insect or stone or anything has ever done that. Heaven is just a nebulous dream imagined from the quagmire of earth. *Allahu akbar!* (Notwithstanding). I have heard that Pope Francis, born Jorge Mario Bergoglio, has hinted that even dogs might go to heaven. This is a dangerous path to tread. Think of all those mangy curs and snapping brutes, malamutes and pye-dogs, all wanting in. I happen to like dogs. He surely did not mean only dogs owned by humans. If he did is it not unfair to wild dogs, stray dogs, and the occasional 'reformed' hyena? Oh fallible Pope!

Even Muhammad drank wine. So it is recorded in our holy book. Much argument is made about the precise meaning of words. The scribes argue about whether the drink was unfermented or fermented, *this* proves *that* they say, no *this* was meant, not *that*. Grapes, dates, raisins, barley, wheat and honey were all used to make intoxicating drinks.

Dinner was served at eight-fifteen. Madame Madeleine Saintoissant looked resplendent, even allowing that the evening was in memory of my mother. She wore an appropriately dark blouse, with white pearls luminous and alluring, hung from her long neck. My uncle looked the part too, with white shirt, dark suit and bow tie, all of which made me feel as if my dress was too casual, in my single pair of jeans, and one of the few shirts I could consider as 'smart' – something I might have worn to dinner at college. I had worn few suits in my life but as a boy in Iran I did sometimes get a new one to wear just for *Nowruz*. Monsieur Alphonse was also smartly dressed in a handsome, navy coloured jacket, made from a type of material I believe is known in English circles as 'barathea'. His wife, Madame Daudier, whose first name eludes me, but I think it is Didina, and then my beloved sister Bahar, completed our table, with one empty space left for Margot, if she got back in time.

Surprisingly, we had dinner in the kitchen, a large room split into two parts, the food served on a wooden table. We started with a duck confit and a salad of chopped wild mushrooms, cherry tomatoes, celery and walnuts served on a bed of crispy romaine lettuce. Madame Saintoissant had prepared the most delicious French dressing, and there was freshly-baked country bread, and a slab of creamy unsalted butter. The bread was to my liking; I did not especially miss my own kind of 'village bread', which we bake in the oven in big pieces on a bed of small stones, often collected from rivers. When the flatbread is cooked, there are round 'bubbles' in the bread made by the stones. We call this kind of bread *sangak*.

The main meal was a kind of beef stew; I suppose you could call it boeuf bourguignon of sorts with a twist, because Bahar had brought some herbs, along with some dried limes or *limu-omani*. She had persuaded Madame Saintoissant to add some – for the piquancy they give (especially to many Iranian dishes).

Did I forget to mention the wine?

Bahar smiled. She had been watching the expression on my face as Monsieur Daudier slowly filled my glass. The colour was dark ruby. '*Voilà*, Monsieur Reza,' Alphonse said. '*Laissez-nous boire à votre mère bien-aimée!*'

'So,' I said, 'to my beloved mother, and all good things that came to our family through her.'

'To your dear mother,' Madame Saintoissant said, looking at me with affection, 'and your sister Bahar, and Dr Arvani.' I let the wine swirl in my glass for a moment; I could already detect the bouquet, my nose not unaccustomed to Bordeaux wines, though I had tried only one good wine before, and that was the one I drank with Margot in the field with a picnic table. There is a French saying about wine that I remember now: 'Burgundy for kings, champagne for duchesses, claret for gentlemen'. As always in life it's easy to find a contrary view. Dr Johnson remarked that 'claret is the liquor for boys; port, for men'. I looked in my glass, and suddenly wondered if Ghorbali Khan had been at our table with us, what he would have done. I felt sure he would stand up proudly, wishing '*Salamati*' to all.

I thought I was a king then, never mind the Burgundy, with the Margaux in my glass. From the very centre of the Haut-Médoc region, this was certain to be sensual, seductive – sufficient to make all the djinn in the world, whether good or evil ones, salivate at the mere thought of tasting it or be consumed forever by apoplexy. The first sip captivated my senses. By the second sip I could write poetry to show to Rumi or Hafez. By the third I remembered my mother, and swallowed hard. I put down my glass, and everyone seemed to be looking at me.

'Reza is thinking,' Bahar said solemnly.

'I am thinking,' I said, reverting to my Iranian heritage where we like to expound or expatiate volubly, if there is a willing audience, 'of the greatness of this wine, and not forgetting all the hard work involved to create it and to fill our cellars. And, you know, the grapes, yes, the grapes – such a little masterpiece God created in this small matter – like the flesh and liquid – to make this fine drink – fit not just for kings and queens, but everyone!' I reached in front of me to pluck a red grape from a dish. I held it in my right hand between thumb and forefinger. 'In Iran we call this *angoor*.' I could see my uncle was getting worried in case I might say something wrong or offensive but I was not intimidated. 'From these *angoor* we get not only wine but also *kishmesh* – raisins – and all the other sweetnesses like currants and sultanas. These are riches too! In my country we have our marvels, Persepolis, snow-capped mountains, the Caspian Sea, carpets made by hands that worked much harder than in any vineyards. The story of the vine is the story of civilisations, of humanity, and in many, if not all, of the great songs of the poets.'

Holding up my glass I turned to Alphonse. 'Wine master, *azizam*, this is *your* creation. It is, exactly as you said, *absolument sublime!*'

Everyone was still looking at me. Monsieur Alphonse (I had called him 'my dear' in Persian) got up from his seat, his smile widening with I suppose appreciation of my praise, and perhaps unsure what to say. Without hesitation, he raised his glass of Margaux, and said, '*A toi, Reza! Bon santé monsieur le poète.*'

In turn, I was not sure how to respond though everyone stood up to 'toast' my health. '*To Reza, bon santé,*' was the cry that echoed round, just as we heard the chiming from the ormolu clock in the hallway.

I felt as if my mind were spinning not from the wine but from the hospitality of this family, and to be truthful, from Monsieur Alphonse's tribute to me. Poets in France have a special place in the hearts of French people, like painters scraping a living on 'La Rive Gauche', the left bank of the Seine, or on the side streets under the Sacré-Coeur of Montmartre, the Sacred Heart of Paris. I knew this from my studies. Rimbaud and Éluard, Ronsard and Baudelaire, at a pinch Verlaine, I knew them all (not from my home town in Iran but from the libraries beneath cupola and casements of that city where I cast my *tokhmeh* on the waters).

These poets were all like Baudelaire's albatross. Giant wings, once caught on ships in the bitter gulfs, when they tired and sought to land, these wings of giants, wings on giants, giants on wings, prevented them from flying, or even walking, hobbled to planks of wood in the far oceans – even though only moments before they were as princes of the clouds, parrying tempests, laughing at the archer who might shoot them down.

I had no words to express my thoughts just then, though when I glanced down at the ruby Margaux in my glass, I imagined, stupidly, wantonly, like a marooned albatross abandoned on the plank of some bitter deck, from a tree cut down from a sacred wood, as if Hafez had heard me, and like a djinni he was rising in my glass, caught in the swirls, but surfacing from the bottom of my glass to speak: *Come, let's scatter roses and pour wine in the glass...*

For dessert there was apple and *alou tarte* with armagnac and cream. When a maid brought small cups of black coffee, there were sounds of a delivery in the courtyard outside. Ten minutes later Margot appeared with a clutch of creamy white roses, I guessed for her mother. She strode in confidently, her hair tossed lightly aside by a flick of her wrist. '*J'ai deux barriques,*' she announced proudly, '*Et ces roses douces pour Maman, bien sur.*' The sweet roses were for Madeleine. Bahar got up to greet her, my uncle too standing ram-rod straight, despite his years. Alphonse was smiling, his wife also.

There was something about Margot that captivated her immediate audience. I know I risk using a word that was originally French, namely the cliché, but 'a breath of fresh air' came towards us, enveloping in its warmth and sincerity. Margot was *being* exemplified. She took command but did not request it. It flowed naturally from her. In France, there is much chit-chat on social occasions. I heard it, I heard them. I introduced my uncle and my sister Bahar, and then I felt perhaps I might slip quietly away. I was sure more armagnac would follow, so I politely excused myself. I wanted to keep my head clear, to be able to think. To my surprise, they let me go, without too much fuss. Perhaps some of them thought I was in love, I don't know.

I crashed out of the main door because to be fair, I had been assaulted, in both cases willingly, first by the beautiful wine, the Margaux, the sleek Margaux, the wondrous Margaux, the enticing Margaux, and then – by the sight of Margot returning, flush with her success with the barrels, and her indomitable youth and energy, and I being a man, must say, by her striking beauty. So I went out into the night to feel the air close to me. I was alone with the benisons of the French night, the rustic and the sylvan, the bucolic and verdant, with the vines in their long serried rows, all breathing the same air, anchored to the soil by their roots. I felt my roots were there too, in that green countryside, in all that green breathing, perhaps hidden by the season, but ineluctably present, and I felt it was my time to stamp on the soil, and declare it as my brother, that I belonged to this Bordeaux magic. My time had come.

Twenty-One

LATER, I FOUND MYSELF IN MY ROOM, SLIGHTLY ASHAMED TO have left the evening's gathering. Was it selfish of me? How could I be sure of anything? How could I know that Margot was for me? It was no use suggesting to myself that Allah would take care of us, of me, of her, of our being together. Suppose Allah did not approve? He did not disapprove of Muhammad marrying a young girl who was only nine years old; if Allah had disagreed, Muhammad surely would never have been allowed to continue spreading his message.

Oddly, I wondered to myself if there were seasons in *Jannah*. Was there a moon even, several, or none? Is there night and day? Does it never rain? I like the cooling rain, rain that nourishes, brings growth. Are there tears in *Jannah* – to express our joy? If you were happy in *Jannah*, as supposedly one must be, would there be no sorrow, the healing of tears falling, tears that make things new again, on earth?

Too much happiness is just as bad as too much pain. Imagine the ever-joyful eternals, those who crossed the sandbar, made it home to *Jannah*; think how there would be no lilac buds in spring, no summer roses, no golden autumn leaves; no dates from date palms to eat by a certain date. Oh, how dull! No achieve of, no mastery, since all must be perfect. You must be asking why I use the phrase 'achieve of'. Why did I not write 'no achieving'? Because another great English poet used it in a

211

poem, so I borrow it from him. It is no heresy for me to mention it, even though it is addressed 'To Christ our Lord'. Just as we exclaim, '*Allahu akbar*', that is God is greater, or God is the greatest for all kinds of reasons, even for seeing beautiful things in the world – like a windhover in the early morning. It is reasonable. Isa has many devotees, and in Islam he has his place, and we revere him along with other prophets who came before Prophet Muhammad, peace be upon him. The poet's 'chevalier' might not be ours but we can understand the poet's great vision of 'the falcon', just as we know that Allah sees everything.

The fact is that the world turns in all sorts of circles, I mean socially. I remember being more than a little nonplussed to read that Elizabeth II, Queen of England, is a descendant of our great Prophet – his 43rd great-granddaughter, and this from the *ne plus ultra* of texts on royal lineages, *Burke's Peerage*. Is it not 'God save the Queen' but 'Allah save the Queen'?

Where is *that* table? The one of which it is said, 'All options are on the table'. Sometimes we have to take no notice of what's on the table but make 'a clean sweep', and push all away, make a fresh start. One of the best things in life, I am sure, is the choice we have to 'start all over again'. By which I mean clean up the mess, put certain habits to bed, and wake up to a new day (and all these musings from a few glasses of Margaux!).

How different life would be, I thought, if there were no night and day, just low level 24-hour light. How much harder it would be to make a new beginning.

A new day comes and you can start over. Of course, you'll probably make yet another mess of your life but you can go to bed and resolve to make a new beginning in the morning. This can go on day after day, year after day, year after year. After a binge night out, enthusiastic love-making, indulgences, all can be consigned to the bin as soon as your head hits the pillow.

One can concentrate again on work the next morning, have a shave, face the *qiblah*, recite some prayers, polish the shoes you had allowed to get dirty.

For these reasons it must hardly be paradise in *Jannah*. Endless indulgence with libidinous virgins, relaxing on silk couches, day after day after day – and who knows whether there *is* night and day in paradise? Would a believer having entered *Jannah* still be required to pray to Allah, with the five (three for Shi'as) daily prayers? The scholars say that *Jannah* is a place of reward not obligation. Acts of worship would therefore be waived (how kind). Of course one would be entirely free to remember Allah if one so desired but the scholars have no knowledge of 'the unseen', so they cannot offer guidance, other than that while one is permitted to eat and drink at will, there would be no need to wipe noses, to urinate or defecate. According to one report, food eaten will harmlessly turn into burps, and sweating from the exertions of overeating will evaporate like musk. As I sought answers from the scholars, by reading articles from Islamic forums, many summarily ended with 'And Allah knows best', as if that would be the end of the matter.

It was no wonder I said 'screw the *qiblah*'! Don't question the teacher, as teacher knows best. If Allah knows best, and here I excuse myself if there is any suggestion of disrespecting Allah, why has he allowed such *an imponderable mess* here on our own dear Earth! If he knows best, he might have known better.

There was a sudden knock at my door. It was Margot, with Bahar standing next to her. 'Are you all right, Reza?' Margot asked. Bahar did not look cross or secretly angry, and it was soon clear that she and Margot had made friends. 'No really,' I replied. 'Everything is good.' They left quietly, wishing me good night, and both gave me a hug in turn, my sister first, then Margot who squeezed me with affection. Suddenly they were gone.

Should I have told Margot I loved her? That I felt I was stepping in the footsteps of one of my great ancestors, Ghorbali Khan? That my fate was somehow inextricably also to be hers, linked together by the Bordeaux destiny, from a prince, a *khan* of Persia as the great Ghorbali Khan was, all the way down to me, to join with the chestnut-haired daughter from the grand estate that had given birth to the glorious Chateau La Comtesse de Margaux? It was better to hold my peace, quite difficult for an Iranian as we are normally very impulsive.

Before I managed to sleep I searched on my phone for comments about a Muslim marrying a Christian. I found, 'Is it bad for a Muslim to marry a Christian?' Other search terms to show were:

Is it bad for a Muslim to have a dog?
Is it bad for a Muslim to say merry Christmas?
Is it bad for a Muslim to date a Christian?
Is it bad for a Muslim girl to have a boyfriend?
Is it bad for a Muslim to smoke weed?

I suppose there are much the same with Jews, Catholics and others. So much for the Enlightenment today. Few have the courage to dare to know for themselves, and most cower in the dark, fearing the poisonous rebukes of sick trolls.

Still less did I wish to get out my small prayer mat; instead I fell on it, and lay there thinking if Allah could see me. My mind clouded and then a stream of thoughts followed. The back of my head rested comfortably on the prayer mat and I could see the dark night through the window of my room. If Allah does see everything I mused, through cloud and storm, from pole to pole, and all earth round, if he has paid more attention to the earth since Muhammad began to praise him from his cave at Hira on Mount Jabal al-Nour, when visited on the Mountain of Light by the angel Jibreel…and if he has been closely watching all humans day by day, night by night, and year by year since only then – it must have been like the most horrific film one could ever imagine, dismembered bodies, piles of dead bodies like Boschian or Bruegelian visions of Hell. The never ending wars, the remnants of cars and warhorses of lost battles, I meant those poetic 'cars' with brazen axles that carried the sun-god Apollo, the dust and plastic, the bombs and savage killings, the gouged-out eyes and torn-up limbs, the death and destruction enough to turn God towards insanity, to tempt him to madness. How could God but decide after this film that the Devil had won the battle long ago, and to believe otherwise would be nothing more than babbling foolishness?

Or perhaps Allah is an optimist, a delusional optimist. But all these things are unknown so it is no profit to speculate. And Allah knows best.

Muhammad, our dear Prophet, peace and blessings of Allah be upon him, I wonder sometimes where he is now. He has had over a millennium and a third to go over in his mind, in his spirit, all his deeds and utterances as revealed to him. I did wonder if he is in *Jannah* now or if that is something that only happens on the Last Day, the Day of Judgement. One Hadith writes that those who enter *Jannah,* who have been chosen by Allah, as attested by his seal 'will be blessed with such bounties as no eye has seen, no ear has heard and no human mind has ever perceived'. How can they talk of things no human has ever seen?

Certainly on earth, all humans have the awful predictability of life: birth, breath, life, mate, death. This inevitability about life is carefully hidden in youth, which is strong and eager for living. However, youth is untested by time, which is also its glory

215

of trying, albeit that one day the young warrior will become old and wizened, as fragile as the bark of an ancient tree, in want of water. No species can progress without the death-harvest at the end of life, and the new shoots beginning all over again. Think of a Ferris wheel; you get on, have as many spins as Allah in his mercy allows, but eventually when the wheel goes back to where you started, a little like blues singer Leadbelly on his last go-round, you are dropped off to oblivion, while a new rider joins, an 'easy rider' of the life to come. Perhaps it is unsurprising that so many mutter, pray and entreat five or three times a day in mosques, or sit or kneel in dark, dank churches, whispering their grief at the awfulness of life.

Some do see *Jannah*, if only in spirit. This is what happens to the dead, lying in the quiet of their graves. The prophets and the martyrs have souls 'in the crops of green birds', and these roam about in Paradise, flying hither, thither, where you will. But to be truly in *Jannah* in body and spirit, one must wait until the Last Day, only then can everyone be with those whom he loves. It is written that the only exception to this is Adam, since he was in Paradise once before, before things went wrong, got out of hand.

In the crops of green birds. When I read this, I had to pinch myself. The birds have their nests in gold lamps or chandeliers hung from trees, beneath the throne of the almighty; there they eat the fruits of Paradise and fly at will down to rivers for water. This especially applies to martyrs, it seems, as if slain in battle in Allah's cause, they are not to be considered as dead, but alive, their souls in the crops of those green birds. They have everything they need there; this message was to be conveyed to the believers on earth so that they would not lose interest in jihad or flinch from war. The green birds, *oiseaux verts* in French, these I could not imagine sensibly in Paradise, just as

216

in Iran I have never seen a *Huma* bird. In Farsi we pronounce the word as *Homā*; perhaps because this mythical creature flies high above the earth all its life, so high as to be invisible. I would prefer to be a soul in the *Bulbul*, the nightingale in my language.

I had to conclude that these ideas were more fanciful than real birds of paradise, more mythical than the phoenix, more fantastical than the fantasies imagined in the wildest bacchanal. We have a name in Iran we use for these fairy tales – *afsaneh*. Like any sensible Iranian, to let these thoughts go from my mind I chewed silently on a few dry *tokhmeh* left on my bedside table. I dreamed of green birds too, flying with me through Persian landscapes, of pomegranates and dates, and orange and almond blossoms in green translucent valleys.

Twenty-Two

I BEGAN TO SEARCH IN MY ROOM FOR MY MOTHER'S JEWEL-
lery. I wanted to see again the fine gold brooch with diamonds
in the shape of a grape cluster. The design was simple enough. I
counted the diamonds. At the top was a tiny ridged band of gold
to represent the vine stem, one small leaf in gold for the vine
leaf, and then 17 small diamonds encased in gold for the cluster,
more diamonds at the top tapering down to the base, just like a
miniscule bunch of grapes.

The next morning my uncle and Bahar were leaving for Paris.
After breakfast, we walked in the cold autumnal air through
some of the vineyards with Margot as guide. '*Amujan*,' Bahar
said to my uncle, 'these vines look so small but they make
such beautiful wine.' 'It is true,' he said. 'It is so true. *Oreah,
vorgahan dostereh.*' My uncle seemed to have lost all inhibi-
tions by then, and his need to direct everything and everyone.
Halfway through the walk quite suddenly he began to dance in
the Persian way – an expression of spontaneous joy in living.
His arms lifted, his hands became twirling wrist circles, and his
eyes sparkled as he danced on the Margaux soil with a strangely fixed enigmatic smile that some people adopt when dancing
publicly, especially if from the East.

Some years later I happened to read about a girl pop star in
Iran. Her name was Gola. She had tried to sing in Iran, her own
country, but if she performed on stage no men must be there,

219

no one was allowed to move in their seats, and she had to stand and not make the slightest movement, such as a sway of her hips, because then the morality police would shut the concert, take her to prison, or simply deny her a work permit. Solo singing for a girl is forbidden – since the 1979 revolution – so she was only allowed on stage with friends who were also singers. Gola went to London to start a new career but she can't go back to Iran. Solo dancing on Instagram is also banned for Iranian women for fear this might inflame men's unruly passions.

Margot was watching. She was both surprised and delighted. I had no choice but to join my uncle, while Bahar clapped and urged us on. I am sure the Margaux soil had not before that day been treated to the spectacle of two Iranian men celebrating with a Persian dance.

Before my uncle and Bahar left for Paris, I was invited, with Margot, to visit my uncle in the spring.

Christmas came and a white carpet of snow mantled the estate but luckily no frost. One day I went out with Margot to the vineyards, wanting to show her the path I had found earlier and the '*passage interdit*' sign.

Perhaps from my stubbornness of character I insisted we go beyond it. The path meandered away until we came across woodland, draped in snow blankets. There was a primal hush, the white silence brought on by the snow. Our steps crunched lightly on soft powdery drifts.

'I have something for you, my sweet *gholam,*' I said (a flower or rose), my breath bringing light misty plumes from my mouth. Under a stand of tall pine trees, before I had time to think, even before I could say a prayer of thankfulness, Margot kissed me. It was a deep, luscious kiss. After all it was a French kiss! I was overwhelmed, that is my senses seemed to be preternaturally alive, capable of infinite levels both of deep, huge understanding joined with enormous complexities and mysteries. When I became more advanced in years, I supposed that a woman should be chaste until a man decides to chase her. A woman should be modest before a man decides she shouldn't be. But then, it was different. I was a novice in the domain of love.

In Iran we say, 'One sin is too much, a hundred prayers are not enough.' For what? At the back of my mind, which was reeling from the touch of Margot, I suddenly remembered one of the Hadiths as recited by our great Prophet, peace be upon him. He said that it was better for a person *to have a nail driven into their head* than to touch someone who is not closely related, for example, a sibling. I was also supposed to 'lower my gaze' before women, so as to avoid the sight of forbidden things. Looking at a woman (even if her head is covered with the *hijab*) is going down a path that might lead to *zina*! It is not good to discuss kissing. It is not allowed to listen to a woman singing alone – it *might* lead to lust, corruption. Body contact, any kind of touching, is *haram*. According to some it is forbidden to squeeze the other's hand. Actually the rules and laws on the subject of sexual pleasures and ways to lower 'the sexual passion' are as numerous as leaves on a tree in summer. In many Muslim countries, as in Saudi Arabia, a man can have a temporary wife – a 'traveller's marriage' known as *al-Misyar*. In this kind of 'marriage' it is therefore permissible to have new sexual partners, to whom the man owes none of the usual marriage obligations; having a temporary mistress in this fashion means being able to bypass the laws against *zina*.

But I was not to be put off by my thoughts. From my jacket pocket I took out the diamond grape cluster on its thin gold chain. It was wrapped inside a handkerchief. I pressed it into

Margot's right hand. Her face shone with delight when she saw it properly, for the first time. She arched her eyebrows.

'*C'est belle, Reza, vraiment belle*. It's so beautiful. Reza, is it really for me?' I told her it was. 'Oh Reza, Mohammad Reza, *mon petit prince*!' She loosened her clothes a little. 'Put it on my neck,' she said.

Margot undid her top a little, enough for me to fit it round her open neck. I couldn't quite see the diamond cluster, so she undid one more button from her shirt, and there it was on her chest. I glimpsed something more, by accident. Please let me say there was no lust on my part, it just happened; it was accidental and therefore more *halal* than *haram*. But I saw them, beyond the valley in the centre, the rising mounds of white flesh on either side, tipped with a pink tip. Like a pink-tipped *tut*, I thought. Yes, that was it. Each nipple like a pink *tut* from a mulberry tree!

I don't think I have ever been so happy. Margot nestled her neck on my shoulder as we walked back to the estate. It grew dark quickly. Several bright stars came out early as if to faintly light our path. I thought of that royal road – the Silk Road – once lit by fire temples along the way, on the road to Samarkand. If anyone had tapped me on the shoulder at that moment, I would have expected to turn around and see the spirit of old Ghorbali Khan! I felt he was walking with me.

'*Bonsoir, mes petites*,' Madame Saintoissant cried warmly as we entered the big house. '*Ça va?*'

'*Ça va bien*,' Margot and I said together.

'*Vous devez manger!*' Madame Saintoissant shouted excitedly, as if this was something terribly important. I had lost my appetite, and I think so had Margot. Who wants to eat when you just want to be beside your loved one? So we had sandwiches and shared a cold beer, which I allowed myself on principle, namely in for a penny in for a pound, or even in for a rial in for a toman. Some *haram* things had troubled me that day; one more would not count for much.

'Reza,' Margot said suddenly, 'Let's talk later.' She smiled, as if imparting an implicit secret, so I just accepted. Madeleine Saintoissant was singing quietly to herself in another room. We went to say goodnight.

'*À demain, mes petites,*' she said, with barely a glance as she seemed preoccupied with some domestic task or other.

In my room about twenty minutes later, as I was looking out of the window towards the vineyards, though I could only see dark shapes in the night, and being not really troubled by my lack of prayers, and my heart telling me to be calm, Margot knocked softly on my door.

For some reason, I remembered 'the Annunciation' to the Blessed Virgin Mary by *Jibreel* – I had not meant Muhammad's first revelation when he was visited in the cave at Hira by *Jibreel* or the archangel Gabriel, according to the cross-worshippers. Gabriel called her 'the Favoured One', and since that time she has been named 'The Queen of Heaven, Mother Inviolate, Ark of the New Covenant, the Second Eve', and so on. The Roman Catholic Church keeps a record of numerous visions or sightings of Mary over many centuries. I found this a curious fact to swallow, perhaps because I had perceived, even from my lowly and unscholarly outlook, that no one ever seems to report sightings of our great Prophet, peace and blessings of Allah be upon him. But no doubt there is a reason for this, and anyway Allah always knows best. It may be that angels and the like have bodies of light only, and Allah has made it impossible for humans to see them, unless the angels take human form. Of course, as someone has sung, if we forget to pray for the angels, then the angels forget to pray for us. No one can claim to have seen the

Prophet, at least when awake and not in a dream. The djinn are different; they have great powers and abilities. As spirits they can take any shape they like, whether animals, humans, even trees but we pray and recite the Qur'an in our houses and then the djinn cannot possess us with their devilish tricks.

Even so I could not understand why Maryam the Virgin has appeared to so many cross-worshippers and nuns of that faith, yet such spiritual visions of our beloved Prophet are forbidden, at least when our eyes are open. I suppose it would only lend credence to baseless delusions if the *Ummah* kept a list of 'sightings', such as 'Our great Prophet sighted on the road to Medina', or 'Apparition of Muhammad seen at such-and-such mosque', or 'Prophet Muhammad vision in Trafalgar Square'. Any 'vision' of Muhammad is more likely in Mecca than St Peter's Square.

Margot came to me. I had my arms open. It was not difficult. We threw ourselves on my bed. Nothing much happened.

Reza? Yes. Do you love me? You know it. Reza? Yes. Kiss me!

The trouble with passion is that it is often so intense. One or two (sweeter than wine) kisses are just the tinder, the kindling. I saw again the diamond cluster of grapes in their new home – between the pink-tipped *tuts*. My lips brushed her neck. Was I behaving as a Muslim should? *I didn't care!* There followed tender embraces, such gentle, sweet sighings in my ears from Margot, and dare I tell you, the tender joining of one soul with another. A most extraordinary melding, a kind of coalescence; in fact it was an utterly new metamorphosis for me, since the two of us became one. The sort of 'touching' involved was the most intimate I had ever experienced, and I had the thought that 'making love' was perfectly normal, like a sacred act, and as beautiful and intense for me as it was for Margot. How shall I describe it? The flame of desire, assuredly I pray it was love, had led me to worship – in a manner of speaking – at the velvet font, where I might offer libations of love, into the living, sweet, some say bittersweet, maw of begotten life, and all in defiance of the laws against *zina*!

I thought of those poor, tortured souls who whip and scourge their bodies to atone for their guilt of sinning, who are ashamed because of the preaching of priests. *Are they not mad? Have they lost their senses?*

After the glorious love-making, and after which I found another reason to pray, and when I had whispered *shab bekheir* or goodnight to my love, we slept like two babies, side by side, and only a slight movement next to me just before it got light informed me while still half-asleep that Margot was leaving.

Later, after breakfast and before lunch, Margot and I decided. We must tell Madame Saintoissant of our intention to become engaged. I went to her alone. 'Madeleine *Khanoum*,' I managed to splutter in my excitement, '*Nous nous fiancons.*' Without hesitation, Madame replied, '*Tu as mes bénédictions. Tous les deux de tout mon coeur.*'

A blessing from Margot's mother was all we needed. The rest happened quickly. We went to Paris in the spring and saw the Seine flowing past Notre-Dame as so many lovers have done. We ran up the stairs to my uncle's flat and that horrible beetle never once came into my mind. I told my uncle we were engaged, and immediately he replied, 'Let us have caviar and vodka! We will remember Ghorbali Khan now.'

We had the now familiar ritual of the vodka shots and the tasting of the caviar on tiny pieces of toast. '*Amujan*, I cried, 'where is it, the family tree?' My uncle rushed to a drawer in his study to find it, and placed it on the kitchen table before us. 'Write your name on this now,' he told Margot, 'on our family tree. It's a little early but never mind. May you have many children together!'

Margot took the pen and wrote her full name opposite mine. My uncle said he would add the actual date of our marriage later. He could not resist one more toast to Ghorbali Khan, and one for us. '*Salamati* to all,' he shouted with great emotion, tears too, falling down his cheeks. It was not typical for my uncle to show his emotions so openly.

I had the thought that humans are like the leaves on trees. When they dry out, they fall down to the ground. So everyone has his day. But true love must mean you keep on loving someone even if your leaves fall off. Yes, that's true love. You never give up on the one you love – whether you win or lose in life – and even if you lose all your leaves!

Quite soon we left my uncle for Bordeaux. I even rescued my old leather suitcase on the way back. I had found my old friend for sale in a Margaux village, in a junk shop or *magazine de charité*, not far from where it was abandoned on my journey to Chateau La Comtesse de Margaux.

***

Three Years Later

WE WERE MARRIED IN THAT SUMMER AFTER PARIS ON A WARM
June day. We had a simple ceremony then the *grand bal* afterwards in the large barn on the estate. Gilles was my best man.
I didn't need to ask him. He volunteered. Alphonse the winemaker presented us with a fine gift, a case of 2015 Chateau La
Comtesse de Margaux to lay down for a few years. There was
much music and dancing, merrymaking. My uncle came too,
bringing the family tree in a briefcase to add the latest date. I
had even invited Alice after making contact with her again. She
loved the *eau-de-vie-de-marc* especially. Madame Saintoissant
glowed with the deep happiness that only mothers know.

Sometimes I think of Allah and then our great Prophet. I can
never completely forget either of them. I will probably recall
both of them on my last day. I still have not tried the noble
Chateau Margaux in our cellars. Margot is having a baby. I will
wait until the birth – and if it is a boy or a girl, and when Margot
is recovered, we shall open a bottle, and 'turn down an empty
glass', for Omar. I expect I will be seduced by the loveliness of
the wine. It is a Margaux memory for me in waiting. It is not a
past memory. It lies somewhere out in the vineyards and in the
barriques or the wine racks in our cellars. Each vintage gives
the possibility of a new Margaux memory in waiting. With just
a corkscrew I can unleash it.

At the first sip I will rejoice as I remember in this peaceful land of Bordeaux, among the vineyards of Margaux, I have
found all that I was ever seeking. Each year a new harvest from
the grapes to add to our cellars, new life and new memories of
Margaux to be rekindled later, if the harvest is good. Portents of
summer will follow with us, like the screaming *oiseaux rapide*
returning to my uncle's flat in Paris.

We shall live with the holy trinity of grape, olive and citrus, and the dark purple *alou* to harvest in August or even September for the apple and *alou tarte*, if I am lucky, with armagnac and cream, and for the *vendange*, the harvest of the grapes, the wine pressings, and the hope of a great vintage for our cellars. The Margaux memory beckons even now, the sturdy vines reaching down deep to garner precious minerals to work their alchemic magic, from stony soil to the glorious grape – and to the glass of Chateau Margaux I am waiting to taste.

The Margaux memory will live on, stay alive with me, perhaps for ever.

God willing.

Inshallah…